RISKY VENUE

SAM CHEEVER

She's got a lot more to lose now...and somebody's determined to make sure she loses it all.

Blaise is at it again. She's still searching for that perfect job. But even when she thinks she might have found a job that could be more of a career than just a 9 to 5 gig, something always happens to get in her way.

Usually, that something involves a corpse...

But this time, Blaise's past comes back to haunt her in a big way. She'd thought she put that whole, *seeing a murder on the beach* thing behind her. But it seems somebody doesn't want to leave the past where it belongs.

And her past problems are about to become her current nightmare.

"Just think of it as a giant party," Blaise's friend, Suz Whatsnoggin told her, grinning.

"It will be just like working at the bar," Dolfe offered, taking a long swig of his icy cold beer.

Tyrese shook his head. "Not really. There are no Bridezillas at the bar."

Dolfe's handsome face filled with worry. "Bridezilla? I don't know what that is but I'm pretty sure I don't like the sound of it."

Blaise winced, imploring her friends with her eyes not to inform her sexy fiancé about the horrors of dealing with a nervous bride. It was the last thing Blaise wanted him to think about on the virtual eve of their own wedding.

Well...if you consider "within the next year" the eve.

Fortunately, Suz caught what her friend was throwing. "It's nothing you need to ever worry about, Honeybun." She winked at Blaise.

But Dolfe was not a stupid man. In fact, he was probably even smarter than he was good-looking, Blaise thought. And that was a lot of smart. "It's just a mean term used for brides who get the jitters," she told him in as offhand a way as she could muster. "Suz is right. You'll never experience that with me. I'm a rock."

He grinned. "A rock, huh?" Being the aforementioned smart hottie, Dolfe was wise enough not to venture any further into those tempestuous seas. He simply smiled, shaking his head, and took another sip of his beer.

Tyrese apparently wasn't smart enough to stay out of the storm. He dove right in, daring the waves to swamp him. "I have no delusions. If Suz and I choose to get married someday, she'll be the queen of bridezillas. My Suz will *own* the term." He shook his head as Suz gave him a quelling look. "I love me some strong woman. I have my own special way of easing her nerves."

When he waggled his brows, Suz rolled her eyes. "Stupidity, thy name is Tyrese."

Ty's leer slid away. "Babe!" He leaned across the table, one long, brown finger tucking up beneath her delicate chin and lifting. "You know you're cray-cray about me."

She leaned in too, her lips a mere breath from his as she released the Kraken. "Dude," Suz said in her sexiest voice. "You know, if we ever did decide to tie the knot, I'd just be marrying you for your last name, right?"

Ty laughed. "What? You don't want to lumber through life with the name Whatsnoggin anymore?"

Suz smacked him on the arm.

Blaise shook her head. "Please tell me you didn't just go there," she said.

Dolfe winced. "We don't make fun of a person's name around here, man. It's not in good taste," said the guy named Honeybun.

Ty's smile withered. "She started it."

Suz snorted. "Really? That's what you're going with? A playground excuse?"

Ty shrugged. "Look, I love your weird name, babe. It's just one of the many funny little oddities that make you special."

Dolfe groaned and Blaise sucked in a gasp. "Ty!"

Suz stared at him for a long moment, her pretty face so lacking in expression it was an expression all on its own. It was a face that said, you are so dead, while simultaneously declaring a total lack of concern.

Tyrese slowly lost his swagger and began to wilt, until he became little more than a handsome puddle in the delicate chair. When he was so puddly he looked ready to slither bonelessly off the chair onto the newly carpeted floor, Suz finally gave him a tight smile. "Just for that, if we ever decide to get married, Tyrese Miller, you're going to take *my* name."

Everybody gasped at that, followed by Dolfe's low chuckle.

"Snap!" Blaise told her friends, knocking dainty knuckles with Suz.

"Come on, girlfriend," Suz told Blaise. "Help me count the new shipment of linen napkins that just came in?"

Blaise stood, winking at Tyrese. "You'd better pull together your best defrazzling game, son. That's one ticked off 'special' girl right there." Blaise grinned as she followed Suz's angrily swaying behind toward the door at the back of the enormous room. Behind her, she heard Dolfe's deep chuckle as Ty whined at him in a voice that sounded like seagulls on a stormy beach.

Suz stopped at the open storage room door and grinned. "That should keep him on his toes for a while."

Blaise laughed softly. "Oh yeah."

Before going inside, the two of them stood in the doorway and looked around at the massive main space. It was a gorgeous room, elegant and clean, with lots of light and clean, simple lines. Blaise was impressed by her friend's vision and decorating skills.

"It's really beautiful, Suz."

Her friend sighed, leaning companionably against Blaise's shoulder. "It is, isn't it?"

Blaise nodded. When Suz had first come to her with the idea of a wedding reception barn venue, Blaise had thought Suz had lost her mind. But her friend had quickly sold the plan, backing up her excitement with lots of rock-solid information that supported both the need and profitability of the venture.

With Blaise's help and Dolfe's investment in time and effort, Ty and Suz had turned the dream into reality in only a few short months.

They'd found a big, dusty barn out in the country on twenty acres of farmland and woods. The property featured a picturesque creek running along behind the main building, a wide lawn with old growth evergreens, and a lovely bridge over the creek that would make a perfect spot for pictures.

Ty and Suz had turned the interior of the metal-sided barn into a beautiful space, with rustic looking cedar walls, a tall ceiling with the original beams, and cream-colored carpet that Blaise couldn't help thinking was going to be Hell on Earth to keep clean.

The public portion of the venue mostly consisted of one, giant room, with an alcove for coats and gifts, two bathrooms, and an open-air patio out back that served both as an outdoor kitchen and smoking lounge. The roof of the lounge was outfitted with industrial-sized heaters for cooler nights, and giant ceiling fans for sultry summer nights. The structure was mostly enclosed, with one wall entirely open so that smoke from cigars or the grill could escape harmlessly out into the night. The view through the open wall included the pretty little creek and bridge, as well as a few acres of grass, flower beds, and evergreen trees.

It was actually a really nice space that Blaise hoped they'd be able to use for future Honeybun parties. It was large enough to accommodate a family as big as the Honeybuns, even as they continued to grow.

The non-public part of the venue consisted of a storage room with a small office at the back, and a caterer's kitchen with restaurant-grade appliances.

The main room held fifty tables that were big enough to seat eight to ten people each, with chairs that Suz had covered in frilly white covers. Overhead, crystal chandeliers looked both opulent and kitschy against the age-darkened wood and were complimented by yard after yard of gossamer drapings, which hung from the rustic beams.

They'd added a small dance floor on one end, with a raised stage and glossy wood floors.

A swinging metal door in the back corner of the main space led to the caterer's kitchen, which contained ample refrigeration, a bank of industrial microwaves for reheating food that was brought in for events, and a couple of long, wide, stainless-steel counters for food prep. They'd added the kitchen space on Dolfe's suggestion, and it had required building a small annex of the main building. But Blaise realized it had absolutely been the right thing to do, and she was happy her friends had listened to her very smart fiancé.

Blaise had been intrigued as the couple turned the ugly building into something straight out of a fairy tale. All her doubts had slowly been swept away as she saw the enormous potential there.

And the last hurdle had been breached when they got their first clients, who were on their way to the venue at that very moment for a walk-thru.

Suz took a deep breath. "This is really going to happen, isn't it?"

Wrapping an arm around her friend, Blaise nodded, "It really is."

"I hope this couple isn't difficult," Suz said, frowning. She chewed on her bottom lip, clearly affected by the whole bridezilla conversation.

"We'll deal with whatever happens," Blaise said soothingly.

Suz nodded, giving Blaise a wide smile. "Have I told you that I'm so happy you're here to help us get this off the ground?"

"Only five times today," Blaise said, laughing. "But remember, it's only for the first few months." The wedding reception venue concept felt too much like working in a bar for Blaise's taste. She was happy to help out, but it wasn't what she wanted to do long-term for a living.

"I know," her friend said on a sigh. "But a girl can dream, can't she?"

"She absolutely can." Blaise swung her arm to encompass the entire space. "Look what happens when she does."

2

*B*laise handed Suz the last wrapped pair of crystal bride and groom champagne flutes as the bell to the outer door tinkled softly. The warning chimes didn't sound in the public rooms of the venue. They were set up to warn employees in situations where they were doing behind the scenes work and received visitors or deliveries.

"I'll tell the guys," Blaise said, as Suz hurried to organize the last of the glassware onto the overburdened shelf.

"Thanks, girlfriend."

Blaise stuck her head out the storeroom door and looked around for the two men. They were no longer at the table where they'd been sitting, and the surface had been emptied of beer bottles and wine glasses.

An attractive young couple came through the door. They didn't see her, but Blaise smiled as the bride's eyes widened in surprised pleasure. "Oh, honey, this is gorgeous!" She clapped her hands, her head swiveling as she took it all in.

Blaise ducked back inside. "They're not out there. Do you want me to stall our guests for a minute?"

Suz had her cell phone to her ear and was frowning at something the deep voice Blaise could hear on the other end was saying. She finally swung her gaze to Blaise and nodded, mouthing, "Please?"

Blaise hurried through the door into the main room, rubbing her grubby palms onto the sides of her jeans. She smiled at the young couple, who were standing in the center of the room, their heads dropped back as they perused the magical drapings high above their heads.

"Hello. You must be Kim and Lawrence." She hurried over, offering the bride her hand. "I'm Blaise."

Kim took Blaise's hand and pumped it energetically, her gray eyes sparkling. "Ms. Whats? I just love this place. Your description didn't do it justice."

Remembering the earlier conversation about names, Blaise fought a grin. Suz had made a decision to shorten the name she used at the venue because she thought their clients might have trouble pronouncing and spelling *Whatsnoggin*. Blaise had tried to talk her out of it, but her friend had spent a lifetime looking for a way to get out from under the name, and once she'd made up her mind, nothing could dissuade her.

Sort of like everything her friend did.

Blaise opened her mouth to clarify, but the groom cut her off. "I'm not wild about the location. It's really out in the boonies, isn't it?"

Blaise stared into the man's dark brown eyes, seeing a hostility there that surprised her. She noted the rigid set of his square jaw that told her as much as his words that the rustic setting hadn't been his first choice.

She gave him her bartender's smile. The one that didn't quite make it to her eyes. It was a warning that most men easily understood. He was welcome to his opinions. But Blaise was darned if he was going to rain all over her friends' enthusiasm by being mean about it. "This venue isn't for everybody," she told him in a casual tone. "But as far as the location, it's really only five minutes from Highway 70. From there, you're twenty minutes to downtown. It's actually very handy."

"It's perfect," said the man's delighted fiancée. She turned to him with such happiness on her face, even *his* belligerence melted beneath it. He gave her a smile that appeared genuine. "If it makes you happy, darling. That's all I want."

She clapped her hands and did a little spin, her

long, dark blonde hair spreading in a pretty fan around her as she twirled. "Let's get the details behind us so I can get back to my 'to do' list." She gave Blaise a look filled with feigned displeasure. "There's just so much to organize. Flowers, the caterer, music..." She sighed, clearly not half as put out by her list as she pretended.

"Well, then maybe we should start our tour in the caterer's kitchen," Blaise told her brightly.

"I'd love that!"

Blaise led them across the big room, pointing out details she thought the young bride-to-be would appreciate along the way. The soon-to-be-groom was a silent, brooding presence behind them. Kim either didn't notice, or she chose not to let ruin her buzz.

Blaise reached for the swinging door into the kitchen just as it pushed outward. She jumped back with a yelp, bumping against Kim and dancing sideways with an apology.

Tyrese came through the door with a sour look on his face, then blinked in surprise and managed to wipe the unhappy expression away just in time to catch Lawrence's eye. "Ah, hello." He grabbed Lawrence's hand and gave it a hearty shake. "I'm Tyrese Miller, co-owner of Wedding Belles." Lawrence frowned, but Ty didn't notice. He'd already turned his copious amount of charm on Kim. "Welcome. What do you think of the place? Everything is brand-spankin' new. None of your friends will have gotten married in a place just like it. It's totally unique."

Blaise had to give the man credit. He certainly knew how to appeal to the millennial bride-to-be.

Kim's pretty face lightened with pleasure. "I think it's just beautiful."

"Have you seen everything?" Ty asked them, sliding Blaise a look.

She shook her head. "We were going to start with the kitchen."

"Excellent choice," Ty said. He glanced toward Lawrence. "And after the kitchen, I have something I'd like to show *you*," His grin widened. "I think it might just sell you on using Wedding Belles."

Ty ushered the two into the kitchen ahead of him and glanced toward Blaise, lifting expressive, black eyebrows. "Thanks for getting them started."

"No problem," Blaise whispered. "Where were you? And where's Dolfe?"

Ty sighed. "Don't ask. Small problem with the generator. But Dolfe's working on it." He jerked his head toward the kitchen. "Best be getting back to them. Cross your fingers I can sell the groom on the smoking lounge. He looks like he's going to be hard to please."

Dolfe woke up with a start, lying perfectly still for a long moment trying to remember what had woken him. Something sharp and painful jabbed into his side, followed by movement on the mattress beside him and a long, low growl.

If the growl hadn't preceded a series of high-pitched yipping noises, he would have been alarmed. Instead, he grinned, reaching down to place a calming hand on Badly's soft tummy. The puppy went very still, took a deep, shuddering breath, and settled into a more restful sleep.

Dolfe hated to interrupt his dream of chasing a squirrel, or a bug, or a spec of dirt, but the dog was getting bigger, and his jabbing back legs were starting to become a liability.

The clock on the nightstand told him it was four o'clock in the morning.

Too dang early to get up.

Yet he'd have to get up soon anyway. They'd learned recently that their other dog, a cute little ball of spunk and fire they'd adopted less than a year earlier, suffered from seizures. The realization had devastated them. It had especially worried Blaise, who treated the devoted little dog like a baby and thought, as any mother would, that she needed to remove all obstacles to her furry little baby's happiness.

Unfortunately, she couldn't take the seizures away. The vet speculated little Miss Ivy had suffered head trauma at some point during her five years. All they could do was give her the prescribed medications, which lessened the symptoms and reduced the numbers of the attacks.

Morning, noon, and night doses.

They'd really had to work at making sure Miss Ivy got her mid-day meds, but they'd divvied up the four AM and eight PM meds so that Blaise could sleep in, and Dolfe would be free to do any late-night stakeouts his job required.

Sure, that meant Dolfe lost out on sleep. But he didn't need as much as Blaise anyway. And he didn't have to be married to know the truth of the old adage...when mama's happy...

Badly yipped again, having apparently found his way back to his dream, and his powerful back legs jerked straight, the tiny feet slamming into Dolfe's lower belly, way to close to more important things for his comfort.

Dolfe glanced at Blaise to make sure the dog's nocturnal activities hadn't woken her. She was curled around Ivy, their noses almost touching, both immobile in sleep.

He grinned at the sight. Ivy had one of her tiny legs thrown over Blaise's arm as if hugging her, and Blaise smiled in her sleep as if even in slumber she felt the pleasure of snuggling with her pet.

Dolfe carefully pushed the covers back and slid out of bed. He hit the button on his alarm clock to keep it from going off, and headed toward the door, yawning widely.

Behind him, a soft thump told him Badly had followed, and he waited for the little dog to patter through the door before closing it so the girls wouldn't hear them moving around the kitchen.

Badly licked the top of Dolfe's foot, grinning up at him, his tail wagging.

"Good morning, Mr. Bad. Did you catch the squirrel?"

Badly's tail increased its tempo to frantic levels, and the little furball took off running toward the kitchen. Dolfe followed more slowly, his body stiff from climbing around Ty's generator the night before. He'd finally gotten it working, but it had taken several calls to his cousins to figure it out.

There were eight of them, brothers, and with their variety of skills and interests, he could usually find one of them who could solve whatever problem he encountered.

The one exception to that was plumbing. Nobody seemed to know anything about plumbing. It was disappointing. And he was tempted to ask his aunt Wanda Honeybun to adopt a plumber prospect.

It seemed a reasonable request to Dolfe. What

was one more male in a family that was already way over the recommended limits on male offspring?

Badly stood at the back door, his entire back end wagging enthusiastically. Dolfe flipped on the backyard lights and let the puppy out to do his morning duty.

Badly surged out into the yard, disappearing past the arc of the light to visit his usual spot at the back corner of the yard.

They'd fenced in the whole back yard so they wouldn't need to worry about the dogs wandering off and getting into trouble. Or, more importantly, the occasional coyote that found its way into the residential neighborhood looking for easy prey.

He dropped a pod into the coffee maker and went to get a glass of water, drinking most of it before setting it down and grabbing the freshly brewed mug of coffee. By the time he'd taken his first sip, Badly was back, scratching softly at the door.

As Dolfe pulled it open, his cell phone rang. He frowned. A phone call at that hour of the morning did not bode well. He quickly answered, not surprised to see Detective Brita Muldane's name on the screen. "What's wrong?"

She didn't seem surprised by his assumption that she was calling with bad news. "Where's Tyrese?"

Dolfe's frown deepened. "I would assume he's home in bed. It's four in the morning."

"Believe me, Dolfe, I know what time it is. He's not answering his phone."

Dolfe heard the note of weariness in her voice. "Dispatch contacted me a little while ago. Called me out to Wedding Belles."

Dolfe relaxed slightly. Nobody he cared about was hurt. "Why?"

There was a beat of silence before she spoke again. "Somebody broke into the place."

"Robbers? Why'd they call you?" It was a fair question. Brita was a homicide detective. Though she filled in where needed when the uniforms were busy.

"They called me because they are aware that I know the owners..."

Dolfe nodded, sipping his coffee. "How much damage is there? Did they break through the front door? I told Ty he needed to get the security lights set up. He's going to explode into a billion pieces when he finds out he's been robbed..."

"Honeybun?" Brita interrupted. "Take a breath. You didn't let me finish."

Alarm made his pulse spike. "Finish what? What aren't you telling me?" he asked too loudly before he caught himself.

"Not for lack of trying..." she said dryly. "Tyrese is definitely going to explode. The storage area has been trashed. Stuff's broken, littering the floor and huge pieces of wall have been ripped out."

"I don't understand. You think somebody was searching for something?"

"It sure looks that way. I'd ask the guy who was here when I arrived, but, unfortunately, he's dead."

3

*B*laise stood well away from the door with Suz and Ty. Brita had insisted they stay outside the storeroom in the interests of preserving the scene. She had no idea how bad the damage was, aside from the quick glimpse she'd gotten as the uniformed officer Brita had posted in the doorway stepped to the side to let the morgue guys through with their black baggie covered stretcher.

Suz made a small sound as they caught a glimpse of the thick layer of broken glass and crushed boxes beyond the doorway.

Blaise reached out and wrapped an arm around her friend's shoulders. "Why don't you and Ty go on home? There's nothing you can do until they finish processing the building. It's going to take a while."

Suz turned a horrified gaze her way. "We can't clean it up?" She turned to Ty, fresh tears sparkling in her bright blue gaze. Tyrese reached out and pulled her into his arms, kissing the top of her head. "She's right, Suz. We'll just get in the way. We should get out of here, get some rest, and hit this hard tomorrow." His brown gaze caught Blaise's over Suzie's head, hardening as he saw the truth in her expression.

They most likely wouldn't be cleaning things up the next day either.

But Blaise understood the message in his eyes. One day at a time. At that moment, he needed to get the woman he loved out of there and into a better frame of mind.

"I'll call you if anything changes," Blaise promised.

She watched them leave a few minutes later, after Suz had all but wrung a promise out of her that she'd call later that day with a report.

Dolfe joined her a moment later, fixing the closing door behind their friends with a frown. "How's Suz holding up?"

"She's a mess." Blaise stepped into his arms, needing a hug.

"How are *you* doing?" he asked.

"I'm okay, I guess. But it kills me to think of what this means for them. They've worked so hard, and now everything's ruined."

He rubbed her back, his deep voice rumbling against her ear as she pressed into him. "It's not ruined." He put her at arm's length. "There's nothing that can't be replaced or repaired."

She grimaced. "Except for the fact that someone was murdered here. I'm not sure that's going to be much of an incentive for couples to hire Wedding Belles to host their receptions."

"It will be fine. The way people are nowadays, the first and strongest reaction will be regret they weren't here to take a selfie with the corpse."

Blaise snorted out an unexpected laugh. He wasn't wrong.

"Besides," he told her, smiling gently. "I know of one couple who won't be canceling."

She frowned for a moment, until she realized what he was saying. "Us?"

Kissing her on the nose, Dolfe pulled her back in for another hug. "I'd walk through a whole army of corpses to marry you, future wife."

"Oh," she pulled a face. "That's really... um...disturbing."

His laugh made her smile.

When they separated again, it was Blaise's doing. "Do you and Brit know what's going on?"

He shook his head. "Not yet. The dead guy was stabbed in the throat with a fork."

"Well, that's certainly a new one."

He nodded, glancing toward the stretcher coming out of the storage room with its new passenger. "Unless we're dealing with a serial killer whose chosen weapon is a fork, I'm thinking this is not premeditated."

She thought about that for a minute, then nodded. "You're thinking maybe there were two of them and they had an argument over something?"

"Possibly whatever it was they took out of the wall," he offered.

She rubbed her arms, thinking of the room where she and Suz had spent a couple of carefree hours putting stock away the day before.

"It will be okay, honey. We'll make it right again."

She nodded, knowing he meant what he said. She just didn't know if it was possible to erase the concept of what happened and return the venue to the fairytale spot it had seemed before.

The uniform in the door shifted sideways, and Brita came out of the storage room, pulling latex gloves off her long-fingered hands. Her gaze found Blaise's, and she gave her friend a commiserating look. "Hey. How you holdin' up?" she asked Blaise.

"Good," Blaise said as brightly as she could. Unfortunately, the tone of her voice came off as more hysterical than upbeat.

Brita glanced around. "Where are Ty and Suz?"

"I sent them home," Blaise said. "Suz was losing it."

Brita nodded. "I don't blame her. They did a real number on that room. The good news is that they didn't seem to touch anything in this room, the kitchen, or the bathrooms. The damage is contained."

Blaise knew Brita was trying to make her feel better. But the real damage had just been wheeled outside and placed into a morgue van. "Who was he?"

Brita and Dolfe shared a look which made Blaise stiffen warily. "What?"

"You didn't tell her?" Brita asked Dolfe.

He shook his head. "I thought you'd want to do it."

"Okay, you guys are scaring me now," Blaise said on a frown.

Brita sighed. "I'm afraid Suz and Ty have already lost their first clients."

Her meaning didn't immediately sink in. Instead, an instant sense of dread filled her as her worst fears seemed to be realized. "Kim and Lawrence canceled already? How in the world did they find out so fast?"

Brita continued to stare at her until her meaning sunk in.

"Oh. Oh no! Both of them?"

Brita shook her head. "It's just the groom." She checked the notes she'd typed into her cell phone. Blaise had been shocked when her friend had finally dumped her outdated pda method for keeping investigative notes and joined the rest of the world using a Notes app. "Lawrence Peck."

"I don't understand," Blaise said, shaking her

head. "Why would a client sneak into Wedding Belles in the middle of the night and start ripping out walls?"

Brita shook her head. "I have no idea. But I intend to find out. And, for starters, I have a lot of questions for the bride-to-be."

Blaise thought about Kim. The bright-eyed young woman hadn't seemed to have anything on her mind except planning a wedding. "I met her, Brita. She's sweet and harmless. A typical twenty-something woman who wants all the frills of a wedding that none of her friends have had. I'd be shocked if she's involved."

"I get that," Brita said, slipping her cell phone back into her pocket. "But she's the obvious first step."

Dolfe nodded toward the storage room door. "Do you need someone to watch that today?"

"No. I've got it covered. But thanks." She looked at Blaise. "I know Ty and Suz will want to get in here later today, but I'm afraid they need to stay out until we finish up."

"I know. I already told them. I'll remind Ty of it when I call them later."

"Good." Brita reached out and squeezed Blaise's hand. "I'm so sorry this happened. I'll try to expedite things so you can get back in and start repairs."

"I'd appreciate that. Thanks, girlfriend," Blaise told her with a weary smile.

Dolfe grabbed her hand as Brita turned back to the storage room. "How about I buy my beautiful future wife breakfast before she heads back to the drudgery of snuggling and feeding and playing with her two furry children?"

Blaise was tempted to take him up on the offer. But in that moment, she really needed the comfort of her own home, filled with the man she loved and her adorable dogs. "I have a better offer. How about I make us a big bowl of cereal and a carafe of coffee, and we sit outside and watch those two chuckle-heads chase bugs around for a bit. I think I'd rather be home right now. Do you mind?"

"Mind?" He tugged her toward the door. "Future wife, sometimes I think you can see inside my brain."

"Ugh!" She mock-shuddered. "What a terrifying thought."

B laise didn't call Ty and Suz because she didn't want to wake them up if they were managing to get some rest.

She soon learned the folly of that hope when her phone rang as they entered their cozy little cottage home, and she saw that it was Suz.

"I'll let the little beasts out," Dolfe told her as she answered the call.

"Thanks, future husband," she whispered before greeting Suz. "Hey, girlfriend. I was hoping you two were resting."

"There's no way we could rest after what happened."

Shrill barking erupted from the kitchen, and the soft stampede of tiny paws followed. Blaise smiled at the sound.

"Judging from the canine cacophony, I take it you and Dolfe are back home?" Suz asked.

"Just walked in the door."

"Good. Ty and I are about five minutes away. We'll see you soon?"

Her friend's voice was so hopeful Blaise didn't have the heart to turn her away, though she'd really been looking forward to some quiet moments with her little family to sort through what had happened at the venue. "Sure. See you in a few."

When he rejoined her a beat later, Dolfe took the news in stride. He nodded and started for the kitchen. "I'll make the coffee."

Blaise realized it would be cereal for four instead of two. Then she grimaced. It wasn't a very special breakfast for company. She'd have to cut up some fresh fruit to have with it. And she thought she might still have some muffins left over from the day before.

A few minutes later, Dolfe came in, frowning. He

was holding his cell phone in one hand. "Is something wrong?" she asked him.

He shook his head. "I'm not sure. That was my dad's assistant, Coop. He said Brick wants to meet us for dinner on Saturday."

"That will be fun. Why the long face?"

He stared at the phone for a beat and then seemed to shake himself out of his thoughts. "Nothing. Except, well, he mentioned that Brick has been under the gun lately and needed to get out of Washington for a while."

Blaise agreed that sounded a bit ominous. "I'm sure it's nothing. I mean, that entire city is a poisonous viper pit. Brick can certainly hold his own, whatever they're trying to throw at him."

Dolfe nodded. "I'm sure you're right. It's just that Coop sounded worried. I've never heard him sound that concerned before."

"Why don't you call Brick and ask?"

"I will later. Once we get Suz and Ty settled down and figure out what's going on at the barn."

ive minutes in the back yard watching Badly try to tackle his much faster, much more agile sister was enough to finally get the haunted look out of Suz's blue gaze. She nibbled on her muffin, eyes alight as Badly stalked Ivy. The little dog obviously thought his sister was too engrossed in the fly buzzing around her enormous ears to notice his clumsy approach.

But Blaise's little girl was clearly playing him. As he finally gave up the less-than-stealthy approach and bounded heavily in her direction, she shot sideways at the last moment, and he landed on his head, his fuzzy little butt in the air for a beat as he tumbled into a messy summersault just beyond where Ivy had been sitting.

Blaise and Suz erupted in giggles at the baby's ungainly landing. He jumped up, big ears flopping as he happily bounded toward his delighted audience, a mischievous light in his brown button eyes.

"Toes!" Blaise screamed as his fat little paws hit the concrete and he yipped gleefully, sharp little teeth gleaming in the morning sun. He headed straight for Suz's feet, probably knowing with a devil's uncanny instincts that she would least suspect his attack, and she jerked them off the ground just before he could pounce on her toes and start nibbling.

Hysterical with laughter as he bounced straight up into the air, tongue swiping wildly at her calves as he tried to get to her feet, Suz finally threw a chunk of muffin across the patio in a desperate attempt to distract him.

As always when dealing with a dog that has any amount of dachshund in it, the ploy worked like a charm. Though Blaise knew the rebound was going to be considerable.

"You know he's going to get your whole muffin now, right?"

Suz's eyes widened. "But I love this muffin."

Returning from the kitchen, Dolfe handed Suz a glass of orange juice. "You'd better eat as much as you can as fast as you can, then. Because he's going to be back in one, two..."

The puppy whipped around and bounced gleefully in her direction once again.

Suz took a giant bite of her muffin and threw it

over his head, causing him to flip around so fast he fell over. Unfortunately for him, in the seconds it took for him to untangle his stubby legs and too-long body from a messy pile, his sister snagged the hunk of muffin and disappeared under Blaise's chair with it.

"Awe," Blaise said, seeing his crestfallen reaction. "Here bad baby." She held out a chunk of banana from her fruit bowl, and he bounced happily over, taking the treat carefully from her fingers and then jumping into her lap to beg for the rest.

Blaise sighed. "No good deed goes unpunished," she murmured.

Ty emerged from the house a beat later, his brown gaze filled with sadness. He laid his cell phone on the glass table where they were having breakfast.

Dolfe turned to him. "Was that Brita?"

Ty nodded.

"What did she say?" Dolfe asked.

"They can't find Kim Vitters. The bride." He shook his head. "Brita's going with the assumption that she was there last night too and that either she was the one who killed Peck or she's on the run from the person who did."

Ty sipped his coffee, looking thoughtful.

"What do you know about them?" Dolfe asked the other man.

"Not much. Only that he's got...or had...a lot of

money to spend on the wedding. I got the impression it was family money rather than his own. He apparently wanted to get married somewhere in the Caribbean but he was humoring his bride with the rustic venue thing."

That certainly made sense, Blaise thought, given the man's attitude as he'd toured the barn.

Suz nodded, watching as Badly begged and bullied his way through the last of Blaise's fruit. "Alex knows them. Or at least Peck's family."

"Alex?" Blaise asked, frowning.

"A friend of Suz's father," Ty clarified as Suz nodded.

"Dad's a silent partner in Wedding Belles. He asked us to consider the couple as a personal favor to him."

"I wondered how you'd found them so fast. Have you spoken to Alex yet?" Dolfe asked.

Ty's frown deepened. "I just can't bring myself to pick up the phone. Not only did we kill off Alex's friends, but the investment in Wedding Belles probably just took a nose dive."

Seeing the effect of Ty's words on Suz's pretty face, Blaise spoke up. "Stop that, Tyrese. You didn't kill anybody. And the venue will be fine. We can fix everything that was damaged. You need to keep a positive spirit, my friend."

He shook his head. "It's a little hard to be positive right now, brown sugar."

Dolfe stiffened slightly at Ty's nickname for her. She reached over and clasped her fiancé's big, warm hand, giving it a squeeze. "Nobody said it would be easy," she reminded Ty. "But we have to do it. This is no time to give up. We *all* need to stay positive."

She stared at him until her message sunk in. He turned to Suz and forced a smile onto his face. "I'm sorry, babe. I'm just feeling sorry for myself."

She nodded. "Me too. But Blaise is right. We need to face this head on and fix it. Wallowing in despair isn't going to do anything for anybody."

"You got it," Ty told her, some of the tension sliding from his handsome face. Then he looked at Dolfe. "What's the plan for figuring this murder thing out?"

Blaise snickered. "Murder thing?" She shook her head. "You're a tool, Miller."

He spread his hands, his trademark cockiness returning. "Hey, brown sugar, you and the hulk there do the murder stuff, while me and Suz figure out the business stuff. You feel me?"

"I'm gonna feel you with my fist if you don't stop calling my fiancée brown sugar," Dolfe said in a too-pleasant voice.

Tyrese laughed, shaking his head. "I thought she might take exception to BS instead."

Blaise snorted. "Some would think BS was a good nickname for me."

Dolfe raised her hand to his lips, giving the back of it a lingering kiss. "Then, *some* would be wrong."

Alex Cox had a suite in a building a block off Monument Circle in downtown Indianapolis. The building had dark granite floors, and walls painted a creamy gold, with brass finishes on all the doors and black granite walls around the elevators.

Huge pots of exotic flowers turned the space into a garden in the midst of a concrete jungle and perfumed the air as they read the large brass sign which listed all the building's businesses.

Cox Beauty Industries had the entire top floor to itself.

Blaise blinked several times when she saw the name of the company. "How does Ty know this Alex guy?"

They rode the elevator to the fourth floor and stepped out into a long hallway, which led to a series of glass walled spaces that looked like training areas. Even at the relatively early hour, the spaces already hummed with young women and men performing a variety of beauty and training exercises. The place smelled like expensive beauty products and flowers.

Alex Cox's office was at the end of the hallway.

Dolfe smiled, heading for the single desk in the

lobby of the offices. "Through Suz's family. Remember?"

"Ah, that's right." She shook her head. "Seeing all this, I thought for a moment he might have a whole 'nuther secret life."

"Like selling beauty cream?" Dolfe asked on a grin.

She snorted. "Well, he does have really good skin."

The woman behind the short, curved desk in the business office stood as they came through the door, her close-lipped smile looking a bit strained. She was on the tall side, with slightly bulging brown eyes and heavy lips she'd painted a dark burgundy that went well with her skin tone. She shoved at the cap of straightened black hair framing her narrow face and looked down her nose at them. "Can I help you?"

Dolfe pulled his credentials out of his pocket. "Dolfe Honeybun Investigations. We'd like to speak with Alex Cox."

The woman frowned, crossing curvy arms over a flat chest. She shook her head. "I'm afraid that isn't possible. Unless you have an appointment?" She lifted midnight black brows, her gaze filled with something that looked like hostility.

Blaise couldn't imagine what they'd done to annoy the woman. Until she took note of the woman's lip curling when she looked from Dolfe to her.

Ah. Problem identified.

Blaise let a wide smile transform her face. "We're here at the behest of Detective Brita Muldane. She thought it might be easier on your boss to speak with us here instead of having to come down to the station. Of course, if you'd like us to call and tell Detective Muldane we can't get in to see your boss…"

Dolfe cleared his throat, studiously avoiding Blaise's eye. Okay, it was a tiny lie, but she was confident Brita would back them up if push came to shove.

Besides, watching the other woman slide a hostile glare over her fiancée, Blaise thought it might come to shoving sooner than expected.

Dolfe didn't seem to notice. But Blaise knew better. He didn't miss anything. "Are you sure Alex can't give us a few minutes," he asked in a pleasant voice. "I assure you it will be much less painful in the long run."

The woman's upper lip actually curled. Finally, she inclined her head, the movement tight. "I'll see if she can squeeze you in." She stalked away, disappearing through a door marked with the words, *Employees Only*.

Dolfe looked at Blaise and grinned.

"Don't enjoy this so much, Honeybun. I'm about to rearrange her hateful face."

"She's not worth it," he said, wrapping an arm around Blaise's shoulders. He pulled her in for a long, lingering kiss. Blaise's toes curled inside her pumps, and the temperature in the room seemed to spike.

The door opened again as Blaise's world started to tilt and she totally forgot about the woman for a long, delicious moment.

Until the receptionist made a sound of pure disgust.

Dolfe let the kiss linger a few more beats before slowly lifting his lips.

Blaise's knees wobbled a bit as he turned to the receptionist. "Any luck?"

The woman's face was like a granite mask. Her full lips pursed with clear rage. Rather than respond verbally, she pointed down the hall. Then, without a word, she walked away from them and left the office.

Dolfe lifted a golden eyebrow. "Ladies room?"

"She's probably in there sharpening her claws. Harpies need to do that every once in a while."

He chuckled, indicating the door the hostile receptionist had left open. "After you, future wife."

"Why, thank you, future husband."

"Come in."

The voice that called out to them when Dolfe knocked on Alex Cox's door was decidedly more feminine than Dolfe had expected. He and Blaise shared a look as he pushed it open.

The woman sitting behind the glass-topped desk was tiny, the hands wrapped around the soggy tissue were veiny and misshapen, probably from arthritis. If he hadn't looked at her face, Dolfe would have assumed the woman was well into her seventies. But her features were smooth, the deep blue eyes carefully made up, with no visible bags underneath, and her narrow shoulders were squared, her back ramrod straight. She dragged the soggy tissue beneath her nose and nodded in their direction. "Please, have a seat. You're from the police?"

Dolfe placed his hand in the small of Blaise's back and urged her forward, his speculative gaze locked on Alex Cox as they approached. Given the treatment they'd suffered in the outer office, he wondered if the problem came from the top or was just the receptionist's problem.

He saw nothing in Alex Cox's well-drawn features to indicate anything but curiosity. She reached across the desk and took Blaise's hand, squeezing it as she gave them an apologetic smile. "Forgive me for not standing. I'm afraid I hurt my knee playing golf last week. It takes me so long to stand up it's not even worth it."

"Oh no," Blaise said, instantly solicitous. "Did you break something?"

Alex shook her head. "It's just a bad sprain. But it hurts like the dickens." She flushed prettily. "I'm afraid I've never been very good with pain."

Dolfe waited for Blaise to sit down and then sat in the white club chair next to her. "Ms. Cox, I'm Dolfe Honeybun..."

"Brick's son, right?"

He blinked in surprise. "You know my dad?"

"We've had dinner a few times."

Dolfe didn't even try to hide his surprise at that. "Dinner? Should I be worried about this?"

She laughed gaily. "Don't flatter me, son. I'm a good two years older than your father." Her eyes twinkled. "Give or take a decade." She looked at the tissue in her hand and made a face, dropping it into a small trash can beneath her desk as if deciding she was finished with grieving. "I lobbied him when the new beauty school regulations were being developed. I'd hoped to head off the train wreck. Unfortunately, the train was hurtling out of control down the mountain already." She shook her head.

"Train wreck?" Blaise asked.

"Politicians deciding what's best for the beauty industry without talking to the people who understand it." She sighed. "It's bad enough I keep losing my girls to the sunny southern climes, now I have the federal government micromanaging my business."

Blaise smiled. "Losing your girls? Where are they going?"

Alex nodded. "My trainers are the best in the business, Ms. Runa. Many of them do catalog modeling on the side. There's a lot of business for them on the white sand beaches of Florida."

Dolfe sat forward, recapturing the woman's tear-reddened gaze. "You heard about Lawrence Peck?"

Her face fell, and she nodded. "Poor boy."

"Do you know why he might have been in that building last night?"

"I have no idea, son. I've been sitting here wondering that myself."

"Do you know who might have wanted him dead?" Dolfe asked gently.

She blinked rapidly, her eyes glistening with the tears she was fighting to contain. She sniffled and then looked up at Dolfe. "This is the point where I'm supposed to tell you that everybody loved Lawrence. That nobody would even think about hurting him."

Dolfe widened his eyes in question. "*Is* that what you're telling me?"

Her lips twisted as if she were chewing the inside of them. She seemed to be carefully considering her response. Finally, she shook her head. "No. I'm not telling you that because it would be a lie. I liked the boy. He's made me tens of thousands of dollars over the years. But he was a bit of a shark. He made enemies, Mr. Honeybun. Lots of them. I wish I could say I was surprised he'd been murdered. But I'm not surprised in the least."

"In this long list of enemies," Dolfe asked. "Does anyone stand out from the others?"

"Not really, no."

"Would you be willing to compile a list of the people who held a grudge against Lawrence?"

"I can do that. It might take me a couple of days though. My schedule's pretty full."

"I understand," Dolfe said. "But this is kind of important. Lawrence's fiancée might be in danger."

Her charcoal gray brows lifted. "Kim? Why would that sweet girl be in danger?"

"The police can't locate her. They're afraid she was there with him when he was killed."

Alex held his gaze for a long moment and then expelled air, chuckling softly. "Oh, what a relief."

Dolfe frowned, perplexed. "Excuse me?"

"Kim couldn't have been with him last night."

Blaise and Dolfe shared a look. Blaise leaned forward. "Do you know where she is, Ms. Cox?"

"Of course, dear. Lawrence packed her off to Miami yesterday afternoon."

5

"*M*iami Florida?" Dolfe asked.

The woman's eyes narrowed slightly. "I don't believe there's a Miami in Ohio or Illinois...but I could be wrong."

He gave her the smile she'd earned. "I'm sorry for seeming a bit daft. It's just that I'm surprised to hear he sent her away. We just saw them yesterday afternoon. Do you know if this trip was planned?"

"I don't know, for sure. But I got the impression it wasn't. Lawrence was in quite a tizzy in the morning. He wasn't at all happy about Kim's desire to get married in *that* place."

Blaise stiffened slightly, drawing the astute woman's gaze. "I've offended you." It wasn't a question. Alex Cox was a keen judge of temperament.

"A little, yes. My friends own Wedding Belles."

"We've been helping them get it ready for business," Dolfe said, squeezing Blaise's knee and giving her a smile. "It's a beautiful place."

Alex flapped her fingers dismissively. "Don't pay any attention to me, kids. I'm a bit of a snob, I'm afraid. That's what happens when your parents have more money than God, and you grow up thinking the world is yours." She chuckled softly. "With age comes wisdom, of course. But I'm still stuck in my old patterns. I actually checked it out when Kim told me about it. You're right. It is beautiful. But I can also see why Lawrence had his aristocratic nose out of joint. His family and mine are...shall we say...of a similar bent?"

"He comes...came...from a wealthy family too?" Blaise asked.

"He did. His granddaddy and I were in the same class at Yale. We've been friends for a long time." She looked thoughtful for a moment. "Actually, I'd thought the two of them were a strange match when Lawrence told me they were dating. I'd believed he would fall for Kendra Baxter, our cosmetology educator. Kendra was a little rough around the edges, but she had big ideas about where she wanted to end up, just like Lawrence." She chuckled wistfully. "And she was definitely his type. He liked them blonde and blue-eyed."

Dolfe nodded thoughtfully before speaking. "Ms. Cox..."

"I'd be very grateful if you'd call me Alex."

"Alex...the man you describe doesn't sound like someone who'd break into a wedding venue and rip out some walls."

"Or get himself killed while doing it," she added, nodding. "I agree."

"You can understand our confusion. I was really hoping, since you know him so well, that you could shed some light on what he might have been doing there."

"The only thing I can come up with is sabotage."

Blaise and Dolfe shared a surprised look.

"Sabotage?" Blaise asked, clearly perplexed by the suggestion.

"Yes, dear. Lawrence had his heart set on getting married at Indianapolis Museum of Art, or on a yacht in the Caribbean. He envisioned them wallowing in old money and luxury. But I'm afraid Kim is a very down-to-earth girl."

"It sounds like they were mismatched," Dolfe said.

"Possibly," Alex agreed, pursing her lips thoughtfully. "Whatever that boy was up to, he loved Kim more than anything. He would have given her that barn for their wedding if he couldn't have found a way around it." She leaned forward, resting her elbows on the desktop and clasping the gnarled hands. "But Lawrence was a very resourceful young man. It wouldn't surprise me at all to find out that he'd been thinking of trashing that place so he wouldn't have to get married there."

They decided to stop by Ty's Place for a sandwich before heading back to Dolfe's office to try and locate Kim. Dolfe knew a couple of cops in Miami, and he figured they could help him in the search.

Blaise called Brita on the way to see if she could meet them for lunch to discuss what they'd learned from Alex Cox.

She sounded a bit harried but agreed. "If I don't come meet you guys I'll probably just work right through lunch, and then poor Percy'll have a hangry fiancée to deal with at dinner time."

Blaise grinned, knowing her friend wasn't lying. "With seven troublesome brothers, I'm sure Percy knows how to handle one hungry woman. Plus, he's a Honeybun, he's probably done *something* to deserve a little abuse."

Brita laughed. "I can think of five things just since he woke up this morning. I'll see you in a bit."

Blaise hung up with a smile on her face and turned to catch Dolfe giving her a look. "What?"

"He's a Honeybun, so I'm sure he deserves abuse?"

"That's not exactly what I said," she waffled, fighting to keep from laughing.

"Close enough for government work."

She leaned across the console and gave him a kiss on a bristly cheek. "Present company excluded, of course."

He harrumphed. "Is she meeting us?"

"She is."

"Good. I'd like to run this Miami thing past her before we talk to the fiancée."

"It seems a little random, doesn't it?" Blaise agreed. "They must have family there or something."

He nodded. "I'm hoping Brita can find that out for me."

Dolfe had to stop for gas and, by the time they walked into their friend's bar at a little after noon, there was already one rowdy table harassing Suz and Tyrese.

Several faces turned to stare at them as Dolfe and Blaise came into the bar, still blinking from the transition of the sunny day outside.

A wolf whistle made Dolfe's fingers tighten against her back. Blaise shook her head. "Don't be such a jerk, Honeybun." She wasn't speaking to her future husband.

Dolfe's cousin, Clovis laughed, unrepentant.

Dolfe expelled a breath, steering Blaise toward the table of three men and two women, his usual good humor missing in action.

Clovis Honeybun stood and pushed a chair out as they approached. "Have a seat, beautiful. And hurry, there's something big and ugly right on your heels."

Ignoring the chair, Blaise rolled her eyes and leaned down to give Clovis's fiancée Emma a hug. "Hey, girlfriend. How's my beautiful little niece?"

Emma's six-year-old daughter Cilla was technically not Blaise's niece, but Emma had taken to referring to all the Honeybuns as either Aunts or Uncles. Little Cilla, short for Pricilla, was spoiled to death and generally had the whole family, men and women, tightly wrapped around her tiny finger.

"She's perfect. A brat of course. But what do you expect when she has twenty people at her constant beck and call?"

Blaise dropped into the seat next to Emma and glanced across the table, where Brita was having an enthusiastic argument with her very own Honeybun, Percy. She gave the other woman a little finger wave, and Brita returned it before smacking Percy on the arm. "Where are your manners, Honeybun?"

Percy grinned at Blaise. "Hey, Blaise. How many dogs are you up to now?"

"Only two," Blaise said, pouting theatrically as Dolfe eased into the chair next to her. "Don't encourage her, cuz. If it was up to her, we'd have ten of the things scurrying around."

Suz settled a basket overflowing with fries and

an enormous burger in front of Brita. The cop plucked a french fry from the basket as she nodded. "Tell me about it. Percy's trying to talk me into getting a sixth dog."

"What's one more when you have five already," he said, winking at Blaise.

"It's six. That's what one more is," Brita told him, stealing an onion ring from Percy's basket. "And it would be the straw that broke this camel's back," she finished, holding the ring behind her so he couldn't take it back.

A big hand came out of nowhere and snagged the treat from between her fingers. Brita turned with a cry of outrage.

Edric shoved the onion ring into his mouth. "Thanks, sis."

Brita reached for her gun and grimaced when she realized she didn't have it. "You're lucky I practice good gun safety policies."

Edric turned a chair around and dropped into it, his gray gaze sparkling with humor. "I'd kill for a fry."

She put her hands over her food basket, blocking him. "You'll *be* killed if you try to take one of my fries," she told him.

Chuckling good-naturedly, Suz settled two big glasses of water in front of Dolfe and Blaise. "What can I get you two?"

"Grilled tenderloin and fries for me," Blaise said.

"Same," Dolfe agreed before returning his attention to Clovis. They were discussing the new Veterans facility the Honeybun family was sponsoring, a favorite project for the whole family. After meeting the man who'd inspired their second puppy, Badly, Blaise was thrilled with the effort. And she was happy Dolfe had suggested using their friend Kyle Reese for a consultant.

After he'd gotten the vet a job at Tyrese's Bar.

She glanced up and smiled as a big, warm hand found her shoulder. "Hey, Blaise."

If she hadn't seen him recently, Blaise wouldn't have even recognized Kyle. The vet had cut his dark hair short, and it was freshly washed. He was dressed in a clean blue t-shirt that framed his broad shoulders and his sculpted torso. His eyes had lost a lot of the haunted look she remembered from the first time they'd met. The soldier suffered from PTSD and had struggled to find a way to deal with it. That is, until Dolfe came up with the idea of getting him another dog.

"Hey, yourself. How's Lila?"

He flushed with pleasure. "She's getting so big and fat." He laughed. "She's always hungry."

"Dachshunds are like that," Brita said, smiling at him as he glanced her way shyly. "They'd eat until they exploded if you let them."

He nodded. "I have trouble saying no to her."

"Puppies are supposed to be chubby," Brita told

him. "But don't let her get too fat after she turns one. They can have back problems if they carry around too much weight."

He looked thoughtful for a moment, measuring her words, and then nodded. "Thanks. That's good to know. Jack hardly ate anything, so I'm not used to this." He chuckled. "Food was love when I was growing up."

Blaise chuckled. "Around this group, food is war."

As if to prove her point, Edric snatched a fry from Brita's basket.

"Hey!" She pounded her fist into his knee, and he didn't even blink. "You snooze you lose, sis."

"I'm not your sister. I don't claim you."

He snagged her around the neck with a long arm and pulled her close, kissing the top of her light brown head as Percy chuckled. "Sorry, I won't let you ignore me."

Kyle was drawn into the conversation about the veteran's center, his tanned face becoming animated as the other men asked him for his opinions.

"I'll go get Edric's food so he'll leave you alone," Suz told Brita.

"Thank you!"

Before Suz could walk away, Blaise grabbed her hand. "Hey, how are you doing?"

"Good." Suz's assertion was weak, but she followed it up with a smile. "I promise. I'm okay. Ty and I are just anxious to get back in there and start repairing the damage."

"We want to help, okay?" Blaise told her friend.

"All of us," Brita added as she huddled protectively over her basket of food.

Heads bobbed around the table. Blaise felt something warm blossoming in her chest. She'd felt it many times before when she'd watched the Honeybun clan come together to help someone who needed it.

Tears sparkled in Suz's eyes. "Thank you. All of you. That means a lot to us."

Edric took advantage of Brita's moment of distraction to dive for another fry. She gave another squeak of outrage. "You can thank me by getting this big, ugly raccoon his own food so he'll leave mine alone."

Laughing wetly, Suz saluted. "Ma'am, yes, ma'am."

Clovis inclined his chin as she walked past. "Good work, soldier."

"Where are Bella and little Matilda?" Blaise asked Edric.

"With gramma," he flushed with pleasure. "She's taking them out to lunch and to the play area for Tildy's almost-birthday."

"Almost-birthday?" Emma said, pulling a face. "Is that a thing?"

Edric sighed. "It is now. If my mother thought

she could get away with it, she'd probably have a party for every single month of that child's life."

"She's so thrilled to finally have a little girl to spoil," Brita said, wiping catsup off her lips.

"Well, hopefully, Angie will have a girl too and take some of the pressure off little Tildy."

"Yeah, because she's just hating being fussed over, fed cupcakes and forced to play on the climbing thingy," Percy said.

"Ha ha." Edric leaned back as Suz placed a basket of food in front of him.

Brita didn't even wait for it to hit the table before her hand was knuckles deep in his fries.

Dolfe didn't get around to speaking with Brita about the murder until everyone had finished eating and the other Honeybuns had left to return to their respective jobs.

When he finally had her alone, he didn't waste any time. "Have you talked to Mr. Whatsnoggin yet?"

Brita shook her head. "I was thinking about that. Since you're friends with his daughter, it might go over better if you two talked to him first."

Blaise nodded. "I agree. He's very protective of Suz. He's not going to like the fact that a man he sent to the venue broke in and was murdered there. He's likely to blame Tyrese. I don't think you'll get beyond that with him. But we might."

Brita nodded. "I agree."

"We spoke to Peck's boss, Alex Cox," Dolfe told their friend.

Brita wiped her greasy hands on a napkin. "What did he say?"

"She. Alex Cox is a woman I'd guess to be in her mid to late sixties. Apparently, Mr. Peck was her star salesman who came from money and was a bit of a snob."

She dropped the napkin into her empty basket and leaned forward, crossing her arms on the table in front of her. "Is that pertinent?"

"I'm not sure. Alex seemed to think it might be. Peck apparently had visions of an elegant wedding and Ms. Cox didn't think it was beneath him to sabotage Wedding Belles to get it."

"I take it he didn't want to get married there?"

"Stupid man," Blaise said, frowning.

"I'm afraid Lawrence and his lovely future wife weren't on the same page. At least according to his boss."

"He had his nose up in the air the whole time they were taking the tour," Blaise said.

"Ms. Cox believes *that* was his motive for being there last night?" Brita asked.

"She didn't really know. But she offered that as a possibility."

Brita studied her short, unpainted nails for a minute, frowning slightly. Finally, she shook her head. "I'm not buying it. He was looking for something in that storeroom. I'd stake my badge on it."

"I tend to agree," Dolfe said. "Which leaves us with the big question. What was he or the person who killed him looking for?"

"I think the bigger question is, did they find it?" Blaise offered. When Dolfe and Brita focused on her with questioning gazes, she added. "Because, if they didn't, they might be back."

asil Whatsnoggin lived in a big house in the upscale Indianapolis suburb of Carmel, Indiana. The big colonial style home was at the very end of the street, set back from the road on a perfectly manicured ten-acre plot with tall, wrought-iron fencing and a gated driveway.

The gate was open, probably because Blaise had called ahead and was told Mr. Whatsnoggin would be expecting them. When they drove up, he was standing on the wide, front porch, looking small beneath the fourteen-foot-high ceiling that ran across the entire front of the large home.

He started down the steps, hands shoved into his pockets and expression tense as Dolfe stopped the truck in front of the house.

Blaise didn't wait for Dolfe to come around. She opened her door and stepped out quickly, stepping into the older man's outstretched arms. "How are you, my girl? Suz worries about you doing all this investigative stuff." His deep voice held only the barest hint of the English accent he'd developed in his birth country.

Blaise found herself hunching a bit so she wouldn't tower over the diminutive man. But, as usual, he didn't seem to notice. His worried expression was locked on hers. "I'm fine. I have lots of protection." She turned, smiling as Dolfe walked over and took the older man's hand.

"Mr. Whatsnoggin."

Whatsnoggin gave Dolfe's hand a firm shake and then dropped it. "None of that, now. Call me Basil. I know it's a silly name, but you of all people should understand it."

Dolfe chuckled. "It's like my mother named you."

Basil guffawed. "How *is* your lovely mother?"

"She tells me she's great. She spends most of her time on a beach in Cancun. I haven't seen her for a few months."

Basil nodded. He'd been a good friend to them when Dolfe's parents were going through their divorce. "And your father?"

"Brick is good. He told me to tell you he's ready for another round of golf. He plans to be in Indianapolis next week."

Basil nodded, smiling. "Excellent. I'll get in touch and we can set a time." His smile slid away, and his handsome face turned serious. "Suz is safe? They only let me speak to her once. She said someone broke into their new place." He shook his head, reaching up to scratch the dense crown of wavy blond hair, so like his daughter's. "It sounds like a bad thriller movie."

"They're upset," Dolfe assured the other man. "But they're safe."

Whatsnoggin nodded. "Come inside. I've made some fresh lemonade."

If any other wealthy single man had told her he'd made lemonade, Blaise would have been skeptical. She would have assumed a housekeeper had actually made it, or that he'd purchased it from a fancy grocery store. But she totally believed Suz's father would squeeze his own lemons and make fresh lemonade. He might be a successful entrepreneur, selling some kind of widget that had to do with computers or something, but he'd been a single dad for longer than he'd been an entrepreneur. Suz's mom had died of cancer when Suz was ten years old. He was very good at playing the part of both parents.

Basil's home was sparsely furnished, the highly polished dark wood flooring of the living room and hallway sporting only a few rugs, a small catchall table beside the front doors, and a couch, two chairs and a matching table set in the living room. The house was cool, almost uncomfortably so, but Blaise knew from hanging out with Suze for years that the Whatsnoggins ran hotter than most.

"Come on into the kitchen," Basil directed them, leading them down the wide hallway that was lined on both sides with dozens of pictures of Suz and him. He'd captured every age, showing her progression from a chubby baby to an adorable toddler, to a sweet-tempered girl, to a beautiful young woman. The early years had also included Suz's mom. She'd been a stunning strawberry blonde who could have graced the pages of any fashion magazine.

Suz had inherited her mother's beauty, but she hadn't gotten her height from her mother. At only five feet four inches, she'd taken after her dad in that department.

Despite the slightly dated dark cabinets and dark flooring of the kitchen, the large picture window framing the breakfast nook turned the space into a place of light and beauty. Beyond the glass, endless flower gardens and perfectly sculpted shrubbery brought to mind the English gardens from another time, which reflected Basil's family history and showcased his favorite hobby.

"Please, sit." He motioned toward a marble-topped table in front of the windows and they obliged, sliding into two of the four sun-dappled chairs.

A large, red maple tree was strategically placed

about fifteen feet from the glass to block the worst of the sun and, as a soft breeze made its branches dance, had the added benefit of sending a play of stippled light across the windows that was truly enchanting.

Blaise looked up as Basil placed a frosty glass of lemonade in front of her, complete with a thin slice of lemon on the edge. "This is beautiful. Thanks, Basil."

He nodded, settling a matching glass in front of Dolfe. "It's lemonade weather for sure." He reached to pull a plate off the center island, adding it to the collection of glasses on the table. "Orange cranberry scones. My mother's recipe. They're really quite delicious."

Dolfe snagged one and bit into it. "Mm, this is great," he mumbled around a mouthful.

Basil smiled, settling himself into a third chair. He wrapped his hands around his glass but didn't drink from it. "I assume you're here to ask about young Lawrence."

"We are. How do you know him?"

Basil glanced at Dolfe. "Know him? I don't. Not really."

"Then why did you recommend him to Suz?" Blaise asked.

"My friend Alex told me one of her employees was getting married and I knew Suz needed clients for her new venture so..." He frowned. "I didn't think

too deeply on it, I'm afraid. As it turns out, I probably should have."

He looked so miserable. Blaise reached over and
gave his hand a squeeze. "There's no way you could
have known."

Basil shrugged, his face filled with worry. "That's
just it. I probably should have. Alex is a bit of a..." He
shook his head, seeming to decide against saying
whatever he was going to say.

"A bit of a what?" Dolfe nudged.

"I don't know. She's kind of a mess, actually."

That surprised Blaise. "Really? My impression of
her was that she was very sharp."

"Oh, you've met Alex?" Basil asked, smiling
fondly. "Yes, in business she's very sharp. And she's a
kind person...deep down...but she has no idea about
people. She has no instincts for picking the good
from the bad. I should have known when she
encouraged me to contact Suzie about the boy that it
was a poor idea."

"Do you have any idea why Lawrence Peck might
have been at Wedding Belles in the middle of the
night?"

"Not a clue," he finally said. "I understood from
Alex the boy wasn't taken with the place. But his
fiancée apparently loved it."

"When did you speak to Alex?" Dolfe asked the
other man.

Basil glanced at the round clock on the wall. "It's

been a couple of hours, now, I think."

Dolfe and Blaise shared a look. "And she didn't tell you she'd spoken to us?" Dolfe asked, his tone incredulous.

"No. She didn't." Basil shook his head. "That's odd, isn't it?"

"Yes, it's very odd," Blaise agreed.

"Y ou know what else is odd?" Dolfe asked her later as he drove toward his office. "When we spoke to Alex Cox, she had her nose firmly in the air about Wedding Belles. Now we learn from Suz's dad that she practically begged him to present them to Suz as clients."

"On the surface, it does seem odd. But don't forget Basil is Suz's dad. Alex wouldn't have wanted to bad-mouth the place to him," Blaise said. "I find his comment that Alex is a mess very interesting, though. She didn't seem a mess to me."

"No, she didn't."

When they reached Dolfe's office, there was a strange car sitting in the small gravel lot Dolfe had added off the driveway. It was one of those miniature cars that always reminded Blaise of a clown car.

It had Georgia plates.

"Rental car?" Blaise asked Dolfe.

He nodded. "Probably."

"Were you expecting a client?"

"Not until later." Dolfe did a quick visual scan of the area and then glanced at the car again. Even from where Blaise sat, she could see it was empty. "Wait here." He slipped out of the truck and tugged his Glock 9 from the holster he wore in the center of his back. Dolfe approached the small car from the rear and avoided a direct line of advance to the windows.

He peered inside, frowning.

A beat later, Dolfe walked back to the truck, pulling open her door and offering her a hand down.

Blaise had resisted his old-fashioned manners at first, but she'd grown to love the fact that he liked to treat her like a lady. She slipped her arm through his, and they headed toward the freshly painted front door of the mid-century brick ranch Dolfe had rehabbed into the office for *Honeybun Enterprises Private Investigations*.

Dolfe kept his gun out, holding it down by his side as they approached the building.

At the door, he motioned for her to hang back and turned the knob, lifting his gun as the door opened without a key. He shoved the door inward and stepped inside, his gun in both hands.

Tension turned her muscles to iron as Blaise watched him enter. He never left the front door unlocked. Whoever had driven the strange car into the lot had apparently broken into the office too.

Although, it occurred to Blaise that they'd be pretty stupid to leave their car parked in front if they were up to no good.

Dolfe's grim expression lightened, and he lowered the gun, finally sliding it into its holster as he shook his head. "Are you stupid? I could have shot you," he told the petite woman sitting in a hard-plastic chair in his waiting room. But he was smiling.

He offered Blaise his hand and she took it, allowing him to tug her through the door.

She came out of the afternoon sunshine just as the small woman with long, golden-brown hair and amused brown eyes dropped a magazine on a table and unfolded herself from the chair. "Honeybun. I see you're still freakishly tall."

Dolfe strode forward and wrapped the tiny woman in a welcome hug. "And I see you're still cartoonishly short."

Dolfe wasn't kidding. Blaise figured the tiny cop couldn't be much more than five feet tall. And that was in two-inch heels. She hurried forward and claimed her own hug. "JJ! How are you? And what the heck are you doing in Indianapolis? Florida's heat finally get the best of you?"

Joanna Granger, a.k.a. JJ for her nickname Jumpin' Jo, stepped back and lost her smile. "I wish I was here for pleasure, but I'm not." She looked at

Dolfe. "It's come to my attention that you're looking into the murder of Lawrence Peck."

Dolfe skimmed Blaise a look. "We're helping Brita out on it, yeah. Why?"

She shoved a small hand into the heavy curtain of wavy hair around her face. "I've got a connected case in Miami."

Blaise realized what their friend was going to say at the same time Dolfe did.

He expelled air, looking down at his shoes. "Kim Vitters."

JJ nodded. "We got a call early this morning. Room service brought her the breakfast she'd ordered the night before and found her dead in her bathtub. Stabbed in the heart."

Blaise's knees softened under her, and she had to lower herself to a chair. "That poor woman." She thought of the bright spark of life in Kim Vitters's eyes. The obvious excitement about her upcoming wedding. And the delight in the venue as she looked around. "How horrible."

"Yeah," JJ agreed. "Everybody I've spoken to loved her. Nobody has any idea why someone would want to do this."

"I have to ask..." Dolfe said, skimming a look toward Blaise.

JJ shook her head. "No signs of sexual assault."

He nodded. "No idea why she was killed?"

JJ hesitated just a beat too long. But it was the

way her gaze skimmed away from Dolfe's that had Blaise's heart rate spiking. She was suddenly sure she didn't want to hear what JJ was about to say.

"Unfortunately, I have a suspicion. And it's ugly."

"What is it?" Dolfe asked, suddenly impatient.

Blaise wondered if he was harboring the same horrible thought she was.

"Lawrence Peck has connections with some pretty seedy and dangerous people," she told them.

Dolfe arched an eyebrow. "Obviously."

JJ shook her head.

"Just spit it out, JJ," Dolfe barked.

She stared at the toes of her scuffed boots for a moment and then sighed. "I'm afraid he was related to our old friend."

"Blanchette?" Dolfe said through stiff lips.

"His cousin."

Dolfe held her gaze for a moment and then nodded toward his office. "I think we'd better sit down. You need to tell me everything you know, JJ. Because if Blanchette's back in action, Blaise is in serious danger."

A while back, before they became engaged and, in fact, when they were broken up, Blaise had witnessed a woman being murdered on a Miami beach. Being in the wrong place at the wrong time had turned Blaise into a target for the man she'd seen commit the murder.

Blanchette was a powerful man. A man without scruples or even common human decency. A man who'd looked at Blaise and seen a commodity to be sold to the highest bidder.

A man Dolfe Honeybun had fought to send to prison for the rest of his miserable life.

Unfortunately, Austen Blanchette's powerful friends had gotten him released from custody despite the horror of his crimes, and those same powerful interests had dragged the trial out so long Dolfe was convinced some of the parties had forgotten why they were even going through the motions.

Through it all, Blanchette had turned an uncon-cerned smile to the world, his manner relaxed and congenial in every television interview. And there had been many of those. Each and every time he'd been asked if he'd murdered that beautiful young woman on the beach on a sultry Miami night, he'd looked directly into the camera and frowned as if so bothered that anyone would think such a thing of him. Then he'd professed his innocence, smoothly reminded everyone he had connections in the gover-nor's office, and topped off his statement with a slightly smug smile that Dolfe always felt was directed at him.

Fast forward to the present. It had only been a

little over a week since it was reported on the national news that Blanchette was missing. Speculation was that he'd climbed onto one of his extravagant yachts in the wee hours of the morning and disappeared across the vast blue ocean.

A lukewarm search quickly turned intense as the Lieutenant Governor was reminded by a cocky young TV reporter that he was running for the top job in Florida and letting his friend, a possible murderer, escape justice on his watch was not going to sit well with the voters.

To that point, Dolfe had managed to keep the news from Blaise. She'd been busy with the venue opening and tied up in enjoying her dogs and the house and hadn't made more than a passing mention of the fact that he'd been doing his best to keep her from watching the news.

But Dolfe had known it was only a matter of time before she found out.

And he'd also known he'd see terror on her beautiful face when she did. Exactly the look of abject fear he was seeing right at that moment, as JJ's news started to sink in.

"Blanchette's free?" she asked as JJ dropped wearily into the blue leather visitor's chair in his office. "How is that possible? How could the DA's office let this happen?"

JJ crossed her legs, sighing. "I wish I could explain it, Blaise. I really do. But I'm shell-shocked.

Blanchette must have something really ugly on someone to have managed this. The only consolation I had was my belief that he'd gone to Cuba or somewhere far away from you."

"And then Kim Vitters was killed," Dolfe said, dropping onto the front edge of his desk. He crossed his arms over his chest to keep Blaise from seeing the tension in his muscles and his clenched fists. He was striving to keep his expression neutral for her sake.

But she was looking at him as if she knew his thoughts. And the fear on her face was twisting his gut into painful bands. "How did you tie her death to Blanchette?"

"A man matching his description was seen going into her room. When we pulled up the security feed, we saw a man who looked a lot like him."

Dolfe grabbed onto hope. "Looked like him? You aren't a hundred percent certain it was him?"

She shrugged. "No. But sure enough." She leveled her intense brown gaze on Dolfe. "When you factor in that his cousin was just murdered, it's too big of a coincidence to think he isn't involved somehow."

"Nobody else went into that room?" Blaise asked. She dropped heavily into the chair next to JJ as if her knees had given out on her.

JJ shook her head. "No."

"Could someone have come in through the sliding door?" Dolfe asked.

JJ frowned. "She was on the tenth floor. Why does it sound like you're trying to clear Blanchette of this murder, Honeybun? I'd think you'd be first in line to take him down for it. After all, it will be hard for the DA or Lt. Governor Demitre to let him walk after this."

Dolfe wasn't sure how to answer her question because he didn't know why he was trying to find another explanation himself. Except that the whole thing just didn't fit. "Blanchette isn't that careless, JJ. He'd have known about the cameras. Don't forget he was part owner of one of the ritziest hotels in Miami. It just doesn't feel right. Why would he expose himself like that?"

Blaise shuddered, rubbing her hands down her arms as gooseflesh pebbled her smooth skin. "It sounds about right to me. You forget I watched him calmly pursue that poor woman on the beach and shoot her. And when he saw me, he intended to kill me too. He's a sociopath, Dolfe."

"I'm not disputing that, honey. He's a killer and a pig and everything else you've ever thought about him. But this goes to intention."

"What do you mean?" JJ asked.

"I have to ask myself if he intended to be seen killing his cousin's fiancée. And if he did, why?"

JJ stared at him for a moment, looking

perplexed, and then her face cleared as she grasped his meaning. "You think this killing was a message to someone?"

"Yeah," Dolfe confirmed. He did. And he was afraid he knew who the message was intended for. "I think he was connecting the dots for us, just in case Lawrence Peck's murder didn't do it for us."

JJ paled. "He's coming after you," she breathed.

"I believe that he is, yes."

Rage brought heat to Dolfe's face, and he gave up trying to protect Blaise from it. He sat forward, his fists on his thighs. "I won't let him hurt her, JJ."

Blaise sucked air as she no doubt realized what he was saying. He was admitting to his friend the cop that he would embrace vigilante justice if Blanchette came near her.

"Dolfe..."

He shook his head. "Don't ask me to stand down, Blaise. The system failed us once on this. I'm not going to sit back and trust it not to fail us this time."

The man was a cold-blooded, unrepentant murderer. And if he was involved in what had happened at Wedding Belles, Blaise was in terrible danger.

Dolfe's message was clear. He had no intention of letting Blanchette walk again.

7

*B*laise sat mutely staring at the floor in front of her feet. She was sitting forward with her arms resting on her knees, fighting nausea as déjà vu swamped her. Months had passed since she'd had to run for her life in Miami, Florida. But in that moment it felt as if it were just yesterday.

She could feel Dolfe's worried gaze on her. He'd given up trying to pretend he wasn't concerned and that troubled her more than anything. His first instinct with her was always to protect. It annoyed her sometimes because he treated her like glass. But the fact that he wasn't even trying to keep the terrifying reality from her in that moment was the most terrifying thing of all.

It meant he thought she'd be safer if she was scared. It meant he believed things were about to get real.

A large pair of boots appeared in front of her, and she looked up to find him staring down at her. "We're going to get this guy, honey."

She nodded, but she didn't really believe him. Blanchette was the worst kind of killer. He was totally devoid of scruples or fear. He'd been protected by money and connections all his life and figured he could get away with anything he did. Even if they took him down, the collateral damage was destined to be bad. It had already taken at least one innocent life. Maybe two.

"Those people are dead because of me," she whispered, her eyes burning with the tears threatening to spill.

Dolfe crouched down and wrapped his arms around her knees, hugging them into his broad chest as his hands found her hips and branded them with heat. "None of this is your fault, Blaise. I won't let you take the blame for what Blanchette has done."

She shook her head, sniffling. "He's the worst kind of monster."

The words were spoken so softly she didn't expect him to hear them. But Dolfe leaned close, placing a kiss on her forehead. "Yes, he is. But the fact that he's targeted you doesn't make you a monster too."

No, she thought, it made her something worse — a victim.

Blaise could hear JJ's voice in the outer office. It sounded like she was calling her boss in Florida. Brita sat at Dolfe's desk talking on her cell and jotting into one of the binders Dolfe kept for case notes.

Blaise was keeping Dolfe from doing what he needed to be doing. She knew he chafed to be moving forward. Then she had a sudden thought. "Suz and Tyrese!" She grabbed his shoulders, her pulse spiking so hard and fast she saw stars. "They're in danger."

He nodded. "I already contacted Alf. He's putting together a protection detail for their home. You, Badly and Ivy can stay with them until we catch Blanchette."

Aside from her relief that he'd been two steps ahead of her as always, Blaise was already shaking her head before he finished talking. "I'm not going to go hide somewhere while you take this on, Dolfe. Don't ask me to do that."

"Honey..."

She shook her head again. "If you ask me to run away and play victim, I'll never forgive you, Honey-bun. Do you understand what I'm telling you?"

Dolfe held her gaze for a long moment. It was clear he understood completely. But that didn't mean he had to like it. Finally, he sighed. "Okay, you're right. You deserve to be part of this. But Blaise, I'm telling you right now, if you get yourself hurt..." His voice broke, and he slammed his lips closed.

She leaned closer and pressed her mouth against his, giving him a tender, lingering kiss meant to reassure. When she broke the kiss, he touched his forehead to hers for a beat and then stood, grabbing one of her hands and pulling her up with him. "Okay, let's get going. We have a lot to do."

Wedding Belles was dark and quiet when Dolfe pushed open the front door. He stood in the open doorway for a moment, listening. Hearing nothing, he lifted the crime scene tape and glanced at Blaise. "Stay here."

He ducked under the tape and moved into the darkness, reaching for the light switch with his gun down by his side. Before he could find it, a warm body moved up behind him and he sighed. "Are you ever going to learn what the word *stay* means?"

Blaise placed a warm hand on his shoulder. "I got lonely."

"You were out there by yourself for three seconds."

She shrugged, a grin tugging at her lush lips. "Should I turn on the lights?"

He sighed, nodding. If Blanchette was lurking in

the barn, he'd already know they were there from the whispered conversation.

The overhead lights flashed on, the chandeliers putting off a soft, flattering illumination that didn't reach all the corners and nooks.

Dolfe reached back and grabbed her hand, moving forward with her pressed tightly against him. He tried to stay a bit in front of Blaise, but she knew what he was doing and kept moving forward. "You are a difficult woman, future wife."

She nodded. "You knew that about me before you gave me this." She flashed the diamond engagement ring on her long, slender finger and he grinned.

"Life *is* boring without a little challenge in it."

They did a slow, careful check of all the spaces, ending in the storage room, which was still closed off behind yellow crime scene tape.

Dolfe and Blaise stood in the doorway, looking at the devastation beyond. What was there was much more than evidence of a tussle. Someone had taken out a significant amount of rage on the shelves full of supplies.

Every glass in the room had been scooped off the shelves and lay broken on the floor. Boxes of silverware, pretzels, and crackers mixed with boxes full of drink mixers and packets of coffee, soup, and sauces. The result was a gloppy mess that had dried to something that looked like puke-green concrete on the floor.

Linens had been slashed and stomped on until they were beyond repair, and rolls of gauzy drapings were spread around the room, torn and splattered with bleach, foodstuffs, and other unrecognizable things.

The sour stench of urine told Dolfe that someone had relieved himself all over the mess he'd created on the floor.

"This is as much about rage as anything," Dolfe murmured to himself.

Blaise shuddered. "It was Blanchette."

He didn't bother disabusing her of that notion because he believed she was right. If not Blanchette directly, it had been done under Blanchette's orders.

Dolfe's phone rang and they both jumped. He hit the *Answer* button. "Honeybun."

"Hey cuz." He turned to Blaise, mouthing the word, *Alf*.

She nodded, moving past him into the room.

"Alf. Are they secure?"

"Snug as four bugs on a Pug."

Dolfe rolled his eyes. "Good. Thanks. You have someone watching them?"

"Full-time surveillance. If your guy shows up, we'll snag him."

The worry twisting Dolfe's gut lessened. "I owe ya one."

"You owe me several. But not for this. I'm doing it for Clancy. He's kind of fond of Ivy and Badly. He won't be happy with me if I let anything happen to them."

Dolfe grinned. "And Suz and Ty?"

"They're darn lucky they're with the dogs."

Dolfe chuckled. "Nice."

"Seriously though, I'd save Suz any day. I like her. But Ty's just annoying. He *is* lucky he's with Suz and the dogs."

"Got it. What's next?"

"We're running backgrounds on all of Suz and Ty's neighbors just in case. I want to know what we're dealing with there."

"Okay, keep me posted."

Dolfe disconnected and entered the storage room. He found Blaise standing near the back wall, where a gaping hole in the drywall spilled torn chunks of insulation and a bulging strand of electrical wiring.

Blood stained the wire and dotted the clumps of insulation on the floor. There was a puddle of it on the floor in front of the hole. "Honey?"

She twitched at the sound of his voice but didn't turn. "Why were they here?"

Dolfe moved up behind her, careful not to step on the debris between them, and wrapped his arms around her waist, kissing the side of her neck. "We're going to get this guy. You don't need to worry."

She sighed, finally nodding. "Are Suz and the dogs okay?"

Apparently, *nobody* cared about Ty. "Alf is personally overseeing the guard detail."

Some of the tension drained from her taut form. "Good. That's good."

Dolfe nodded in silent agreement. "We can focus on finding this guy. And the first step is to figure out what was so special about this room. This spot."

He moved around her and peered down into the hole, pulling a small flashlight from the back pocket of his jeans to illuminate the space.

It was empty.

Just to be sure, Dolfe shone the light to the left and right of the space, finding nothing.

He stepped back. "Whatever was here, the killer must have taken it with him."

"But what could it have been. You saw this space before we started renovating it. This was just two-by-fours and bare metal. If something was hidden here, it had to have happened during construction." She gave a violent shiver as the idea blossomed full-blown into her mind. "They were here all this time."

Dolfe didn't like the idea either, but she was right. If something was planted inside the walls, it happened during the construction of the interior space. "The bigger question is why *this* place. We're twelve hundred miles from Miami, out in the countryside, in a space that was an old country barn a few months ago. Why target this place?"

There was only one possible reason.

"Me," Blaise said softly.

"Us," he corrected gently. "Unless we're wrong about Blanchette being involved," Dolfe said. "Maybe the girl's death in Miami is unrelated. It's possible this had to do with Ty or Suz."

"That seems unlikely," Blaise told him, almost angrily. "Don't twist yourself inside out trying to make me feel better, Dolfe. If we're going to work together on this, you have to trust that I can handle whatever we find out."

He held her gaze for a moment and then nodded. "You're right. I'm sorry, honey. It looks like it's Blanchette. And that means it's about us. Not just you. He's not any happier with me than he is with you."

She tensed again. "We need to assume Peck's death was a message for us. Maybe there never was anything in this wall. Maybe Peck was sent here on a fake mission so he could be killed right in the heart of our world. The destruction of the room might have just been staged to throw us off balance."

"That makes as much sense as anything. Except for one thing. Peck knew there was something coming. He must have known he was in danger because he sent Kim away."

She frowned. "Yeah. He'd have been stupid to trust Blanchette. Even if he *was* his cousin."

"Stupid yes. But this goes beyond just not trusting the man. If Peck sent her away, that implies an active threat."

"Which would explain why Peck was so unhappy when they toured the place. If he knew there was something going on here..."

"Exactly."

She shrugged. "Okay, so what's next?"

"Let's take a quick look around. I just want to make sure the police didn't miss anything."

8

*U*nfortunately, they didn't find anything new inside the venue. The main room, the office, the restrooms, and the caterer's kitchen were all clean. Nothing damaged, nothing moved as far as Blaise could tell. As they finished up with the kitchen, Dolfe opened the door leading from the kitchen to the outdoor space.

"Where are you going?" she asked.

"Kim and Lawrence toured the smoking lounge, right?"

Blaise nodded, "But they wouldn't have needed to break into the building if what they wanted was out there."

"It's worth a look," he told her, holding the door as she slipped outside. "Maybe they weren't sure where whatever they were looking for was hidden." The heat hit them as soon as they stepped through the door. It was turning into a really hot spring day, and beyond the low front wall of the lounge area, birds flitted happily from tree to bush to grass, busily going about their business.

The overhead fans were off, but it was probably cooler under the ten-foot-high ceilings even so.

"I'll take the outdoor kitchen."

"I'll check under the tables and chairs and around the walls."

Fifteen minutes later, Dolfe joined her as she searched the last segment of wall. There wasn't much to search, but they'd built a bench around the entire space for extra seating and the roof's extra long eaves kept the benches across the low front wall as cool as the rest of the lounge.

"Nothing?" Dolfe asked as he joined her.

"Not a dang thing." Blaise dropped onto the bench and sighed, shoving a strand of her curly black hair off her sweaty cheek. "A total waste of time."

Dolfe's gaze was locked on something over her shoulder. And a beat later he started walking. "Maybe not a total waste."

"Where are you going?"

He wasn't listening. He was focused on something in the landscaped gardens leading from the lounge to the creek.

She slid off the bench and started after him, jogging a little to catch up as he approached the pretty little bridge over the creek. "What do you see?"

Dolfe pointed toward the mulch at the side of the path. The pathway itself was formed of large flag-stones, with river rock in between the stones. But on either side of the path were curving mulch beds filled with young flowering bushes and small trees that would someday provide shelter and cooling cover to the walkway.

She squinted at the bed, not seeing anything except a slightly churned area that looked as if a small animal had been digging. "What am I looking for?"

Dolfe moved forward a few feet and then stopped, crouching down and pointing to what appeared to be an unmistakable footprint in the mulch. "These lead from the lounge. And if I'm not mistaken, I think they're going to take us to the creek."

Blaise squinted toward the sparkling ribbon of shallow water. "You think someone escaped this way?"

"I'd bet on it."

"It could just be from one of the gardeners," she argued, unconvinced.

He shook his head. "I don't think so. The prints are too small."

Dolfe stopped at the bridge and looked carefully

toward the water below. The footsteps led directly to the water and then disappeared.

He pointed. "She stepped into the water there."

"She?" Blaise frowned. "But Kim Vitters was in Florida."

Dolfe caught her gaze. "She was. But these prints were made by a woman. I'd stake my license on it."

"Do you think this is the killer?"

"It's possible."

"But you don't believe it?" Blaise said.

He shook his head, pulling out his phone. "I'm calling Brita. I want to know what they can tell me about those footprints."

"The prints came out a ways down the creek and headed into that copse of trees over there," Brita pointed to a small wooded area across the barren field. "There are tire tracks back there. Some kind of recreational vehicle if I had to guess. We sent the tire impressions to the lab."

"Could they determine if it was a woman?"

"Either a woman or a small man," Brita responded. "Weight would be around one sixty, which is within the range of either. The shoe is small, but it could be a man's shoe. We're running the tread patterns through the computer right now."

"Hey, guys!"

They turned to find Ty and Suz heading their way. They'd walked around the building, and both wore worried expressions on their faces.

Ty stopped in front of Brita, looking angry. "Your people wouldn't let me inside my own building. What's going on?"

"Please tell me you haven't found another body," Suz said, her gaze looking haunted.

Blaise dropped an arm around her shoulders. "No bodies, Suz." She frowned at her friend. "But please tell *me* you didn't come here without protection."

Suze sighed. "Our guard dogs are around front."

"I'm afraid this is my fault," Dolfe told them. "We came out to look things over one more time and found a set of footprints coming from the kitchen through the lounge and along the pathway to the creek."

Brita slanted a look at Suz. "You haven't walked along that path recently, have you?"

Suz frowned. "How recently are we talking? I was out here last week with the gardeners."

Brita shook her head. "This happened after the rain. Sometime last night."

Ty's eyes widened. "You think this was the killer?"

"We don't know yet. But we're considering it a possibility."

Nodding, Ty frowned. "Wait. You're asking Suz,

not me. Was it a woman?" He slid his gaze to Dolfe. "Maybe the bride *did* kill him."

"Talk about Bridezilla," Suz murmured.

"She didn't," Brita said. "She was in Florida at the time."

"Florida?" Suz glanced at Ty. "But we just spoke to her yesterday afternoon."

"Peck apparently suspected there'd be trouble and sent her away to keep her safe."

Blaise winced and Suz noticed. "What?"

"It didn't work," Blaise told her. "Dolfe's friend, JJ, a cop from Miami, said Kim Vitters was murdered late last night in Miami."

Suz's knees seemed to buckle out from under her. Ty caught her with an arm around her waist before she fell. "What in the world is going on?"

"We're going to find that out, girlfriend," Blaise said soothingly.

"In the meantime, is there anybody else you know of who might have had a reason to cause you and Tyrese problems here?"

Ty and Suz seemed to avoid looking at each other. It was so obvious, Blaise noticed. "What's up, you two? You need to be honest with us if you want us to figure this out."

Suz sighed. "I'm sure it's nothing."

"*What's* nothing?" Dolfe urged.

Ty looked down at his shoes for a beat, then lifted his head. "It's just a crabby neighbor. He doesn't want the venue here, and he's been sending us threatening notes."

"What kind of threatening notes?" Brita asked, frowning.

"He says he'll drive all our customers away. Stuff like that," Ty answered shrugging.

"Oh my gosh!" Blaise exclaimed. "Why didn't you tell me?"

Suz shook her head. "He's just a bully. We decided that ignoring him was the best thing. I didn't want to worry you."

"Tell me his name," Brita said.

"We don't know his name. He never gave it to us. But I followed him one day when I saw him on the street, and I know where he lives."

Brita looked at Dolfe. "I need to get back to the station and oversee this evidence collection. Do you think you could go talk to the neighbor?"

Dolfe nodded. "Happy to. If nothing else, maybe this guy saw someone he didn't recognize riding around on a recreational vehicle."

The house was a typical farmhouse. Faded and chipped white paint covered buckled and dented siding. An ugly layer of green mildew stained the surface along the front of the house and the small porch on the front canted slightly, as if the ground beneath it had fallen inward.

The mailbox looked as if it had recently been replaced, the post beneath it unpainted lumber that stood rigid in the hard-pack dirt alongside the road. The name on the box was Smythe.

A rusty pickup truck, probably as old as Dolfe, was parked in the rutted drive under an ugly carport. He pulled up behind the truck and stopped his own truck, staring at the unassuming property with a sense of foreboding. "I'll just go talk to them. You can wait here."

She blew a raspberry. "Fat chance, Honeybun."

He sighed. "I'd tell you to stay, but you don't seem to know the meaning of the word."

"Maybe because I'm not a dog," she said, arching a fine, black brow at him.

"Not in any sense of the word, beautiful." Dolfe gave her an apologetic grin. "Stay behind me then, okay? I have a feeling we're not going to find happiness and rainbows in this place."

Blaise's response was to roll her eyes.

He stepped out of the truck, his hand going to the small of his back to feel the reassuring heft of his Glock 9. Pulling his t-shirt back down over the gun, Dolfe opened Blaise's door for her and gave her a hand down.

There was a soft squishing sound as she placed her foot down.

He would have laughed at the look of horror on her face, except she would have belted him for it. Instead, he formed a sympathetic grimace and said, "Dog poop. Unfortunate."

"Ya think!" She tugged her hand angrily from his. "This was a really big dog." Blaise stepped into the grass and did her best to rub the poop off her shoe.

Right on cue, a deep rumbling sound filled the air. Dolfe turned slowly as Blaise's head snapped up.

An enormous black dog stepped around the unsightly white truck in the carport.

The dog's lip was curled menacingly, and its throat vibrated on a constant growl. It started forward, and Dolfe pushed Blaise behind him, reaching for his gun. But the dog jerked to a stop with a yelp, a rusty length of chain keeping it from reaching them.

"Aw, Dolfe its chained." Blaise's pretty brown eyes turned shiny with tears.

His jaw tightened with disgust. He hated to see dogs chained outside alone. He always told himself the owners were probably at work or away and would bring the dog inside when they got back. But looking at the conditions the dog appeared to be living in, he doubted the people who lived there were sensitive to its discomfort or loneliness.

A door slammed, and Dolfe looked up to find a woman standing there, her dark gaze filled with distrust and a little fear. "What do ya want?"

Blaise stepped around Dolfe. "Do you keep this dog chained all the time?"

The woman blinked in surprise. "Uh, my husband won't let him in the house."

"Then you should give him to a rescue organization. He deserves to be treated better."

The woman stared at Blaise for a moment, clearly caught off guard by her line of questioning. Finally, she frowned. "That ain't none of your business, lady. Now get off my property."

Blaise nodded toward a beat-up metal bowl, overturned in the weed-strewn grass. "He has no water, and it's hot out here."

The woman's gaze turned soft as she looked at the dog. "I'll fill it when you leave."

Dolfe felt Blaise winding up to argue, so he placed a hand on her arm. "Mrs. Smythe, we were wondering if we could ask you a few questions about Wedding Belles."

She frowned, clearly not placing the reference at first. Then her expression cleared. "Oh, you mean that barn business up the road?" She shook her head. "That's a real sore subject around here, mister. You should get on now."

"That's what we wanted to ask you about," Dolfe pushed. "We wondered just how mad you were about the business coming?"

"Plenty mad. Do you have any idea how much noise that place is going to cause when it opens? The streets are gonna be full of jerks driving around drunk and rowdy." She glanced over her shoulder. "This place don't look like much, but it's my home. I got a right to protect it."

Dolfe's pulse spiked at her words. "Exactly how far would you go to protect it?" he asked.

She frowned, crossing skinny arms over her chest. "What do ya mean?"

"I mean, would you be willing to kill to stop it?"

She flinched as if struck, her glance jerking toward the house. Dolfe caught the tremble of a curtain in the front window.

"Is your husband home, ma'am?"

The door behind her swung inward, and a man stood behind an old aluminum storm door. He was a big man, almost totally filling the narrow door. As he shoved the door open and stepped outside, Dolfe thought he would be plenty strong enough to have stabbed someone in the neck with a fork.

The man Dolfe assumed was Smythe stepped out and glanced toward his wife. "You go on inside."

She threw one last glance toward Dolfe and then fixed Blaise with a pleading look that could have meant anything, before disappearing back into the house.

Dolfe felt Blaise's fingers on his arm and reached to cover them with his, giving her a silent assurance that they'd get to the bottom of everything. He nodded toward the man on the porch, pulling his license out of his pocket with his left hand and holding it up for the man to see. "Dolfe Honeybun, Honeybun Investigations. How are you today, sir?"

The man fixed an intelligent gaze on him. "What would you be investigating around my house, I wonder?"

Blaise opened her mouth, but Dolfe squeezed the fingers under his hand in warning. "There was a murder at Wedding Belles down the street. We believe the killer escaped on a recreational vehicle and we wondered if you'd seen anybody you didn't recognize on the road around that time?"

"That depends, what time would it have been?"

"Around two this morning?"

Smythe frowned, appearing to give it some thought. Then he shook his head. "I had a breech calf at one o'clock. I was in the barn."

"Maybe you heard something?" Dolfe asked.

He looked at Dolfe as if he weren't right in the head. "I wasn't payin' attention. I had my hands full tryin' ta save the cow."

Dolfe nodded, glancing toward the ramshackle red barn behind the house. It was a distance from the road but not far enough that the noise of a small vehicle or its headlights wouldn't have been noticed in the quiet of very early morning. "Did you by any chance see tire tracks you didn't recognize on your property?"

That seemed to get the man's attention. "Now

that you mention it, I noticed someone tore up the ground around my creek. I figured it was that kid again. He likes ta pester me."

"Kid?" Dolfe asked.

The man pointed a thick finger down the road, to a distant red brick home on a manicured yard with a medium-sized outbuilding. "The Markum brat. He doesn't like that I chain the beast out here and he's always sneakin' over to spoil him."

Good for him, Dolfe thought.

"Dogs shouldn't eat people food. It makes 'em soft," the man said.

"Really?" Blaise said. "It doesn't seem to have softened you any."

The man jerked a glare at Blaise. "Mind your own business, lady."

Dolfe squeezed her hand again and then stepped forward. "Why don't you show me those tracks, Mr. Smythe. I'd like to see if they match the ones we found at Wedding Belles."

The man glowered one last time at Blaise and then jerked his head toward the back of the property. "This way."

Dolfe threw Blaise a warning glance before following Smythe away. Blaise easily read the caution in his gaze. He wanted her to stay put and try to keep out of trouble. The keeping out of trouble was going to be an issue for her. Because she wasn't going to walk away from that poor dog without trying one more time to help him.

And he already knew how good she was at staying put.

Blaise headed for the house, climbing the three worn concrete steps and knocking loudly on the screen door. After a few seconds, Mrs. Smythe's soft footsteps sounded inside the house. She pulled the inside door open and stopped, staring at Blaise with a mixture of wonder and pique.

Blaise lifted her hands. "I'm sorry, but I couldn't help noticing that you're afraid of your husband. Do you need help? If so, I know people who can help you."

The woman stared a bit longer and then opened the screen door, stepping outside. "It's nothing like that. He's never raised a hand to me. But the dog's a sore point. I begged him to get Beast. I was lonely when he was gone all day. And the first time the dog had an accident in the house, he threw him out. It's breaking my heart."

Blaise followed her gaze toward the dog, which

was lying in the shade beneath the carport, his gaze locked wistfully on the woman.

"You know it's not fair to leave him out here by himself?" Blaise said gently.

A single tear slid down her cheek, and she shoved it aside with a roughened, red hand. "I know."

"It would be a kindness to give him to someone who could love him like he deserves."

She sniffed again, her gaze sad.

Voices drifted to them from the back of the house. Male voices. Still a distance away but coming closer. Blaise reached out and clasped the woman's work-roughened hand. "I can give you the name of someone who could help."

She shook her head and Blaise's spirits fell.

"He won't let me give the dog away. He says he's good protection for me when he's gone."

Blaise dropped the woman's hand, her heart breaking. "Oh."

"But I have an idea."

Blaise's gaze snapped back to hers.

"If you're willing..."

9

*B*laise was sitting in the truck when Dolfe and Mike Smythe returned to the front of the house. Dolfe's opinion of the man had softened a bit as he'd walked the property looking at tracks. Smythe had a true love of the land and his life within it that was wholesome and pleasing to Dolfe's way of looking at life.

In some ways, the Smythes' lifestyle wasn't that much different from Blaise and Dolfe's. They both enjoyed working with the soil, growing stuff, and cherished their time alone in their little house, enjoying their privacy.

Of course, there was a vast ocean of difference in how they treated their dogs. Miss Ivy and Badly were pampered and spoiled. Poor Beast was neglected and borderline mistreated.

It was hard to look beyond that difference to appreciate the shared values in other areas.

Walking back to his truck, Dolfe thanked the man for taking him around back and warned him the police would be there later in the day to get pictures of the tracks around his creek.

"Mind you talk to that boy down the street. He's a shifty one. I wouldn't put it past him to have been sniffin' around that place."

"Why would he do that?" Dolfe asked, his hand gripping the door handle.

Blaise hit the unlock button on the door, drawing his attention inside.

She ran a finger over her throat and widened her eyes.

He frowned.

"Oh, didn't I tell ya? He tried to buy that barn for his own little business. The bank wouldn't give him the loan 'cause he was too young."

"You don't say?"

The doors locked and unlocked again and the windshield wipers waved across the glass, spraying Dolfe with wiper fluid before he had a chance to dance back away from it.

He threw a warning glare into the truck. To his surprise, Blaise slashed a finger across her throat again and jerked her thumb toward the road.

Something big was stuck in her craw.

"Okay, I'll talk to him. Thanks for the info, Mike."

Smythe lifted a hand over his head in a wave, heading into the house.

Dolfe opened the door and slipped into the truck. "Have you lost your mind, woman?"

"Let's go. Hurry."

"What's up?" he asked, narrowing his gaze at her.

"Nothing, I just..." Her gaze shifted and she looked embarrassed. "I really have to pee."

"I'm sure the Smythes would let you use..."

"No! Let's just go. I can wait until we get back to the office."

He stared at her for a beat longer and then started the truck and backed it out of the drive. "The tracks at the back of the property look a lot like the ones we found at Wedding Belles." He got a whiff of sour air and his nose twitched.

"You think the killer crossed the road and left through those fields out back?"

"It wouldn't be a bad way to stay out of sight. Though the acres behind the house are fenced and full of cow bumps. It would be a rough route."

Another sour wave of air assaulted him, and he suddenly remembered that Blaise had stepped in dog poop. He glanced her way. "You might want to give your shoe another cleaning when we stop. It smells foul in here."

Her face split in a grin, surprising him. "Yeah, okay."

"You don't mind if we stop up at the end of the

road and talk to that neighbor kid, do you? Mike thought he might have been hanging around the barn."

"You don't think an eighteen-year-old kid killed Lawrence Peck, do you?"

She sounded so affronted that Dolfe gave her a surprised look. "Not necessarily. But it's happened before."

She adamantly shook her head. "He's a good kid. He wouldn't do that."

He slowed the truck, staring at her. "How do you know he's a good kid, honey. Have you met him?" The idea that Blaise would know some random eighteen-year-old was a bit disconcerting. Dolfe thought he knew her better than that. He thought he knew all her friends and acquaintances.

She chewed her bottom lip. "Sally told me."

"Sally?"

"Mrs. Smythe."

"I don't remember Mrs. Smythe giving us her name."

Blaise shrugged. She was looking so guilty he stopped the truck in the middle of the country road, glancing quickly into the rear-view mirror to make sure no one was behind them. He turned and leveled a look on her just as another wave of sour air assaulted him. He covered his nose. "What in the world?"

Something warm and wet swept over his ear.

Dolfe jumped so high he banged his head on the ceiling of the truck. But it was the decidedly unmanly yelp that bothered him the most. He turned to find the Smythe's big dog sitting in his back seat, wide pink tongue lolling and tail snapping happily against the back of the seat. "Blaise!"

She held up a hand. "It's not what you think." She tucked two fingers into the front pocket of her jeans as his face heated with outrage. "I can't believe you took their dog!"

Blaise rolled her eyes. "I won't allow myself to be offended that you would think that about me because..." she pulled a folded piece of paper from her pocket. "To tell you the truth, if Sally hadn't given him to me, I probably would have stolen him." She handed the sheet of paper to Dolfe.

"She *gave* him to you?" Dolfe unfolded the note, feeling a weight simultaneously lifting and crashing into his chest cavity. "Blaise, we can't keep..."

"Just read the note."

He clamped his lips closed and quickly scanned the tidy, handwritten note, signed in a pretty flourish by Sally Smythe.

A horn sounded. A big, black truck swerved around them and whipped past, the driver flipping them off before he shot on down the road.

The remaining weight on his chest lifted. He turned to Blaise and smiled, her reactions of moments earlier finally making sense. "Okay, but let's keep this..." he swept a hand in the direction of the dog in the back seat, "...quiet for the time being. I need to figure out if the Markum kid had anything to do with the murder."

Barely repressing a grin, Blaise nodded.

In the back seat, Beast made a happy little woo-woo sound and swiped his tongue over the back of Dolfe's neck as he sighed, put the truck into gear, and headed on down the road.

Devon Markum was a burly kid with a thick mop of short-cropped hair and the dark shadow of whiskers covering his square chin. He was mowing a straight path through the lush green grass of his yard when Dolfe pulled into the drive and cut the engine.

The teen turned to them, his eyes narrow and dark as he squinted into the sun. He stopped the riding mower and climbed off, striding toward them with a question in his eyes.

Blaise climbed out as Dolfe walked around the truck, smiling at the boy...no the man...who offered her a square hand with callouses.

"Hello? Can I help you?"

Blaise carefully examined his face, seeing only kindness and curiosity. "Devon Markum?"

He nodded. "Do I know you?"

Blaise shook his hand as Dolfe joined them. "I'm Blaise. This is Dolfe."

Dolfe inclined his head in greeting, staying silent to let Blaise take the lead.

"We work at Wedding Belles down the street."

The boy nodded, his expression neutral. If he knew about the break-in and murder, he was hiding it well.

"We spoke to your neighbors, the Smythes," she told him, "Mike Smythe said you'd been interested in the barn?"

The boy's expression darkened when she mentioned Smythe. "I can just imagine what he told you," Devon ground out.

Dolfe shifted on his feet. "We're looking into the source of a set of recreational vehicle tracks on the barn property. The tracks lead across the road and toward the back of Smythe's property. He thought they might be yours."

The kid stared at Dolfe for a long moment before responding. "I wouldn't ride my ATV on Smythe's property. He'd call the cops on me."

"You and Mr. Smythe don't get along?" Blaise asked, though she already knew the answer to her question.

The kid snorted out a laugh. "You might say that. If you enjoyed massive understatement."

"What's the general problem between you?" Dolfe asked.

Devon shrugged, but instead of answering Dolfe's question, he offered them one of his own. "Why are you people here?"

"The barn was broken into last night. Vandalized. We were wondering if you knew anything about that," Dolfe said, his tone brusque.

Devon Markum's face lost some of its color. "And I'm assuming Smythe told you I did it?"

Dolfe just held his gaze, not responding.

The kid sighed. "I *did* want to buy the building. I'm trying to start a small engine repair business and that space would have been a good fit for what I have in mind."

"You don't think that barn would be too big for a small engine repair shop?" Dolfe asked.

"A little. But sometimes I work on boats and RVs too. Fixing them up and reselling them. It would be perfect for housing larger projects."

"That's an ambitious plan for someone your age," Blaise said, trying to sound more impressed than skeptical.

"I'm no kid," Devon said, glowering at her. "I'm almost nineteen, and I've been working since I was thirteen, saving my money. I have a business plan and everything."

Blaise was impressed. The kid was sharp, clearly driven. But was he a killer? She glanced toward the large, red-brick ranch, thinking the apple didn't fall far from the tree. His parents had obviously done well for themselves.

"Don't assume that I'm blogging in my parent's basement in my underwear just because I still live with them," Devon said on a frown. He'd misread Blaise's glance toward his parents' home. "I'm only staying here for now because I've been saving up for my new business. But I'm moving out in a few days. Into my new barn."

Her eyes went wide. "You found another place."

He nodded. "About twenty minutes from here. The barn's smaller, but I think it will still work. And there's already an apartment built over one end. It's perfect. So, you see, I have no reason to cause trouble down the street. I've moved on."

Blaise nodded, feeling better.

But Dolfe wasn't entirely convinced. "I'd like to see your recreational vehicle if I could," he told the kid. "I need to look at the tires."

Markum bristled. "Do you have a warrant?"

Blaise was surprised by his question. She thought that most nineteen-year-olds would just capitulate to be rid of the questions and intrusion.

Unless he had something to hide.

"I can get one today," Dolfe told him. "But if you make me go that route, I'm going to have to look more closely at you for last night. I'll probably have to take you down to the precinct for more questions."

The kid tensed, his gaze sliding toward the outbuilding at the back of the property. Finally, he shrugged. "Help yourself. I didn't do anything, so I have nothing to hide."

But the way his gaze shifted from side to side, avoiding Blaise's, told her that was probably not true.

The kid might not be their killer. But there was definitely something he wasn't telling them.

"What are we going to do with this dog?" Dolfe asked as the big hairy beast swiped the back of his neck with another wet doggy kiss. Dolfe grimaced and Blaise giggled.

She reached over the seat to scratch the big dog on top of his head. "First we're gonna give him a bath." Her nose wrinkled. "He stinks."

"You know you're going to give your little furry bedroom slippers a heart attack when they catch sight of this guy, right?"

She grinned. "I think you're underestimating the power of small dog syndrome. Miss Ivy might need a minute to consider how best to subdue him, but she's not going to let him get the best of her."

Dolfe frowned, a niggle of worry coming

forward. "We don't really know this dog, honey. He might hurt them."

She shook her head, smiling as Beast slathered her palm with kisses. His muscular tail slapped rhythmically against the back seat. "He's a big sweetheart."

"With us, yes. But dogs are different with other dogs."

She was silent for a moment, telling him all he needed to know. She had her own doubts that she didn't want to acknowledge. He knew Blaise better than she knew herself. And right at that moment, all she wanted to do was adopt the big ball of black and white fur in the back seat and make his life better. Dolfe wouldn't mind taking on a big dog. In fact, he'd always thought of himself as a big dog kind of guy. But he'd grown fond of their two little furballs and didn't want them hurt. "I'd like a big dog some-day," he told Blaise. "But it would be better to intro-duce one as a puppy so Ivy would have time to cow it into submission before it got big enough to hurt her."

Blaise didn't speak, drawing Dolfe's gaze to her as he turned down their long drive.

Her eyes glistened with tears. Dolfe felt immedi-ately sorry for making her cry. He reached over and patted her knee. "We can try it and see how they do."

She sniffled, blinking hard and scraping at the escaping tears with the back of her hand. "Let's just see what happens. Ivy and Badly aren't here right now, so we have time to get to know him better."

Dolfe parked in front of the garage and climbed out, his hand grasping the gun in the small of his back as he pulled open Blaise's door and helped her out. "Wait here while I check the house. I'll bring a leash out so we can walk him around the property."

She blinked in surprise before nodding. With the excitement of getting the dog, she'd clearly forgotten the threat of Blanchette and his people.

Gun drawn, Dolfe did a quick but thorough search of the house, including the small, unfurnished basement, all the closets and even the sunny porch off the kitchen. Everything looked normal.

He grabbed one of the thin leashes they used for Ivy and Badly and grimaced. It would be like leading Beast around with a thread. He hoped the dog had good leash manners.

He found Blaise and Beast standing in the open door of the truck, her fingers tucked loosely around the dog's leather collar.

Beast stood quietly, gazing lovingly up at her as she talked softly to him as if he were one of her friends. "Dolfe and I planted all these pretty plants around the house so make sure you don't dig any of them up. I won't be mad if you do," she assured the big dog as he dropped to his butt on the gravel. "But I'd be sad for the plants."

Dolfe grinned. He really hoped Beast was well-behaved with Ivy and Badly. He seemed like a nice dog, and Blaise was already bonding with him. He clipped the leash onto the dog's collar and wrapped it around his hand a couple of times to shorten it. "Okay, let's check out the yard, big fella."

Beast eagerly started forward, immediately hitting the end of the leash and yelping as it jerked against his throat.

Blaise's hand flew to her mouth, and she gave Dolfe a worried look.

"That shouldn't have hurt him," he told her. He bent over the dog, running his fingers through the thick fur around Beast's collar, and frowned when he discovered the problem. "There's a second collar here," he told her, anger making his chest tight. "It's spiked."

He'd inadvertently hooked the leash onto the collar that pinched when it was tightened. Dolfe's carefully probing fingers felt some old scabs, and he discovered fresh wounds beneath the spikes. "Dammit," he said softly. "Sorry big fella," he told Beast, running his hand over Beast's head and wide nose. "Let's get this off you." He quickly transferred the leash to the other collar and removed the pinching metal link collar.

When Blaise saw it, she tensed angrily. "How can somebody do that to a sweet dog like this?"

"People don't know any better. They think they're exerting control. They don't consider the pain element. Especially for a dog who's left outside alone all the time. He probably got the chain wrapped around a post and hurt himself trying to get to his water bowl."

Dolfe flung the offending collar toward the door, intending to throw it out when they got back. Beast bounced up on his back legs and put his big paws on Dolfe's chest, scouring his neck with a big, wet kiss, as if to thank him.

"He's happy to have that thing off," Blaise said with a smile.

"I don't blame him."

"Let's go, boy," Dolfe said. "Let's check out the boundaries."

They walked down the drive in the lush grass and Beast tried to pee on every dandelion and long blade of grass he saw. By the time they turned at the sidewalk, he'd run out of liquid. Tail wagging, his nose found the grass as he followed the scent of a squirrel who'd debunked to the old oak tree alongside the street and was currently chirping indignantly at them.

Blaise grinned up at the angry critter. "Sorry, buddy. We're just passing through. I promise."

Beast tried without success to anoint the trunk of the oak tree, marking it as his own before trotting off again to explore other scents in the grass. Several trees and bushes later, they were almost to the far corner of their property when Dolfe saw movement beyond the tall hedge separating their property from the neighbor's. He threw out an arm to stop Blaise and gave the leash a gentle tug to halt Beast.

He stared at the nose of a shiny black car sitting along the curb. Nothing moved. After a moment he thought maybe he'd imagined seeing someone there.

He turned to Blaise, smiling. "False alarm."

But she wasn't looking at him. She was staring at the dog, her arms wrapped around herself.

Dolfe glanced at Beast, whose big body was rigid, tail stuck straight up in the air and quivering slightly. The fur along his back stood straight up and his ears were pinched back. A low, constant rumble filled the air. Dolfe quickly realized it was a growl.

He was staring at the black car.

"What is it, boy?"

Beast's tail gave a quick wag, but he kept a laser gaze on the street.

"Maybe we should go back," Blaise said.

Dolfe didn't disagree. "You take Beast and go. I want to check out that car."

She reached out and grabbed his arm, her long fingers like a slender vise on his flesh. "No, stay with us."

Dolfe handed her the leash and pulled out his gun, lowering his voice. "I'll be right behind you, beautiful. I promise." He jerked his head toward the house. "Go on, run."

She hesitated another moment, her face filled with fear, and then gave him a quick nod. "You'd better stay safe, future husband."

"You have my word, future wife."

She nodded and tugged gently on the leash, "Come on, Beast."

The big dog reluctantly gave up his watchful pose and, when she started to run, took off with her, staying close to her legs as if he'd been trained to heel.

Dolfe watched them until Blaise was close to the house and then turned toward the waiting car, moving in close to the hedge before taking a direct line to the street. He stopped at the end of the hedge and glanced around, scoping out the car. The windows were too dark for him to see inside with the sun shining on them.

The car appeared to be empty. But that didn't make Dolfe feel any better. It was parked too far from the neighbor's drive to be one of their visitors. And the house across the street was set too far back from the street, with a gated driveway. If they had visitors, they wouldn't be parked at the corner of Dolfe and Blaise's property.

Which begged the question...why was the car there?

The out-of-state plates didn't make him feel any better. It was clearly a rental car — a Chrysler 300.

Nice car. He wondered if Blanchette would send his guys in a car that nice. Or if he'd come himself.

The thought made his skin crawl with dread.

He slipped around the dense wall of green, moving close to peer in the windows of the car. It was empty, with fast food bags strewn around on the floor and back seat as if someone had spent a lot of time in the vehicle.

Had he and Blaise been followed from the barn? His face in the reflection of the darkened glass folded into a frown. Had he been careless? He'd had trouble wrapping his mind around the possibility that their old nemesis from Florida would come all the way to Indiana, risking their home turf and all the support they had there, to get another chance at Blaise.

Blanchette had been home free. He'd gamed the system and made his escape. There was no longer any reason for the high-priced thug to fear what Blaise knew. The only reason he'd have for risking everything to pursue her was pride. And revenge.

She'd been the one to get away. In more ways than one. And Blanchette was an evil man with too much pride.

Behind Dolfe, the hedge rustled softly, and he turned, seeing nothing.

A gentle breeze touched the sweat moistening his neck, making him shiver.

He was jumping at spooks. There was nobody

there.

Then he had a terrible thought. If there was nobody there...where were they?

A familiar scream rent the silence, brittle with fear, and Dolfe's pulse spiked, his heart suddenly slamming against his chest.

He took off running, blind fear spearing him into an impossible speed as he rounded the hedge and took off toward the house. From inside the home, a deep, excited barking told Dolfe he'd messed up.

He'd searched the house. But he'd missed something.

He'd missed a killer.

And Blaise was about to pay the price.

Shoving the thought away so he could focus on getting to Blaise, Dolfe dug his toes into the thick grass and ran on, his heart pounding so loud and fast he was surprised he didn't pass out.

He approached an enormous walnut tree and slowed, realizing he'd be doing her no good to go thundering through the front door.

He skidded to a stop and started to turn. He'd go in through the porch and catch them by surprise.

Something flashed in his peripheral vision. He jerked around, gun raised, and pulled the trigger as a rifle butt drove toward his face.

There was a burst of pain, a disconcerting crunch, and the sky swung wildly by as the ground rushed up to slam into him.

laise's first awareness of trouble was when she let go of the leash and turned to close the door behind her. Beast trotted away from her, his tail high and the hairs still standing at attention on his wide back.

She started to kick off her shoes as she reached for the door, giving it a shove so it would close just enough to keep Beast inside. She didn't bother closing it because she fully intended to throw on some sneakers and go back outside. There was no way she was leaving Dolfe out there by himself.

Then Beast started to growl.

Blaise went very still, her pulse spiking. She hurried toward the kitchen and jerked to a stop in the doorway, her eyes wide.

A man stood in front of the island at the center of the large, sunny room. He had white-blond hair that was gelled to spike straight up on his small head. He was tall, with long limbs and narrow shoulders, but there was no mistaking the taut muscle in his forearms as he bunched his fists.

Blaise gasped when she saw his hands. He was holding a large knife, the blade pointed toward the ceiling, and his icy blue gaze was locked on Beast.

The big dog stood a few feet in front of Blaise, his body rigid as he gave the man a deep-throated warning.

Nobody moved for a long moment, but then the man's gaze shifted to Blaise and he smiled. "If you like this dog, you'd better call him off, lady." Quick as a wink, he threw the knife into the air and caught it, blade down.

Blaise stood uncertain for a beat, unwilling to withdraw her only protection, but having no appetite for seeing the dog hurt in saving her.

She slowly crept forward and placed her foot on the trailing leash. "Beast," she said softly, without taking her gaze from the man.

The dog's tail twitched to show he'd heard her. Blaise slowly reached for the leash, keeping the man in her sights. "It's okay, Beast. I've got you." She felt silly reassuring the dog. He was far better equipped to defend himself than she was. She was counting on him holding the man off until Dolfe got back.

That thought had her shifting her gaze toward the window. The crisp white cotton curtains were pulled back to show the lawn and trees of the front yard. In the distance, the driveway wound gently toward the gray ribbon of the road.

But Blaise didn't focus on any of that. Her gaze was riveted to the sight of Dolfe walking along the hedge.

And the man standing hidden behind the tree at the center of their yard with a deadly rifle trained on her honey.

Blaise forgot how to breathe. Stars burst before her eyes.

Dolfe was going to be killed!

He had no idea the man was standing there with a gun trained on him. He was going to walk right into the trap.

But if she screamed to warn him, Dolfe would come running, and he'd have even less of a chance because he'd be focused on her.

She couldn't do that. But she had to warn him.

What was she going to do?

The man by the counter shifted, and she jumped, the dog giving a snarl as the man moved.

But as her eyes met his, Blaise knew he wasn't going to let the dog stop him. The evil curve of his lips and the blizzard-like cold of his gaze were all the proof she needed of that.

With a quick intake of breath, the man shoved away from the island, knife raised over his head.

And Blaise screamed as Beast lunged toward

him, teeth bared, ripping the leash right out of her hand.

Brita stared at the small detective from Florida. JJ held her gaze, not even shuffling her feet or looking discomfited over what she'd just shared. Finally, Brita shook her head. "That's beyond astounding."

JJ shrugged. "Welcome to my world."

"Is everybody corrupt in your government?"

"Pretty much. It's amazing what a little fear and greed will do to bend a politician to your will. Blanchette wasn't worried for a moment that he'd go down for his crimes. The only question was how long it would take for him to walk."

Brita's head was shaking again. "Doesn't that make you crazy? All your hard work to bring him in..."

JJ nodded, hunching her shoulders as she dropped her backside onto the edge of Brita's desk. "I'm getting used to it. Still, it is frustrating. But on the positive side, the arrests on most of his men will stick. At least we got some of the scum off the streets."

Brita frowned, crossing her arms over her chest. "Unfortunately, the head of the snake is still out there. And now he's threatening my friends."

"Yes," JJ said, her voice filled with determination and a little anger. "But he doesn't know what he's up against this time. He has no idea about the Honeybuns, and about Blaise. People continually underestimate her."

Brita gave the other woman a look. "I wasn't under the impression you knew Blaise that well."

"I don't. I mean, I haven't known her long, but it didn't take me long to figure out she's a pretty impressive woman. She seems like a ditz—a party girl—but she's strong and resilient. And that's before you even add in the Honeybuns. A force of nature all on their own."

Brita couldn't help smiling. "Well, that's true at least."

"Anyway, we're going to get him this time. And since he's in Indiana..."

Brita gave her a long, slow smile. "He's away from his corrupt champions."

"Exactly." JJ unzipped a computer bag decorated with different sizes and makes of guns and reached inside, pulling out a manila folder covered in scrawls and stickies. She handed it to Brita. "This is all the information I gathered on this guy when we were looking into the disappearances."

Brita scanned the pictures of the women inside, remembering Dolfe telling her about the case the year before. Blanchette had been the manager/owner of one of the ritziest hotels on the Miami shoreline. He'd also run a party cruise from a fancy yacht owned by the hotel.

JJ had been looking into the disappearance of several women when Blaise came to town. They'd had no leads. No idea what had happened to the women who'd gone missing.

Then Blaise had seen a man kill a woman on a beach in the wee hours of one morning around Christmas, putting her directly into the man's crosshairs.

It was Blanchette's attempts to add Blaise to his long list of successful sex slaves, abducted right off the pretty party yacht in the international waters off the Florida coast, that had eventually landed him in jail.

But it hadn't been enough to keep him there, apparently.

"Here's the woman from Indiana."

Brita looked up as JJ turned her laptop screen so she could see it. The crime scene photo had been taken from some distance away, probably near the door of the large hotel bathroom. Brita could tell by looking at the oversized soaking tub, the marble floors, and the upscale finishes in the bathroom that it had been a pricey hotel. "Where was she murdered?"

"The Grand Palm."

Brita grimaced. "Wasn't that Blanchette's hotel?"

"Yes." JJ stared at the screen, her gaze narrowing.

"I can't get beyond that fact. It's just too much of a coincidence." She looked up at Brita. "What are the chances a guy from Indiana would send his fiancée to Florida because he figures trouble is heading his way, and he just happens to send her to the one place where Blanchette is sure to find her?"

"Except Blanchette wasn't supposed to be there, right?"

"No. He wasn't. But nobody knew where he was."

"Maybe the guy figured that would be the last place Blanchette would go. I mean, if the police were keeping an eye on him, they'd start there."

JJ's gaze dropped to the picture, showing the slim, pale arm hanging over the side of the tub and one, narrow foot sticking up over the end, burgundy polish covering the delicate toenails.

Brita could just make out a thick strand of dark gold hair floating on the surface of the water.

If she hadn't already known that the woman inside the tub was dead, Brita wouldn't have realized the scene represented a crime. Nothing seemed out of place. Nothing looked disturbed. "I'd love to know why Lawrence Peck chose the Grand Palm to send his girl. I mean, why send her to Florida at all?"

"I don't know. He's got family in the Keys, but they claim they had no idea she was coming."

"Have the Miami PD located Blanchette?"

"No. But the *Grand Lady* has disappeared."

"The Grand Lady?"

"The Palm's yacht. It was in drydock after Blanchette was arrested. But somehow it made it back into service, and he's apparently debunked in it."

Brita shook her head. "There's nothing worse than a crooked politician."

"Tell me about it. The Coast Guard is searching for the yacht now. When we find it, I'll let you know."

"Good. Thanks." She pointed to the crime scene photo. "Can you send me that picture for my files?"

"Sure. And I thought we could go through my records from before. Maybe there's some connection we can use in there to find Blanchette now."

"You read my mind." Brita dropped the thick folder to the conference table and pulled out a chair, sighing. It was going to be a late night.

11

"No!" Blaise screamed as the man's hand jabbed downward, the big knife stabbing toward Beast. The dog launched off the ground, his forefeet slamming into the man's chest as the knife slipped past, leaving only the meaty sound of his fist connecting with Beast's broad torso, and then he went down.

Blaise rushed them, not sure what to do, but knowing she couldn't just stand there and watch the intruder kill the dog.

Beast's teeth were bared and he was snarling, sending spittle in angry ribbons slicing through the air around his muzzle.

The man hit his head hard on the floor when he landed, but he shook it off and lifted his hand again, clearly intending to use the weapon against the enraged dog.

Blaise kicked out hard, her sneaker connecting with the man's arm. The deadly blade slammed into the island and flew out of his hand, skittering across the floor.

With an angry shout, the thug used his fist, slamming it into Beast's muzzle and the dog yelped in pain, rearing back as the man shoved to his feet. He spun to find Blaise, standing behind the island and looking frantically around for something to use against him.

The only things within easy reach were a set of knives and a heavy frying pan, which hung from a holder over the island.

He lunged for her and she dodged sideways, her arm coming up and sweeping the block of knives off the counter to crash against the floor so he couldn't get to them.

As he started toward her again, Blaise threw her arm up and wrapped her fingers around the handle of the heaviest pan, jerking it off the hook.

He dodged the other way and she ran away from him, realizing too late that she was leaving him access to the knives. Blaise took off running toward the door, praying she could make it outside before he got to her.

To Dolfe.

It occurred to her that Dolfe should have been there by then and the thought turned her belly to ice. *No!* She couldn't think about him being hurt. She wouldn't. He had to be all right. All she had to do was get to him.

A hand snaked out and grabbed her by the hair, yanking her backward.

She screamed in pain and fear and spun on her heel, slamming the pan into white hair's midsection before he could use the deadly blade he held in his hand against her.

Her attacker grunted, stumbling backward, and bounced off the wall, somehow keeping his feet and coming right back at her.

Blaise didn't think. She didn't look for options. She realized she wasn't going to be able to outrun him. Instead, she ran right at him, shrieking like a banshee, and swung the pan as hard as she could toward his head.

The iron pan slammed into his skull. The impact reverberated down her arm and into her shoulder. Pain blossomed from the impact and her fingers went numb. The heavy pan crashed to the floor at her feet with a resounding clang, barely missing her toes.

The thug's head snapped back and smacked hard against the wall. She watched his eyes roll back in his head as he slid bonelessly toward the ground. Out cold.

Beast whined and Blaise started toward him.

Agony stabbed through her ribs. She looked

down, shocked to see a bright splotch of blood staining her shirt.

The white-haired thug had slashed her with the knife. She sucked in a shocked breath and eased back against the wall, her breath coming in pain-filled gasps as the full awareness of the wound hit her. A quick examination told her it wasn't very deep or long. Blaise pressed her hand against it and went looking for the dog.

Beast met her at the kitchen door, head hanging low and tail drooping.

She dropped to her knees. "Oh, poor baby. Are you okay?"

Beast whined softly and pressed his head into her middle, drawing a hiss of pain that Blaise forced herself to breathe through. "It's okay. Come on, let's go make sure Dolfe's all right."

As she said the words, panic swelled, taking her breath away.

He had to be okay. Suddenly she remembered the sound of a gun going off. She'd been so focused on surviving her own crisis she hadn't realized at the time what that meant.

Tears burning her eyes, Blaise grabbed Beast's leash and started running toward the door. She peered into the yard before going out.

Relief filled her when she saw that Dolfe's body wasn't lying in the grass. She dove through the door, her eyes going to Dolfe's truck. It was parked right where he'd left it.

The truck was empty.

She ran toward the spot where she'd seen him last. Beast's throat rumbled on a fresh growl as they neared the trampled grass under the tree. He put his nose down into the grass, whining.

The spot was smashed and torn in one spot.

Blaise's gaze shot to the car at the curb.

It was gone!

Beast whined softly and dropped to his belly in the grass. Blaise looked down and saw him sniffing a small area covered in something glossy.

Something red.

It looked a lot like blood.

Dolfe swam slowly back to consciousness. Pain throbbed in time with his heartbeat, the agony seated in the center of his face. His mouth was dry, his throat sore, and he closed his lips, licking them with a tongue that felt like sandpaper.

But he couldn't breathe with his mouth closed.

He groaned as he tried, agony shooting from his nose to pierce his sinuses. He pried his eyes open, seeing only a blurry mix of gray and black that slowly swam into focus.

Concrete. Metal. Filth.

He pressed his eyes closed again and reopened them.

Nope, it still looked like a dungeon. His body swung as he turned his head. His toes scraped the moist concrete and a new agony blossomed in his arms.

He looked up to find his wrists twined with heavy rope, blood running down his forearms from the friction burns.

Water dripped in the distance, the sound melodic, rhythmic, and desolate.

Above his head, footsteps thumped past, muffled and indistinct except for their cadence.

Dolfe tugged on the rope, ignoring the bright tang of pain from the rope and the answering pulse of discomfort in his benumbed arms. He stretched his legs to press his toes against the gritty floor and tried twisting his arms, using the slickness of blood in an attempt to pull free.

A door slammed overhead and Dolfe stilled, his gaze locked on the stairwell across the basement room.

Heavy footsteps descended toward him, slow and methodical, creating tension in his belly that made him want to strike out at something. Anything.

After a moment stretched taut with ugly expectation, a hated foe strode into view from behind the stairwell wall.

Perfectly dressed, carefully coiffed, and looking out of place in the moldering basement environment, Austen Blanchette smiled when he saw Dolfe. "Ah, you're awake, Mr. Honeybun. Wonderful."

Filled with remembered rage, Dolfe jerked hard on the rope, his body swinging wildly at the frantic movement.

Blanchette's teeth gleamed white against the smooth brown of his skin. His dark hair was swept back, away from a handsome face with sharp cheekbones and angular features. He was wearing a charcoal gray suit, perfectly tailored to his lean form.

"If you touch her, I'll kill you, Blanchette," Dolfe growled.

The other man laughed lightly. "You're not in any position to make threats, Honeybun." Blanchette's Cuban accent was a soft lilt behind his words. Dolfe was surprised, Blanchette usually didn't allow it to emerge. He must be feeling very comfortable with his position.

Blanchette stepped closer, but not close enough for Dolfe to reach him. He cocked his head. "I must say our beautiful Blaise has only grown lovelier since I last saw her. This godforsaken state seems to suit her."

Dolfe bit back the surge of rage that threatened to turn him into a madman. He clenched his bloody fists and clamped his lips together so he wouldn't growl and foam at the mouth. He wouldn't give Blanchette the satisfaction.

When he thought he could speak without losing control, he finally said, "What is it you want, Blanchette? You're a free man. Why don't you just go live your wretched life and leave us alone?" *Fat chance of that*, Dolfe thought. He wouldn't rest until he saw Blanchette behind bars.

Or sucking dirt in a cemetery.

Blanchette looked at his perfectly manicured nails. "Why do you assume I'm behind this?"

Dolfe frowned at the strange question. "Cut the crap, Blanchette. What's the plan here? If you think you're going to add Blaise to your stable, you're delusional. I'll rip the black heart out of your chest if you touch her or hurt her in any way."

Blanchette shook his head. "You're starting to repeat yourself, Honeybun. It's boring." He looked pointedly at the ropes around Dolfe's wrists. "Besides, you don't appear to have the means to follow up your threats." He turned away. "My plans are mine alone. I just wanted to stop by and say hello. And goodbye. You and I won't be seeing each other again." He stopped with one highly polished dress shoe on the bottom step. "I have one more stop to make, and then I'll be on my way." His mouth curved upward, the perfect teeth looking impossibly white against his hated face. "It will be good to have female companionship for my long trip. *Adios*, Mr.

Honeybun. Have a nice life. Though I understand it might be a short one."

Dolfe didn't wait for the other man to climb the stairs to start trying to get loose again. He jerked and twisted against the ropes, gritting his teeth against the pain in an effort to loosen them. The door at the top of the stairs opened and Dolfe stilled as another voice addressed Blanchette, listening carefully in an attempt to identify the speaker.

But it was too low, the tone angry and the words spoken in Cuban Spanish. Dolfe couldn't tell what they were discussing. But someone wasn't happy with Blanchette.

Someone else besides him.

There was a shout and something slammed into the floor up above. But it was the sound of a gun going off that had Dolfe working harder to get loose, his fear for Blaise like a lead ball in his belly.

Blood ran freely from beneath the ropes as he struggled against them. He'd managed to work the rope a bit looser by the time he heard footsteps hurrying across the floor, followed by the slamming of a door. Sometime later, after what felt like hours, Dolfe pressed his hands together and twisted them hard, his body swinging violently with the effort.

With a final grunt of pain, he wrenched them free.

His feet hit the ground and his legs collapsed underneath him. But Dolfe shoved upright again, looking around for something he could use as a weapon.

There wasn't much in the basement, aside from the bloody ropes hanging from a beam in the ceiling. He checked the darkened corners and found a chunk of broken brick. It would have to do. Enclosing it in his hand, he grimaced as it slipped over his bloody palm.

Wiping his hands on his jeans, he palmed the weapon again and headed for the stairs.

In his bare feet, Dolfe was able to move silently until one of the steps creaked under his weight. He stilled, gaze locked on the door and ears attuned to the upper floor.

Silence.

He started up again, praying there wouldn't be any more surprises. At the door he stopped, pressing his ear against the scarred wood.

More silence.

Dolfe carefully eased the door open and peered through, seeing an empty room with filthy, stained mattresses on the floor and rodent droppings on the thin carpet.

He pushed the door open a couple more inches and it stopped with a dull thud.

With a final glance around, Dolfe eased through the space and pressed his back against the wall, his hand still clutching the sharp-edged brick.

Nobody moved. No sound came to him. Beyond

the picture window at the front of the long, narrow room, an empty driveway made his pulse quiet.

They'd left him alone.

Then his gaze slid toward the floor behind the door and his pulse shot back upward.

Not totally alone.

They'd left a very dead Blanchette to keep him company.

"Can you get into Dolfe's truck and come to the station?" Brita asked Blaise.

Blaise's hand was shaking so hard around her cell phone she almost dropped it several times. Her palms were sweaty and her chest heaved with fear. "There's no time. You need to come *here*, Brita. We need to find him!"

A beat of silence told Blaise Brita was looking for the right tone in the face of her near hysteria. "I understand. I'm going to do that." Brita finally said in a voice appropriate for dealing with PTSD patients. "But I need to know you're safe. It's the first thing Dolfe will ask me when I find him. You know that, girlfriend. I don't want him to thump me upside the head for not securing you first."

Despite her numbing fear, Blaise relented. "Okay, I'll come to the station, but only if you promise to leave now. Don't let his trail get cold."

"I promise. I'm walking out to my car now."

"Good. Okay. I just need to grab the dog..."

"Wait? What dog?"

"Oh, yeah. I'll tell you about that later. In the meantime..."

"I know, I know. I'm coming."

Blaise ran back to the house, yanking the screen door open. She suddenly remembered the unconscious bad guy and stilled, going quiet. What if he'd woken up?

She eased the metal door wider and saw Beast sitting in the kitchen doorway, his gaze locked on the man on the floor. "Beast," she whispered.

The big dog turned to look at her. "Come on, boy."

But the dog simply laid back down, resting his big head on his paws. He wasn't giving up his guard duties.

Sighing, Blaise started into the house but stopped when she heard tires on gravel.

Brita had arrived. "That was fast," she murmured. Throwing a last glance at the dog, Blaise stepped back through the door and pulled it closed, turning to find a car easing up the driveway.

It wasn't Brita. Blaise nearly turned back around, intending to lock herself in the house.

Then she remembered what Beast was guarding.

It wasn't safe in there either. Instead, she took off

running, hoping to make it to Dolfe's truck before the dark blue sedan got to the house.

She knew where Dolfe hid a key. Blaise wrenched the driver's side door open and dove inside, flinging herself sideways and ripping the floor mat on the passenger's side up to grab the key.

She jammed the key into the ignition and was turning it when a shadow fell over the window on her side. She yelped, instinctively slamming her hand over the lock in an attempt to keep them out. But she was too slow. Before she could scramble sideways, the door was wrenched open and a rough pair of hands grabbed her arm, yanking her back into the seat. She shoved and kicked, earning a few inches of space, but lost her advantage when she jammed her foot down on the doorframe and it slipped out from under her. Blaise slid off the seat and hit the ground hard, agony razoring up her tailbone. The impact knocked the wind out of her. She struggled to pull air into her lungs, the sound a tortured wheeze. Spots burst before her eyes as she fought panic.

There was a sharp pinch on her arm and she struck out, hitting a solid torso with the heel of her hand and taking pleasure from the grunt of pain that resulted.

Her assailant stepped away, staring down at her as if waiting for her to respond in some way. The sun shone into her eyes, making them water and close against her will. She tried to shove to her feet, flailing her arms around for something to use as leverage.

But Blaise couldn't stand. Her limbs turned to water beneath her as she tried to shove off the ground. She collapsed back, noting the pain of the gravel digging into her flesh before everything seemed to go numb.

She stared up at the form towering above her, trying to memorize the features. But the sun hung above her, blaring down to burn her eyes as she tried to see, and she couldn't make out anything but a vague outline.

And then she couldn't see anything at all.

12

"*D*olfe?" Brita pressed speaker on her cell phone and eased her car to the curb, putting it into park. "Where are you? Are you okay?"

"Have you spoken to Blaise?"

Brita shook her head. She wouldn't get a word out of him about where or how he was until he knew Blaise was all right. "She's fine. She's on her way to the station right now."

"Thank, God."

"She's really worried about you, though. She'll be over the moon when she hears you're okay."

His sigh filtered through the phone line. "I was terrified. I couldn't get to her."

"Tell me what happened. Are you hurt? Where are you?"

"I'm okay. A little beat up but I'll live. Can you pick me up?"

"Of course. Just tell me where you are."

"At a gas station on the east side." He gave her the address. "I'll wait for you out front."

"I'll be there in fifteen minutes." As Brita drove, she dialed her partner's phone. Bud Hinks answered after four rings. He sounded breathless. Brita bit back her usual tease about him getting too old and fat to do his job. It wasn't as much fun to tease him about it anymore. Since he'd turned fifty, he no longer thought it was funny. "Hey, Bud. I just wanted to make sure you got Blaise settled and comfortable. Dolfe and I will be in shortly. I'm going to pick him up right now."

"He's okay?"

"Apparently. He wouldn't give me much information. He was too worried about Blaise. How is she?"

There was a pulse of silence. Finally, Bud said, "Blaise isn't here, Brita. When did you talk to her?"

An icy stab of dread speared Brita's belly. "What do you mean she's not there? Maybe she's in the ladies' room or something."

"I'll look around." Bud's voice changed as he kicked into movement.

"Do that. I can't tell Dolfe we don't know where she is. And check the parking lot. She was driving Dolfe's truck."

"I'll call you back in five."

Bud disconnected before Brita could tell him to stay on the line. She was about six minutes out from

Honeybun's location. If she had bad news for him, she needed to prepare.

There was going to be a level five tornado when he heard.

Dolfe disconnected with a muttered curse. Blaise wasn't answering her phone. He wasn't comfortable with that. He dialed Brita again, holding up his hand when the clerk behind the counter glared at him. "Sorry. Just one more call. I promise."

Brita's line was busy. He forced himself not to slam the phone down and caught the impatient clerk's gaze. "Thanks. I'll be back to pay you for the use of the phone. I don't have my wallet with me."

"Sure, man," the greasy-haired clerk said, rolling his eyes.

Dolfe headed outside and anxiously paced the sidewalk in front of the smeared glass door of the rundown station. He glanced at his watch and fought frustration, scrubbing a hand over his jaw and glancing back toward the interior of the station again.

He was reaching for the handle, planning on calling Brita again, when he saw her little rust-bucket of a sedan turning the corner and speeding toward him.

The car barely screeched to a halt before he wrenched the door open with a squeal of metal on metal and jumped inside. "What took you so long?"

Brita caught his gaze, her golden-brown eyes tight with intensity. "There's been a development."

He met her gaze, his gut tightening. "That doesn't sound very hopeful."

"I'm afraid it's not."

Dolfe's hands fisted as terror filled him. "You'd better not be telling me Blaise is...hurt..." He just couldn't bring himself to consider anything worse than that. Hurt would be bad. Hurt would be terrifying. But hurt they could recover from.

"I have no knowledge of that."

Her words...the careful way she said them... turned his belly to ice. "Tell me."

"I spoke to Blaise from the house. She'd fought off the guy they sent after her and was freaking out about you. I convinced her to come to the station..."

"You didn't send help?" he growled out.

"It wouldn't have made sense, Dolfe. Think about it. She had an unconscious thug in the house and they knew where she was. I thought it was better for her to get out of the house right away. I was heading there as we spoke."

He scrubbed his hand over his eyes and nodded. "Okay, I'll give you that."

"But I just talked to Bud and he told me she

never arrived." She frowned before she caught herself and Dolfe noticed.

"What?"

"She was insisting on going back into the house to get the dogs." Brita shook her head. "They're at the house with Suz and Ty, aren't they? Under guard?"

Dolfe swore softly. "It's not the bedroom slippers. She rescued this big beast of a dog from a couple in the country. Near Wedding Belles."

"Rescued?" Brita frowned. "Was it being abused?"

"More like neglected." He shook his head. "Never mind that. We need to get to the house."

Brita nodded, reaching for the switch to flip on her lights and siren. "Strap in. We'll be there in seven minutes."

H is truck was still parked in front of the house when Brita shot into the drive, hitting the switch to shut off the lights.

"Brita..."

Her face tightened. "I see it."

She skidded to a stop near the truck, throwing gravel up in a violent spray that clanged against his truck. She shoved it into *Park* and leaped out, yanking her gun from the holster in the small of her back. "Stay out here."

He ignored her as he wrenched open the door of the truck, quickly searching it. Icy fear filled him when he saw the flipped-back passenger side mat and the key sticking out of the ignition. She'd tried to start the truck.

Then why hadn't she left?

He examined the area carefully and saw no blood. Nothing that would indicate a struggle. Maybe she'd just gone back inside for some reason. Maybe she was in there now, hurt and scared.

He took off running toward the house, easing quietly through the door Brita had left ajar. He moved to the cabinet where he kept his gun. His thumbprint unlocked the cabinet and he reached inside, pulling the Glock 9 out as he heard a long, low growl coming from the direction of the kitchen.

Beast was there. And he was protecting something. Or *someone.*

Dolfe moved quickly toward the door, stopping just behind Brita, who was training her gun on a battered looking man pressed against the cabinets, his hostile gaze spinning between Beast and Brita.

"Tell me where they took her?" Brita said softly, her head swiveling to take in the big dog. Beast's fangs gleamed in the sunlight streaming through the window over the sink.

The tall man with spiky white hair stood with his

arms out, hands spread and arctic blue eyes filled with terror. He was clearly not a fan of dogs. "Not until you call off this wolf."

"I'll call him off after you talk."

But Dolfe knew she wouldn't be calling Beast off. The dog was too intent on keeping the intruder contained. He wasn't going to pay any attention to her. And if she approached him in his current state, she was going to be subjected to a kind of canine attention she definitely didn't want. "Brita?" Dolfe said softly.

She twitched slightly at the sound of his voice but didn't turn. "I told you to stay outside."

"I think you could use some help, don't you?"

"I've got this."

"Are you going to shoot the dog?" he asked softly enough for only her to hear. "Because, if you're not, you might need my help."

She tensed and he knew she didn't want to hurt Beast, though he also knew she was a good enough cop that she'd do it if she had no other choice.

"I think he'll be okay with me. Let me try to grab him," Dolfe tried.

She jerked her head once in the negative. "That dog could kill you, Honeybun."

"He could, yes. But I'm not sure he would."

She half turned, one golden brow arching. "You're not *sure*?"

Dolfe winced. "He was giving me kisses in the car. I'm holding onto that."

"How long have you known this dog?"

He winced again. "Counting this last fifteen seconds?"

She sighed. "Are you sure you want to do this?"

"No. But if anything happens to that dog, Blaise will kill me."

She sighed, probably realizing Blaise would never forgive her either. "Okay, but if he attacks you, I'm going to have to shoot him."

"Just try not to miss and hit me."

She snorted.

"Are you going to get this beast under control or not?" the thug growled out.

Dolfe touched her shoulder, easing her sideways so he could get by on her left, staying out of the way of the gun in case she needed to use it. He eyed the white-haired man as he moved slowly toward Beast. The man had a big goose egg on the side of his head, rising purple and angry from his light hair. Dolfe nearly smiled at the sight. Blaise had gotten in her licks before she was taken. "I'm going to get control of him, but that isn't going to help you. He's on our side."

The man's face tightened with rage. The blizzard-like gaze skimmed toward the floor behind the island. Dolfe's gaze slid that way too, and his pulse spiked.

A large knife lay on the floor, blood glistening on its deadly looking blade.

"Don't even think about going for that knife," he told the man to warn Brita. She moved into the room, toward the seating area at the front corner of the kitchen and started along the island to get behind the man.

His gaze widened with alarm, skipping back and forth from Dolfe and Brita and then to Beast.

Dolfe read the man's panic and realized he might do something desperate. If he lunged on that knife the dog was going to attack and nobody would be able to help him. Then they'd have another problem on their hands.

The dog would be in a whole 'nuther state of mind. One which Dolfe wasn't sure he could manage. "Stand down, man. Just let me get my hand on the dog. If you go for that knife, he's going to go for you. I'm thinking you'll get the worst end of that scenario."

Beast's head suddenly whipped around and he snarled at Dolfe. Glancing from Dolfe to the white-haired man, Beast stopped growling and whined, his body shifting slightly toward Dolfe.

He was clearly unsure.

"It's okay, Beast. You remember me, right? I'm the one who gave you a car ride."

The dog's uncertain gaze slid back to the thug.

Behind the island, Brita shifted a few more inches closer to the knife.

The thug risked looking away from the dog to the knife, his look clearly gauging if he could get there before Brita.

"Come here, Beast. It's okay, boy."

The big dog shifted on his feet, whining again, and then his tail gave a quick wag and, with one last look at the white-haired man, he started toward Dolfe.

"That's a good boy." Dolfe took a step closer, meeting him as he walked over and his big tongue swiped out, catching Dolfe across the face.

Dolfe swiped his hand over his face, reaching for Beast's leash, which was still attached.

He barely managed to grab it before the thug threw himself on the knife, his hand grasping it and one long leg snapping up as Brita dove for him to kick the gun from her hand.

The gun flew upward, hitting the edge of the window and shattering the glass before clattering to the floor. Brita fell backward and immediately pushed off, kicking the thug's knife arm as he reached up and yanked on her leg.

She fell sideways and found herself an inch away from the tip of his deadly weapon, his hand fisted in her shirt to hold her there.

Dolfe reached for his gun as Beast whipped around and shot across the room with a snarl.

"No, Beast!" The leash slipped from between Dolfe's fingers, slicing the skin of his palm with the violence of the dog's movement and Beast went airborne, landing on top of the thug, his snarling teeth mere inches from Brita's face.

13

"Beast, come here, boy," Dolfe said gently.

The dog's tail gave a twitch but he held, his eyes locked on Brita's face. She eased slowly back but stopped when the thug beneath Beast shifted and the dog snarled anew.

"Hold still, idiot," Dolfe growled out.

Brita frowned up at him. "Excuse me?"

He narrowed his gaze. "I was talking to *that* guy."

Brita's shoulders shifted slightly and her hand came around. She'd managed to get hold of her gun again. And she was pointing it in the general direction of the intruder and the dog. She avoided looking directly at Beast while keeping him in her peripheral vision.

Dolfe knew she was still watching the dog because when he moved slightly, her gun shifted back to him. "Beast..." The dog ignored him. He stepped closer, deciding he'd have to take a chance. Reaching down, he touched Beast's shoulder, prepared to jerk his hand away if the dog snapped at him.

The creature's teeth were enormous and white, much scarier-looking than the bedroom slippers' teeth. And Dolfe knew first hand how much even Badly's tiny puppy teeth hurt. "Leave it, boy," Dolfe said with a bit more urgency.

The dog's lip lowered over his teeth and he whined. A beat later, he eased his weight off the thug and looked at Dolfe, tail wagging.

"That's a good boy," Dolfe told him. He reached over and wrapped his fingers around Beast's leather collar, pulling him away as Brita moved quickly to grab the white-haired man's wrists, twisting them behind his back and slapping on handcuffs.

She sat back on her heels and rolled her eyes to Dolfe, her chest heaving. "I thought for sure I was going to have to shoot that dog."

Dolfe nodded, petting the big mutt on top of his head. "He was just being protective," Dolfe told her.

She nodded and stood up, grabbing the man's arm and jerking him to his feet. "If you're keeping him, he'll need training. He's a good dog, but he could be dangerous." She pushed the man backward, holding him against the cabinets as he glared into her face. "Where's Blaise?" she demanded.

"How should I know?"

Dolfe started to move closer and stopped, looking down at Beast. The big dog was staring toward the white-haired man, licking his lips. "Brita, let me talk to him."

She shook her head. "Not a chance, Honeybun."

Dolfe fixed a glare on the other man, noticing the way the man's body stiffened with fear. "I only need five minutes with him. Three if I decide to let Beast have a snack." He was, of course, bluffing but he liked the reaction he got from white hair.

Fortunately, Brita knew him well enough to know he was bluffing too. She looked for a moment like she was considering his offer.

The man shifted forward, a pleading light coming into his light eyes. "You aren't going to let him sic that wolf on me, are you?"

Brita shrugged. "I do need to make a couple of calls. I can go out to my car..."

"Okay! I'll tell you where I think she is. I don't know for sure."

Dolfe slid his hand down the leash and wrapped it a few times around his palm, wincing as it rubbed the lacerated skin there. "Start talking?"

The man shook his head. "I need some assurance of protection. He'll kill me."

"Blanchette isn't going to kill anybody," Dolfe told him. He took a step closer and Beast leaped to his feet, straining against the leash.

"Okay, okay. I think they were going to meet back at the place."

Brita frowned. "The place? What place?"

"That barn."

Brita and Dolfe exchanged a look.

"Why?" Brita asked, seeming genuinely confused. "What is it about Wedding Belles that is so fascinating to Blanchette's crew?"

The man shrugged. "It's not Blanchette. It's the other guy."

"What other guy?" Dolfe asked.

"I don't know who he is. Just some guy from Florida. They call him *El Jefe* for fun, but nobody knows who it is."

Dolfe didn't like the sound of that. He'd thought they knew their nemesis. But it sounded as if they had a whole new player. And whoever it was, he wasn't afraid to kill people. He'd apparently killed Blanchette without a second thought.

Dolfe shifted closer before thinking about how his action would affect the other man.

White hair shifted back, his icy-blue gaze going wide. "I'm not lyin' man. I don't know who he is. I'm new to the organization."

Brita held up a hand. "Calm down. We're listening."

He shook his head, the sunlight through the broken kitchen window casting patterns over his pale features. "All I know is the girl hid somethin' there. Something of Blanchette's. He swore he'd tear the place to the ground if he had to."

"Do you mean Kim? The bride?"

The guy shrugged. "I don't know from no bride. And I don't know her name. I just know Blanchette sent her here to get somethin' and she was supposed to bring it to him. But she showed up without it, and he killed her."

"Are we talking about money?" Brita asked. "Drugs?"

The guy shrugged again. "I told ya. I'm new. He didn't tell me what he was doing."

"I know how this works," Dolfe said. "You guys know things you aren't told. You hear things. You see things. And you put stuff together."

The guy gave Dolfe a belligerent scowl, and Dolfe unwrapped the leash one loop from around his hand.

Dolfe tapped the dog gently on one haunch with the toe of his boot and Beast jerked forward, snarling.

White hair slammed backward, cracking his head on the cabinet. "Okay, man. Geez!"

"I'm not playing," Dolfe ground out. "That was my fiancée you attacked. And because of you, she's in danger. If anything happens to her, I'm holding you personally responsible. And you don't want me holding you responsible for that. It's not going to end well for you."

White hair sighed. "Look, Blanchette had some kind of thing goin' on here. He had some government stooge in his pocket and was tryin' to get some laws changed."

Dolfe remembered Alex Cox talking about new regulations for the beauty industry. Surely that wasn't what Blanchette was working on?

"What kind of laws?" Brita asked. "And why Indiana?"

The guy glanced at Dolfe and then looked quickly away. Dolfe read the meaning in that glance. "He's working on something to take us down," he told Brita. "Me. And Blaise," he told Brita.

"But if he's working with the government…"

Dolfe's eyes widened. "He's targeting dad to get to me."

Dolfe's father was US Senator Brick Honeybun, a multi-decades long veteran in government and a trusted advisor to scores of powerful people. Brick was a high-level target and, along with Blaise, the best way to make Dolfe Honeybun suffer.

Brita didn't look convinced. "Brick would never do a deal with Blanchette."

"No," Dolfe agreed. "But he wouldn't have to. All Blanchette needs is the stench of corruption. The mere suggestion of it. Brick's enemies will do the rest."

Her face tightened with sudden understanding. "The politics of innuendo and smear."

He nodded as he remembered. "Dad's assistant called me yesterday. Brick's going to be in town today or tomorrow. He wanted to have dinner with Blaise and me."

Brita grabbed white hair by the arm. "Then we'd better move fast and figure this out, because I'm pretty sure that, whatever Blanchette's guy had in mind, he's going to set it into motion while Brick's at the scene of the crime."

They bundled white hair into the back of Brita's car, and she hit the lights as Dolfe pulled out his cell phone and called Alex Cox.

The woman's assistant put him through immediately.

"Mr. Honeybun? Have you found Lawrence's killer?"

"We're getting close. I had a question for you, though."

"Anything I can do to help," she assured him.

"You mentioned you'd worked with Brick in an attempt to manage new regulations at the school. What exactly did that consist of?"

"I don't understand the question."

"I mean, did you meet with him outside your

office? Speak to him on the phone? How did he try to help?"

"We had dinner a couple of times. I mostly worked with his assistant Dresden Cooper. Coop was very helpful. He and I worked on writing up a draft of the regulations that wouldn't put the industry on its heels."

"Coop did that?"

"Yes. He even offered to meet me after hours at home to make it easier."

Bingo! "Did he make any promises or offers?"

There was a beat of silence, and then she sighed. "I knew it was too good to be true."

"What was too good to be true, Ms. Cox?"

"It was just a donation. There's nothing illegal in that, is there?"

Dolfe could tell by her tone of voice that she already knew the answer. "How much?"

"A hundred thousand. A small price to pay to save the company. My investor was happy to pay it."

"You mean Mr. Whatsnoggin?"

"No. He's a silent partner. He's not involved in the day-to-day. He actually only invested initially as a favor to me."

"You have another investor?" Dolfe asked, "Who is it?" Dolfe was afraid he already knew the answer.

"*Grand Lady Enterprises.*" Dolfe's heart sank. "It's a company out of..."

"Florida," he finished for her, scrubbing a hand

over his face. "Your partner's name is Austen Blanchette." *Not any longer*, Dolfe thought miserably.

"Why, yes. Do you know him?"

"Unfortunately, yes." Then he had a thought. "Ms. Cox, you said when we spoke to you earlier that the attempt to affect the regulations didn't work." If that was true, then Blanchette would have had trouble pinning a Pay-to-Play charge on Brick.

"Mostly it didn't, that's correct. But we did manage to win one pretty sizeable concession. There was a requirement to actively monitor and track the candidates after they graduated from the schools. It was a nightmarish proposition, requiring that we monitor their employment, compensation, and even general welfare for years after they left us. It would have caused no end of headaches and expense. And you can imagine that the girls hate it. Talk about an invasion of their privacy."

Dolfe frowned. That didn't sound exactly news-worthy. "That's it? That was the only concession?"

"Yes. But I'm afraid we're going to lose even that in the end. Proponents of the original bill are currently fighting to defeat our proposal."

Dolfe wondered why Blanchette would expend political capital on such a small thing. And then it hit him.

All the blood rushed from his face.

Alex's statement about losing girls to sunny Florida.

SAM CHEEVER

Blanchette's previous crimes. He was a sex trafficker. He trafficked in beautiful women.

He was mining his own beauty schools for prospective victims.

And he was trying to tie Brick to the sex slavery ring.

He wasn't trying to embarrass Brick Honeybun. He was trying to get him thrown into prison.

Blaise climbed slowly back to awareness. She tried to sit up but fell back with a groan, wiping an embarrassing stream of drool from the corner of her mouth. The room was dark except for the soft glow of moonlight through a high window. The space was filled with shadows and felt foreign and threatening around her.

Her head pounded and the quick view between her lids told her two things, her vision was wonky, and she didn't recognize where she was.

She struggled to recall what had happened—where she was—but her mind couldn't pull the details together and trying just made her head hurt.

Somewhere in the distance, sirens flared and the smell of something burning sent up a dull warning in her brain.

But her eyes wouldn't stay open, her limbs felt

weighted down, and she was so tired. After a moment of trying to beat it and failing, Blaise let the lethargy win.

Her eyes drifted closed again and Blaise drifted back to sleep.

ive minutes out from the barn, Dolfe dialed his dad's private cell and got voice mail. He left a brief message for Brick to call him just as another call came in.

The ID was for Channel 13 News and he nearly ignored it. But something told him he should answer. He glanced at Brita. "The press."

She grimaced.

"Honeybun Investigations."

"Mr. Honeybun, this is Madeline Sommers..." She hesitated as if waiting for him to acknowledge her notoriety. When he remained silent she added, "From Channel 13 News?"

"Yes. I know who you are, Ms. Sommers. How can I help you?"

"Actually, I'm calling to help you. I thought you

might want to get out ahead of the story we're going to break this evening."

Dolfe's blood went cold. "And what story would that be?" He caught Brita's gaze across the small car, and she shook her head.

There was a beat of silence before the reporter answered. Her tone was filled with surprise, but Dolfe could clearly hear the insincerity in it. "Surely, you've heard?"

He had no intention of playing her game, so he simply waited.

Brita made the turn onto the road where Wedding Belles was located. They sped past the brick ranch house where Devon Markum lived.

Brita made a soft sound as sirens blared behind them and she jerked the sedan to the side of the road as a fire truck shot past.

In the distance, a cloud of black smoke filled the afternoon air.

He looked at her and she shrugged, pulling out behind the IFD truck.

"Mr. Honeybun, Dresden Cooper has been arrested. Your father is being dragged before the ethics committee for his part in a breaking corruption scandal."

And there it was. Dolfe's world rolled sideways and his lungs seized. He suddenly found it hard to breathe. First Blaise and now Brick. He hung his head, blood pounding in his ears, and did the only thing he could do. "I have no comment."

"Really, Mr. Honeybun?"

He smiled grimly. "*Really*, Ms. Sommers. Have a nice day."

"Oh, no!"

He disconnected and looked up at Brita's muttered comment. He sucked in air, the scene outside the car hitting him like a fist to the face.

Three IPD trucks filled the gravel parking lot in front of Wedding Belles, their water cannons vomiting copious amounts of water at the building. Unfortunately, the attempt didn't seem to be having any effect on the flames crawling skyward in twisting columns of orange and gold.

Firemen scurried around the trucks, untangling hoses and pulling on gear as the sky thickened with smoke.

Dolfe was so stunned he sat silent for a long moment, his mind churning with the horror of the scene.

Brita wrenched her door open and the squeal of metal yanked him from his daze, jerking him into the true horror of what he was seeing.

Tucked behind the last fire truck, its shiny black form like a mirage behind a waving curtain of smoke, was the Chrysler 300 he'd last seen parked in front of their home.

Blanchette's guy was there!

White hair's words slid through his mind, turning his blood to ice. *"I think they were going to meet back at the place. That barn."*

With a cry like a feral animal, Dolfe launched himself from the car and ran for the blazing front door, shoving anyone who tried to stop him violently out of the way. He had tunnel vision for that flaming entrance, fully intending to defy nature and his odds and plunge right through it to save her.

"Blaise!" he screamed in a desperate voice he wouldn't have even recognized if he'd been listening to himself. *Blaise, honey! Oh my God! I'm coming...*

A big guy in turnout gear yelled at him, trying to step in front of him and block the door.

Dolfe didn't slow or hesitate. He put his hands out and shoved the guy, barely noticing when the burly fireman stumbled backward. By some miracle of grace or luck, the firefighter kept his feet and stumbled back toward Dolfe, one arm rolling back from a linebacker's shoulders as Dolfe tried to shove around him again.

Dolfe just had time to recognize what the movement meant before a fist as big as his head slammed into him and he went down.

The bite of wet gravel digging into his face was the last thing he remembered.

Something familiar drew her from sleep. Something that made her pulse race and her alarm bells clang. Despite the fear making her muscles tense, it took her a few moments to drag herself from sleep. But when her eyes finally opened, Blaise noticed she felt a lot less groggy than she had the last time she'd awakened in that room. She pushed to her elbows and looked around, taking stock of the strange bedroom, and trying to remember why she was there. The view beyond the room's only window was unfamiliar. The sparsely-furnished space smelled of mildew and neglect and the room was stuffy, probably in large part because of the unyielding glare of sunlight piercing the glass and painting the floor. The first thing she noticed as she pushed unsteadily to her feet was the smell. Someone had been cooking peppers and onions. Or burning them, anyway.

It smelled strangely homey in the place meant to be her prison.

The second thing she noticed was a soft whining sound that made her skin crawl and brought her pulse spiking so high she suddenly felt dizzy.

She pushed straight and scoured the room with her gaze, seeing the small metal crate tucked into the corner, behind the room's only dresser. It was covered with a cloth of some kind, but the soft shifting sound from within sounded very familiar.

"Ivy?"

The whine sharpened and turned into a strident bark.

She ran toward the kennel, stumbling under the lingering effects of whatever they'd injected her with and catching herself on the sharp edge of the tall, wooden dresser.

Ignoring a wave of dizziness that made her sway where she stood, Blaise bent to tug on the towel covering the kennel. Another whine turned her spine to ice.

Badly!

The kennel was small, metal, and there was nothing in the bottom to cushion their tiny bones. If Blaise hadn't been so dehydrated, the sight of her two fur babies huddled together, clearly terrified, would have brought an instant flood of tears.

When he saw her, Badly jumped to his feet, his stumpy feet dancing over his sister as he fought to get through the door and into Blaise's arms.

His sister lay where she was, her warm brown gaze locked on Blaise with accusation. The little dog's silent reproach was like a knife to Blaise's heart.

She flung herself to her knees and wrenched open the kennel door, catching Badly as he threw himself into her arms. She sucked in a gasp as his flailing feet hit the wound in her side, but she didn't pull away. She held the frantically thrashing puppy tight against her chest as he covered her face with kisses interspersed with frenzied whining.

Ivy remained where she was, her gaze never leaving Blaise. But she didn't so much as give her tail a wag. She looked tired, and her eyes were filled with pain.

Blaise hoped it was strictly emotional pain from being kidnapped and locked into a cage for heaven knew how long.

Then she realized that Ivy had missed a couple of doses of her seizure meds and worried the little dog might have had a seizure along the way. It sometimes took her hours to recover fully from one.

"Come here, Miss Ivy. Sweet girl."

Ivy's gaze softened slightly, and she whined faintly in her throat. But she didn't move.

Blaise placed Badly into her lap and, to her shock, he curled up and immediately went to sleep with a big sigh. The poor thing was exhausted.

She reached for Ivy, but the little dog's head snapped up and she snarled, jumping to her feet, her tail straight up in the air.

Blaise jerked away, shock ripping through her and her eyes burning with tears that couldn't fall.

But then she realized her little dog wasn't looking at her. She was growling at someone standing behind Blaise. She turned and jumped to her feet, holding a startled Badly against her chest.

A Hispanic woman with thick, straight black hair and hostile brown eyes stood just inside the door.

"Why am I here? Where's Dolfe?"

The woman smiled, placed a small bowl with water onto the dresser, and turned away without speaking. She was almost out the door when Blaise realized what having the dogs there meant. "What did you do to Suz and Ty?"

The smile dimmed. "That's not your concern. You have a job, Blaise. And if you don't perform it as instructed, you're about to lose everything you love."

Dolfe sat morosely on the tailgate of someone's truck, an ice-pack which was a gift from the EMTs in his hand. He didn't use it on the new goose egg decorating the side of his hard head. He'd deserved the punch. And once he'd calmed down sufficiently, he knew he needed to apologize to the firefighter.

But it wasn't the time.

Night had fallen over the countryside and they were operating by portable scene lights somebody had set up around the scene of the blaze.

Aside from the soft sizzle of burning embers and the occasional crash of timbres from inside the disemboweled building,, the night was silent.

The flames had long been extinguished and

Dolfe was waiting for news of what the inspector was finding inside. It was all he could do to keep from running into the building and demanding answers.

Only the terror of what he might find kept him rooted to the tailgate of the fire investigator's truck like a coward.

He needed to know. But he wasn't sure he'd survive the knowledge.

A black Escalade with darkly tinted windows pulled into the gravel lot and stopped on the outside edge, well behind the one remaining fire truck.

Dolfe recognized the car and climbed down from the tailgate, striding quickly toward the Escalade as the back door opened and his cousin Clovis climbed out, his gaze scouring the area for possible trouble before leaning down and nodding into the car.

The other door opened and another man stepped out, an earpiece tucked in one ear and his dark suit bulging over the spot where Dolfe knew he kept his weapon holstered.

A third face appeared in the open car door and Dolfe grimaced, hoping his father hadn't risked himself just to come out and support his son. Dolfe felt guilty enough for his part in his dad's current problems. He didn't need Brick to put himself in danger on top of everything else.

But as the senator spotted him, Brick frowned,

and he moved toward Dolfe with open arms. "Son. I'm so sorry…"

Dolfe let his father hug him, rage a boiling presence at the bottom of his throat. He briefly returned the hug and then stepped back. "You shouldn't be here. Blanchette's guys are all over the place."

Brick shook his head. "Blanchette's dead. And I needed to be here." He frowned. "Have they found… is um Blaise…?"

Dolfe looked down at his feet, fighting not to snap at his father for the question. Brick Honeybun wasn't the problem and he wasn't the enemy. "No word yet."

"What can I do? How can I help?"

Dolfe opened his mouth to tell him to go home. There was a commotion near the smoldering remains. A group of people emerged from the building, faces streaked with soot and clothes dark with sweat.

Clovis's head snapped up when they appeared and he put himself in front of Brick. But he relaxed when he spotted Brita at the center of the small group.

Dolfe turned and hurried toward them. Fear a lion rampaging in his chest. "Did you find her?"

Brita gave him a look with too much pity in it for his comfort and Dolfe's knees softened beneath him. Stars burst in front of his eyes.

Then she shook her head. "There were no bodies."

Relief was like air to a suffocating man. He filled his lungs with it for the first time in what felt like hours. "Thank, God."

Brita patted his arm. "But we did find evidence that the fire was deliberately set."

The fire investigator, a man whom Dolfe had met a handful of times before and trusted, nodded his head, pulling a soot-stained helmet off his head to scrub short fingers through a sweaty mass of dark hair. "The place was clearly doused with gasoline. The arsonist didn't even try to hide it."

Dolfe frowned. "That makes no sense. We thought Blanchette was searching for something in there. Burning the barn would only destroy whatever he was looking for."

Brita nodded. "I've been thinking about that." She nodded to Brick and Clovis as they joined the group, giving Brick a smile. "Hey, Senator."

Brick winked jauntily. "Detective, are you taking good care of my nephew?"

"She rolled her eyes. He's a Honeybun, sir. He can take care of himself."

Brick barked out a laugh. But the laughter died when Dolfe glared his way. "Lighten up, son. Blaise wasn't in there. That's good news."

He couldn't deny that. "But I don't know where

she is," he ground out through gritted teeth. He looked at Brita. "You were saying?"

"Yeah. Maybe destroying what he was looking for was the idea. Maybe it wasn't money or drugs like we'd assumed." She skimmed a quick glance to Brick. "Maybe it was information."

Dolfe caught her meaning. "Someone was trying to make a play with Blanchette's scam?"

She nodded.

Clovis suddenly stiffened, spinning on his heel as he tapped his earpiece and appeared to be listening. A beat later he nodded. "Bring him in." He turned to Dolfe. "The Service caught a lurker. He says he knows you."

Dolfe turned toward the road as two men in dark suits and bright white dress shirts with nearly matching red power ties approached with a familiar form between them.

Devon Markum glowered past the small group, his gaze locking onto Dolfe. He lifted his hands, which Dolfe noted with a grimace were cuffed.

"Clovis..." Dolfe said.

His cousin sighed. "Take the cuffs off," he instructed Brick's protective detail. "An abundance of caution," Clovis murmured under his breath with a quick glance toward Brick.

Dolfe understood. The Secret Service could be a bit anal when it came to protecting their charge.

Heaven knew Brick had attracted more than his share of bad attention in the past.

The taller agent on the left quickly divested Devon of the cuffs and Dolfe motioned him forward. He noted the way Brick's detail slid their hands into their coats, hands resting on the guns hidden there, and sighed. Dolfe couldn't help thinking how sad it was his father couldn't have a normal interaction with anybody. He didn't know how Brick stood it.

Brick moved forward, extending his hand to the teen. "Hello. I'm Brick Honeybun. It's a pleasure to meet you."

Dolfe nearly rolled his eyes. Every warm body was a possible constituent, after all. He felt immediately guilty for the thought, realizing his father's face held a warm smile and his gaze was filled with interest. "Do you live on this road?"

Markum had tensed when Brick introduced himself. Dolfe felt a brief moment of panic, his own hand sliding to the small of his back. But the kid swallowed hard, looking more nervous than deadly, and nodded. "Senator Honeybun. It's an honor, sir."

Brick covered the teen's hand with his own and his smile widened. "The honor's all mine..." He hesitated, a question in his kind gaze, and Devon hurried to answer the unspoken question.

"Devon Markum. And I do live here." He pointed toward the distant brick ranch. "For now, at least. But not for much longer. I'm moving soon."

"Not because of all this, I hope?" Brick waved a hand toward the still smoking shell that had represented Suz and Ty's dreams. The thought reminded him of Blaise and impatience surged. "What were you doing out there?" he asked the teen, albeit a bit more harshly than he'd intended.

The kid frowned. "Watching the fire. Doesn't everybody watch fires?" He shook his head, flinging Brick's stone-faced detail a glower. "Until I was practically tackled and dragged over here."

"Not everybody watches fires at eleven o'clock at night," Clovis told the kid.

Devon shrugged. "I'm a night owl."

Dolfe took a step closer. "I need to ask you something and it's important, Devon. Do you remember the pretty lady who was with me the last time we talked?"

The kid grinned. "Blaise." Nodding, he added, "she's hard to forget."

Dolfe couldn't argue with that. "She's missing. I believe she was taken by someone driving that car." He pointed to the dark sedan, which was covered under a hazy film of ash. "Did you see her here before the fire? Or did you see this car arrive here?"

The kid shook his head, but his gaze drifted guiltily away.

"Devon, this is life or death. I need your help. If you saw something..."

Brita joined them, her golden-brown gaze

settling onto Devon as she nodded. "You're Devon Markum?"

The teen nodded.

"I'm Detective Muldane. I've just been informed by my partner that tire tracks matching those belonging to the recreational vehicle you were driving were found at the scene of a murder. Do you know anything about that?"

The kid shook his head. Too quickly. And shuffled his feet as if he was considering taking off. Clovis and Dolfe quietly filed in behind the kid and Brick's detail spread wide to cover the wings.

If Devon tried to make a run for it, he wouldn't get far.

He switched from one sneaker-clad foot to the other, seemingly unable to make direct eye contact with anyone.

"If I check into who owns that vehicle, I'm guessing I'll discover it belongs to your dad, Devon," Brita said softly. "I'll have to bring him in for questioning. And if he has any connection at all to the people involved..."

The kid's gaze finally landed on hers and his face hardened. "Leave my dad out of this. He had nothing to do with it."

Brita held that angry gaze a moment longer, no doubt seeing the fear behind the hostility as Dolfe did. Then she nodded. "I'll try to do that. But I need you to start being honest with us."

Devon jammed his big hands into the pockets of his grease-spotted jeans, his face a dark cloud. But he finally shrugged, staring at the ground. "I saw her. I saw the woman. That night. And I followed her." His gaze jerked to Dolfe's. "But I didn't kill that guy, I swear. I didn't even know he was dead. And it wasn't until later...when I heard he was dead...that I figured out she must have killed him."

15

*B*rita sat across the table from Devon Markum, her gaze locked on him long enough to make him squirm. Despite his initial resistance, the kid had been very talkative since she'd brought him into the station. He'd told a story of sneaking over to visit with the neighbor's dog in the wee hours of the morning, when he knew he wouldn't be seen by the owners, and seeing lights and activity at the barn across the road. He'd gone to see what the activity was about, parking the recreational vehicle at the side of the road and running toward the building to get a closer look.

He'd heard a shout. A shrill scream that he'd assumed came from a woman, and had just about decided to call the police—in fact claimed to have his cell phone in his hand—when he heard a door slam in the back and, by the time he'd run around to see what was happening, had been just in time to see a woman running toward the back of the property.

"So, what did you do then?" Brita asked the sulking teen.

"I watched her until she got to the bridge. She started across, her footsteps so light I couldn't even hear them from where I stood."

The woman knew enough to stay quiet, Brita thought to herself. Had she been running from a killer? "She ran across the bridge?" Brita asked.

He shook his head, frowning. "She started to. But then she stopped and turned back." He frowned.

"She ran back to the barn?" Brita asked, surprised.

"No. Just around the bridge. She splashed down into the water and went under the bridge, coming out the other side a minute later and heading through the creek for a ways before coming out in that field over there and heading into the woods."

The fleeing woman had gone into the water? Why? Had there been dogs she was trying to confuse? That just didn't make any sense. Besides, they'd found no evidence at all of any dogs bigger than Dolfe and Blaise's tiny babies. Brita doubted anyone would be using a Chihuahua for a bloodhound. "What did you do then?"

"I knew I couldn't catch her on foot. She had too big of a head start on me. I ran and jumped on my ATV and took off after her."

"Did you find her?" Brita asked.

"No. It was like she disappeared into thin air."

Brita could imagine how it might have transpired. The recreational vehicle was loud. Really loud. And in the silence of an early morning it would seem louder still. The woman had probably believed that Lawrence Peck's killer was coming after her.

Unless she'd been the killer herself and was running from someone she feared might have seen her.

She'd been motivated. And if she and Peck had been smart, they'd have parked a vehicle somewhere along the dark country road where neighbors couldn't tie it to the venue.

"You drove around for a while?" Brita prompted.

"Yes. Then I went and gave Beast the snack I'd brought him and sat with him for a while, hoping she'd turn up if everything was quiet."

"Did she?"

He shook his head. "I never saw her again."

"Mr. Markum, can you describe this woman for me?"

He frowned, clearly trying to remember. "It was really dark."

"Just give me what you can."

"I'd say average height. Maybe five foot six or seven. Long, straight dark hair..."

"Dark as in black or not quite that dark?"

He shrugged. "It was too dark to tell for sure. She was kind of puffy."

"You mean like she was carrying extra weight?"

"I guess."

It wasn't much to go on. But it was more than they'd had before they'd spoken to him. "That's it for now, Mr. Markum. Don't leave the area. I might have more questions for you."

He nodded and stood, hesitating as if he wanted to say something but wasn't sure how.

Brita gathered up her case notes and slid them into the folder. "Is there something else, Mr. Markum?"

"I just..." He scrubbed a hand over his jaw, the telltale scratch of whiskers against his palm filling the silence between them. "I'm sorry I didn't tell you everything. I was afraid whoever killed that guy would come for me if he found out I talked to you."

His words surprised her. "You don't think the woman you saw killed him?"

"I don't know. At first I did. But the more I think about it, the more I realize she seemed scared. She kept looking over her shoulder like she thought someone was chasing her."

Brita figured there was a good chance the woman thought Devon Markum was chasing her. But she kept that to herself.

Dolfe stepped out of the observation room next

door as Brita escorted Devon Markum from Interview.

The two men inclined their heads in silent greeting. "This way, Mr. Markum." Brita indicated the elevator at the end of the hall.

Dolfe fell in behind them.

As the elevator door closed, Brita turned to Dolfe. "Did you get some rest?" She'd offered him a cot in one of the Interview rooms but he'd been unable to sleep. All he could think about was Blaise and what she was going through while he lounged around the police station. "I tried." After a couple of hours, he'd given up and just resorted to drinking a lot of coffee instead. He'd gone out and driven around the city for a few hours, even stopping in at the house to make sure they hadn't missed anything. But he'd found nothing. And a belly full of coffee and no food had just made him feel more antsy and depressed than before.

He'd returned to the station at eight o'clock for Brita's interview of Devon Markum.

Brita and Dolfe headed to her desk in the Detective's bullpen. Her partner Bud Hinks was just hanging up his phone when they approached. He smiled, the lines in his face showing light against his tanned skin. "Hey, Dolfe."

The two men shook hands, exchanging pleasantries, and then Bud turned his hazel gaze to Brita. "Did you break the kid?"

She snorted. "Into tiny little pieces." She dropped the folder onto her desk and sat on the edge, crossing her arms and fixing Bud with a look. "How about you? Did you get proof that Kim Vitters was on a plane that night?"

He turned his monitor to show them a grainy video that was frozen on a pretty young woman reaching across a counter, handing an Asian woman a bill. Kim Vitters was smiling, looking relaxed and happy as she apparently purchased a bottle of water while waiting for her flight to Miami.

"She got on the flight?" Dolfe asked.

Bud nodded. "And we have her renting a car in Miami. She couldn't have been at the scene of the murder."

Brita stared at the lithe form of the pretty blonde, thinking she couldn't look more different from the woman Devon Markum had described running from the scene. "Okay. Thanks. That's good work, partner."

Bud nodded. "I'll keep trying to trace her movements. Just in case she made a stop that might help us piece this together."

"Good. Thanks." She walked around her desk and pulled open her drawer, grabbing her Glock and an extra magazine.

"Where are you off to now?"

"I'm going to pay Lawrence Peck's boss a visit. If Kim Vitters was in Miami when Peck was murdered,

I need to find out who the woman at the crime scene was. Maybe Alex Cox has some idea who it could be." She glanced at Dolfe before heading for the elevator. "You coming?"

A lex Cox was standing beside her assistant's desk when they stepped into her office. She looked up from a sheet of paper she and the other woman were discussing when the door slid open, and Brita and Dolfe stepped out.

Dolfe didn't miss the quick frown on the older woman's face before she schooled it and offered them a smile. "Mr. Honeybun. How nice to see you again." She pulled her shoulders back and offered her hand.

Dolfe shook it, surprised by the strength in the small offering. "Ms. Cox. How are you?"

"Right as rain, Mr. Honeybun." She turned a questioning gaze toward Brita. "Detective."

Clearly, the two women hadn't hit it off well during their follow-up interview. But then, Brita had a badge and the authority of the IMPD to back her up. She didn't need to use charm.

"Mrs. Cox. We were wondering if we could ask you a few more questions?" Brita said.

Alex's lips tightened but she gave them a quick nod, glancing down to the steel-eyed woman behind the reception desk. "I'll need those numbers on my desk by this afternoon."

The other woman nodded without removing her hostile gaze from them.

Dolfe gave her a smile just to tweak her and followed Brita's brisk strides into Alex's office.

Alex led them to a small conference table beneath the window. "Have a seat. Would you like something to drink? Coffee? Water?"

"No, thank you," Brita responded tersely. She sat down and crossed her long legs, looking around the office as if she hadn't a care in the world.

Dolfe didn't sit. Instead, he perused the hundreds of hardcover books lined up on a set of built-in shelves on the back wall. Some of the tomes looked ancient. Dolfe figured Alex Cox had some real money tied up in those volumes.

"What can I help you with, Detective?"

There was a beat of silence while Brita no doubt looked thoughtful. He heard the soft, answering rustle of Alex's pantyhose as she shifted in her chair under the prolonged silence. His back turned to the women, Dolfe smiled.

Finally, Brita tugged a folder from her oversized bag and laid it on the table, opening it to show the airport security camera shots of Kim Vitters. "Is this the woman Lawrence Peck was going to marry?"

Alex grabbed one arm of the cheaters she had hanging around her neck, placed them onto her nose, and pulled the picture closer, examining it carefully before nodding. "That looks like Kim." She frowned, pushing the file back to Brita. "Why do you ask? Is she all right?"

Brita didn't respond to the question. Instead, she asked another one. "The night Lawrence Peck was killed, a witness saw a young woman running away from the scene."

Dolfe turned just as Alex's face lost all its color. "Kim? But I thought she was in Miami. Oh, that poor girl. Do you know where she is?"

Brita stared at the older woman for a few beats.

Alex held her gaze, her small hands fisting on the table. "Detective Muldane, why do I feel like you're accusing me of something?"

Brita shook her head. "I'm not accusing you of anything, Ms. Cox. As I said, I need your help."

"Then please stop treating me like a suspect and tell me what you want my help with."

Dolfe strolled over and sat down, reaching a finger to tap the photo where the time stamp showed. "This says eight PM. The flight left about an hour later, arriving in Miami at twelve oh three. We have Kim Vitters checking into her hotel there a little after two in the morning."

Alex blinked for a moment and then nodded. "She made it to Miami okay?" She took a deep breath. "What a relief. I thought you were going to tell me that whoever killed poor Lawrence got to her too."

"It appears they might have," Brita said softly.

Alex sucked in a gasp. "I'm sorry. I don't understand."

"Kim Vitters was killed in her hotel room at two-thirty AM." Brita turned a sheet of paper over and uncovered the crime scene photo from Miami.

Alex stared at the photo for a long moment, her horrified gaze locked onto the pale limb draping toward the floor.

Something slid through her gaze. Just a blip. But not fast enough for Dolfe to miss it. Strangely, it had looked like relief. "Did you know she'd been killed?" he asked gently.

Alex shook her head. "Of course not! How would I know that?" She placed a shaky hand over her mouth, shaking her head. She appeared to be trying to gather her wits. "What the heck is going on?"

"That's what we were hoping you could help us with, Ms. Cox." Brita sat forward, closing the folder. "Our witness described a woman who was likely two inches taller and fifteen to twenty pounds heavier than Kim with long dark hair running from the scene of the murder at Wedding Belles. Does that sound like anyone you know?"

Alex's confusion turned to anger. "Detective Muldane, do you know how many women I interact with on a daily basis? Dozens. I have ten educators and thirty students just at this location. How could I possibly identify one of them from such a vague description?"

"That would seem impossible," Brita agreed. "Except that not all of the women you know would have interacted with Lawrence Peck."

Alex blinked rapidly as Brita's meaning became clear. "You think Lawrence was having an affair with someone?" She shook her head briskly. "That's impossible. He loved Kim."

"Enough to try to keep her safe while doing something illegal that night?" Dolfe asked.

The older woman nodded. "Exactly. He sent her away that night. That should be all the proof you need."

"Except there was another woman with him in the barn when he was killed. Having another woman there would also be a perfectly good reason for him to send Kim away," Brita offered.

Alex's face darkened with anger. "I can't help you. As far as I know, Lawrence was completely faithful to Kim."

"But you didn't know why he'd break into Wedding Belles either," Brita pointed out. "It appears you didn't know him as well as you thought."

Alex pressed her hands into the table and stood, moving quickly around the furniture. "I think you should go, Detective."

Brita and Dolfe stood together.

"I'll need all of your security footage for the school from the last month," Brita told the older woman.

Alex inclined her head, her movements stiff with anger. "See my assistant Sara. She'll get you what you need."

"Thank you for your time, Ms. Cox."

Alex glared up at Brita, watching the cop stride quickly toward the door into the outer office.

Dolfe hesitated briefly, giving Alex a smile. "Thank you so much, Alex. I'm sorry we had to dredge all this up again."

She took a deep breath and gave him a weary smile. "It's okay. I do want to help find poor Lawrence's killer."

Dolfe nodded. "I'm glad to see your knee's feeling better."

Alex frowned slightly, glanced toward her knees, and then gave a small bark of laughter. "Oh, the golf injury." She nodded, patting him on the arm. "Yes, it's much better. It's so kind of you to remember, Mr. Honeybun. I'm touched by your interest."

He nodded, reaching out to squeeze her hand before turning away and leaving her office. As he strode across the outer office to the spot where Brita stood talking to the crotchety assistant, Dolfe couldn't help wondering if Alex Cox was telling them everything she knew. Or if she was leaving details out to cover for someone she believed was innocent.

His gut told him it was a combination of the two. But that brought another question to the forefront.

Who was Alex Cox trying to protect?

*B*laise listened carefully at the door. Her captors had locked her into the small bedroom on the upper level of the house a few hours earlier and, other than the rise and fall of voices far below, she hadn't heard anything for a while.

It had been about an hour since she started smelling the appetizing scent of food cooking, the delicious smells apparently lifting upward through the vents.

The dogs were curled together on the twin-sized bed, Badly twitching in a dream that probably involved chasing one of the chatty squirrels who lived in the tree closest to their house.

The thought brought a deep sadness into Blaise's breast. She missed her and Dolfe's pretty little cottage.

She missed Dolfe.

She turned away from the door and paced the space between the bed and the door, occasionally glancing toward the undersized window on the outside wall.

It was round, like something builders used to put into the peaks in an attic room of an old Victorian, and set too high in the wall to use for an escape.

Besides, she had the dogs. And there was no way she was leaving them behind.

Badly yipped and jumped in his sleep, drawing Ivy out of her uneasy rest. Her round, brown eyes skimmed to Blaise and held, a question replacing the warmth usually found there.

Blaise's heart broke a little more with each accusing glance from her little dog. Ivy clearly blamed her for their being kidnapped.

And even if Blaise could explain the situation to the little dog in a way she'd understand, Blaise wouldn't be able to deny the truth in that.

It *was* her fault they were all in the predicament they were in. Her, the dogs, Suz and Ty, and Dolfe.

It was all her fault. She should have known Blanchette would come after her. She should have been more careful.

Footsteps sounded on the steps and Blaise jerked around as a key found the old-fashioned lock in the heavy wood door.

She blinked in surprise as the woman came through the door, sending an unfriendly glance her way. "Dinner." The woman slammed the tray she carried onto the top of the tall dresser beside the door and started to turn away.

"Wait!" Blaise was half surprised when the woman did as she asked. "Please tell me if my friends are okay."

The woman stared at her for a long moment, dark brown eyes showing nothing except contempt. Her caramel-toned, oval face would have been pretty under the dark fall of hair, except that it was too hard-edged to be really attractive. She was dressed in a t-shirt and camo fatigues and carried her muscular form like a soldier.

"Please?" Blaise tried again.

For a beat, Blaise thought the other woman might soften and respond. But then her full lips tightened and she frowned. "I don't know."

She turned away and left, closing the door firmly behind her.

Badly woke and jumped to his feet, his little nose scenting the air as he whined. Blaise quickly went to him, picking him up and snuggling his squiggly form against her chest as she buried her nose in his soft fur. "Are you hungry, buddy?"

Blaise had no idea if the dogs had been fed since they'd been taken. She picked up the glass of water on the tray and refilled the bowl the woman had brought earlier. Her poor dogs had drained the first bowl almost immediately. They bounced excitedly as they saw her fill it again.

But she had a horrible thought, hesitating before setting the water in front of the two dogs. What if it had been doctored with something? She took a small sip, holding the water on her tongue to test it against her taste buds for any strange flavors. When she didn't taste anything, she swallowed and then turned back to the tray, taking a bite of the thick stew in the heavy bowl and then dividing it between the bowl and a small plate that had held a roll.

Blaise waited a full fifteen minutes before she was pretty certain the food and water weren't tainted. She set the water down first and watched them share the bowl, thirstily lapping it up and then draining it of the second serving Blaise dumped into it for them. The poor things had probably not had anything to drink for a day or more.

Then she settled the food in front of them and grabbed the roll for herself. She wasn't hungry, but if she was going to get them out of there, she'd need her strength.

Ivy ate a few thick chunks of meat and left the rest to her little brother, who happily wolfed it down, almost without tasting it.

Blaise's eyes filled with tears as the little dog sat down a few feet away and fixed her with another look. "I'm sorry, Miss Ivy."

Ivy's oversized ears swiveled, her brown gaze

sliding to the window, and then she stood and trotted over to Blaise, leaping agilely onto her lap.

Blaise pulled her close, kissing the soft spot between the big ears as they shifted and tickled her face.

Ivy gave her one kiss on the nose and then jumped down, running over to the wall with the window.

When Blaise just stared at her, Ivy pattered back and jumped up, putting her tiny paws onto Blaise's shin, before returning to the window to give a little whine.

Blaise stood up. "It's too small, Miss Ivy. And I couldn't get you and your brother through." She shook her head as if the little dog were arguing with her. "I'm not leaving you behind."

Ivy whined again, jumping up to rest her paws on the wall and giving a little bark.

Blaise frowned. "What is it, girl?" She glanced around, finding a small chair resting against the wall next to the tall dresser, and pulled it over, stepping onto it with the intention of looking through the window.

The chair creaked loudly and the seat shifted underneath her, making Blaise yelp in surprise and fear and slap her hands against the wall.

She stilled, listening for a beat to make sure nobody was coming to investigate the noise.

Down on the floor, Ivy danced around, her eyes bright with excitement.

"Okay, I'm looking." Blaise carefully straightened until her face came level with the round window. She looked out onto a clear blue sky and the sun sinking slowly beneath a distant fringe of trees.

She stretched to see the ground below. Her gaze fell on a silver SUV parked in the dusty grass in front of the house. The woman watching them was leaning down, talking to the driver of the car and blocking Blaise's view.

A moment later, the woman nodded and stepped back, but her muscular form still blocked Blaise's view of the driver.

The car pulled out of the grassy drive, through an opening in the trees and onto a gravel road. Blaise watched it travel down the empty road until all that was left was the bloom of gravel dust in the distance.

If the person in the car had been there to help watch Blaise, his leaving meant that she only had one babysitter.

Blaise slipped carefully off the chair and snatched Miss Ivy from the floor, covering her tiny face with kisses and receiving a few wet smooches in return. "Good work, Miss Ivy. This whole escape thing just got a lot easier." She settled the little dog onto the floor and a black and tan blur shot across the room, tackling her.

Blaise grinned as she watched the two dogs run

and play. Their world was starting to realign. Blaise just needed to make sure it didn't take another turn for the worse. She had to make a plan. And she had to make it fast. Before the second captor returned and their chances got eminently more difficult.

D olfe returned home after talking to Alex, determined to speak to all of their neighbors until he found someone who'd seen Blaise leave. He'd only been mildly surprised when he saw JJ's car in the driveway and found her shaking the hand of the ex-cop who lived next door.

She waved goodbye and headed toward Dolfe as he climbed out of the truck. "Hey. Any word on Blaise?"

His stomach twisted at the question. Too much time had passed and her chances of being hurt or... worse...improved with every passing hour. "Nothing. It's like she just disappeared from the face of the earth."

JJ shook her head. "I heard Blanchette's dead. That's good, right?"

"To tell you the truth, I'm not sure exactly what that is, JJ. If Blanchette had her stashed away somewhere and he's dead, what does that mean for her? Will his men abandon her? Leaving her to die alone and scared somewhere?" He scrubbed a hand over his face as his stomach tried to twist itself inside out.

JJ clasped his arm, giving it a reassuring squeeze. "Blaise has been in tough spots before," she reminded him. "She's not helpless."

No, Blaise was far from helpless. But she wasn't exactly equipped for combat either. He'd been remiss in training her to protect herself. But he'd learned his lesson. If...no...*when* he got her back, Dolfe swore to himself that he was going to remedy that oversight. He jerked his head toward the neighbor's house. "It looks like you and I had the same idea."

She nodded. "Brita's partner and a couple of uniforms canvassed the neighborhood already, spoke to everybody, but I thought it couldn't hurt to talk to them again. Somebody had to have seen what happened."

Dolfe wanted to agree. But the truth was their neighbors pretty much kept to themselves. All the homes were set far back from the street and there were no sidewalks so interaction between the home-owners was limited to the occasional wave from a car or a called greeting across yards.

"Any luck?"

"Not so far. I've spoken to everyone on this side of the street for a four-block distance. Most of them were either at work or inside their homes at that time and didn't see or hear anything."

"Most of them?" Dolfe asked, lifting his brows.

"The woman next door wasn't home." JJ pointed to the house he could barely see past the long hedge. "She just drove up a minute ago. I was going over there next."

Dolfe inclined his head. "Let's go."

Blaise and Dolfe had met the woman who lived next to them a couple of times. She'd brought them a plate of brownies the week they moved into their little cottage and had knocked on their door once to tell them Badly was in danger of escaping the back-yard fence by digging a hole underneath it.

She'd seemed very friendly, though like the rest of the neighborhood she kept mostly to herself. And there was something sad about her that tugged at Blaise every time the two women spoke. Dolfe figured it had something to do with the truck taking up the bulk of the woman's garage. The vehicle hadn't moved since they'd been living there. It was a big truck. A man's truck. And there didn't seem to be a man around to drive it.

Paige Lincoln was tugging a bag full of groceries from the back of her small SUV when they cut through the hedge near the house.

She jumped a little when she saw them and Dolfe apologized. "Sorry to startle you, Paige."

The woman chuckled, shaking her head. "It's fine. I wasn't paying attention. My mind was on other things." She smiled at JJ. "I see you have a visitor, young man."

The way her gaze settled speculatively on JJ, Dolfe got the feeling she thought he was up to no good.

Dolfe quickly introduced them. "JJ's a friend of mine from way back. She's a detective in Miami now."

Paige's light-brown brows lifted. "My goodness, you're pretty far from home, aren't you? What brings you to Indianapolis?"

JJ shrugged. "I had some business here. Plus, I wanted to take the chance to reconnect with this big lug."

Paige chuckled and allowed Dolfe to divest her of the two bags she was holding. "Thank you, Dolfe. That's very kind."

"My pleasure."

"Where's your beautiful fiancée today?" the woman asked, sending a too-bright smile in JJ's direction. "I wanted to tell her how much I'm enjoying the scent of the lilacs she planted at the corner of the house. They're so beautiful and they bring back memories of when I was a young girl. Lilacs were my mother's favorite flower."

Dolfe could barely speak around the lump in his throat. "Actually, that's why we're here. I was wondering if you saw Blaise earlier today? She might have left with someone else?"

Paige frowned. "Oh. She isn't answering her phone?"

"Um, no. It's probably dead again. She tends to forget to charge the stupid thing." Dolfe forced his lips to curve upward, but he had his doubts as to how genuine the smile would look.

Paige's frown deepened. "Something's wrong, isn't it?"

"Did you speak to the police yesterday?" JJ asked the other woman.

"The police? No, why? I've been gone most of the day."

The bags in his arms crunched beneath his grip. "I'm afraid something's happened. We were attacked yesterday, by two men. By the time I could get to Blaise she was gone. I'm trying to find her." Dolfe saw no need to go into the horrific details of being rifle-whipped, hung by a chain in the moldy basement of an abandoned home, and stepping over a dead body to escape.

"Oh my!" Paige looked to JJ as if for verification of Dolfe's story.

JJ nodded. "We think someone might have pushed her into a vehicle and driven off. If we could get a license plate or even a description of the vehicle that would help a lot."

Her gaze slid to the break in the hedge where the corner of Dolfe and Blaise's house was visible about twenty yards away. The lilac bush she'd been commenting on filled the space as if Blaise had deliberately put it there for Paige to enjoy. "She did seem a bit upset."

Dolfe started at her words, glancing quickly at JJ before moving a step closer to Paige in his excitement. "You saw her yesterday?"

Paige nodded. "I was just heading out to run my errands. I'd gone over to enjoy the scent of the lilacs and I saw her. She ran out of the house and jumped into the truck as a car pulled into the driveway."

"Did you see who was in the car?" JJ asked.

"Not in the car, no. The windows were too dark. And when he got out, it was kind of hard to see him. He was standing behind the cab of the truck. But I could see Blaise through the side windows. She seemed to be gesticulating, her arms swinging..." She hesitated as if just realizing that she might have misinterpreted Blaise's movements. "Oh, my." She covered her mouth with her hand, her eyes widening with horror.

"What kind of vehicle was he driving?" Dolfe asked, his words coming out terser, his tone more abrupt than he'd intended.

"It was a small red hatchback. I'm afraid that's all I can tell you about it. I couldn't see it very well from where I was standing."

"You didn't by any chance catch the license plate, did you?" Dolfe asked.

"No. I'm sorry. I'd never think to do that."

He fought despair. There were other things they

could try. If they were lucky, they'd catch the vehicle on a traffic camera and be able to grab the license plate number that way. He nodded. "Thanks for your help, Paige."

The woman frowned. "I only wish I'd realized she was in trouble earlier. I was embarrassed to be caught standing in your yard and didn't want her to think I was spying."

He nodded. "I understand."

"I hope you find her, Dolfe."

Yeah, Dolfe thought. He hoped he did too. Because if he didn't, the people who took her wouldn't have just devastated one life. They'd have ripped his reason for living away from him too. And he wouldn't rest until they paid for their actions with their own disgusting lives.

17

*B*laise searched the drawers of the tall dresser, finding nothing she could use either as a weapon or to unlock the door.

No surprise there. She really hadn't expected it to be that easy.

She dropped to her hands and knees in front of the furniture, dodging Badly's blindingly fast kisses to search beneath it. She saw nothing, but it was dark under there and she couldn't see all the way to the back.

Badly leaped onto her head and stuck his tongue in her ear and she yelped, giggling as she tried to wrangle the little dog away.

A sharp bark just behind her announced the arrival of the party pooper and Badly stopped trying to lick Blaise's eyeball long enough to turn and bark at his bossy sister.

Ivy danced backward, her tiny nails clicking on the hardwood floor beneath Blaise's knees.

Badly bounced twice on Blaise's thigh and then launched himself to the ground to chase Ivy around the room.

Blaise had a few seconds to finish her search before the naughty little dog was back. She shoved a hand underneath the dresser and ran it along the wall, then skimmed it outward to the edges.

Nothing but dust.

Wiping her hand on her jeans, Blaise sat up just as Badly launched himself at her and she caught him, pulling him under her chin to keep him from roto-rootering her nostrils. The tiny dervish twisted and jerked in her arms, wide pink tongue lapping the air near her face in an attempt to get to her.

Blaise kissed him on top of his soft head. "Go play with your sister." She set him on the ground and gave his wriggling backside a push toward Ivy and he was off as if she'd shot him from a cannon.

Blaise hurriedly crawled over to the bed and looked beneath it for a tiny scrap of metal or a skinny stick.

There was nothing but dust balls and a few crumbs covered in green fuzz. She was surprised Badly hadn't hoovered those up already. She grimaced at the thought.

The dogs whizzed past her on a mission only they understood, circling the small room at the speed of light with Badly doing the chasing as they disappeared under the bed and coming out the other side after a brief tussle among the dust bunnies with Ivy doing the chasing.

Blaise couldn't help grinning, even with a tightness in her chest that made it hard to breathe. She was hyper-aware of the passage of time and the danger the second captor would return. Her gaze skimmed to the empty tray on top of the dresser. She stared at it for a minute and then stood, moving over to stare down at the single metal spoon there.

If only they'd given her a fork or a knife. But the people who'd orchestrated her capture were clearly too smart for that.

She picked up the spoon and stared at it a moment, wondering how much damage she could do with it. She could always stab it into the woman's face. It could do some real damage to her eyes.

Blaise winced. Could she do that? She shuddered at the thought.

Then she had another thought that might just prove more useful. She walked over and looked at the doorknob, trying to insert the skinny end of the spoon's handle into the mechanism.

It was too thick to slide inside.

She swore softly, jumping at a soft, wet touch on the back of her calf. She turned around, smiling down at Miss Ivy. "Thank you for the kiss, girl."

Ivy kissed her again as if offering encouragement.

Blaise turned back to the knob, trying again to insert the spoon handle into the lock. It was just too big. And she had no way to whittle it down.

She eyed the door for a moment and then tried shoving the handle into the lock plate between the door and the frame. It went in a fraction of an inch. Not enough to trip the lock.

She flipped it around and inserted the curved front edge of the spoon into the space and found that it slid in far enough to reach the lock. Shoving hard, she wiggled it around, feeling something shift slightly inside the mechanism.

Excitement surged, causing her breath to quicken.

Blaise put more muscle into it, jerking the spoon up and then down until something clicked.

And the door popped open to bounce against her toes.

JJ returned to Dolfe's office to work the Miami end of the investigation. Her partner there had called with information about Blanchette's yacht. Apparently, it had been located in a North Carolina marina and JJ was overseeing the gathering of evidence via phone.

She'd promised Dolfe that if she had to fly to North Carolina to get what they needed she'd do it. But they both knew how long it would take her to get to the scene. Even if they had Godric Honeybun fly her there in his private plane. It would take another couple of hours to get to the remote location where they'd found the boat.

Dolfe had driven to the station and given Bud Hinks a description of the car Paige Lincoln had seen, and Brita had asked her partner to get with the Electronic Surveillance group at the precinct to find the car.

Brita sat next to him in the truck as they pulled away from the precinct, staring straight ahead and frowning.

Dolfe glanced her way. "Something wrong?"

She skimmed him a look. "Everything?" Shaking her head, Brita sighed. "Something's just...off...with all of this. Nothing fits and everything fits. You know what I mean?"

Dolfe knew exactly what she meant. He'd been thinking the same thing. "Yeah. Blanchette supposedly comes to Indiana to exact revenge on Blaise and me. He sets up this elaborate plan to take out Brick and then promptly gets himself murdered. Then I'm attacked and kidnapped but they leave Blaise behind and let me escape. And then they kidnap Blaise." He shook his head. "It's all a mish-mash. And I'm terrified that we haven't heard anything from the people who took her."

Brita nodded, her frown deepening. "To be honest, that's been bothering me too. There's no point in using her as leverage unless you're going to *use* her as leverage."

Dolfe's cell rang and he glanced at caller ID. It was Clovis. He hit *Speaker* and settled the phone on the console between them. "Hey, cuz. You're on speaker with Brita and me."

"Good," Clovis said, his deep voice sounding weary. "You need to come to Methodist Hospital right away."

Dolfe frowned. "Why? What's happened?"

"Just hurry. We need you here. Ty and Suz's house was breached last night and Alf's been shot."

Blaise stuck her head into the hallway and listened, hearing music and the muted interplay of voices that sounded as if it came from a television program.

Something clinked below, like the sound of a glass being settled into a porcelain sink. She'd been unconscious when they brought her to the house so she had no idea what the layout of the place looked like.

She was working completely in the blind.

If it was like most homes, the kitchen would be close to the front door. She couldn't risk trying to make it out that exit.

But maybe there was a back door. In fact, the more Blaise thought about it, the more she realized there had to be another way out of the house.

Her pulse pounded. She hated not having more information.

Blaise hesitated, wondering if it would be safer to wait for the woman to bring another meal and ambush her from behind the door.

She dismissed the idea almost immediately. She couldn't risk having the woman realize she'd breached the lock.

Blaise pressed the door nearly shut without letting the mechanism engage and reached down to scoop up Badly. The happy puppy slathered her cheek with wet kisses as she scooped up Miss Ivy with her other hand. "Okay, kids. We need to be very quiet, okay?"

Miss Ivy gave her soft eyes as if she understood. Badly stuck his tongue up her nose.

Jerking her head away, Blaise sighed. It would be a dang miracle if she managed to get out of that house without alerting the woman downstairs.

She stuck her toe against the edge of the door and pushed it open, easing through and moving as quickly as she dared along the wide hall toward the stairs.

She eyed the scarred wooden steps, remembering hearing them creak a few times as the woman climbed them to bring Blaise food. She had no way of knowing which steps had creaked, so she decided to stay as close to the molding on the wall side as possible, praying the wood was better supported there.

She started down, the sound of a television laugh track startling her to a stop just as a shadow moved across the room beyond the dark wood banister. When no one came for them, Blaise let another moment pass and then risked moving down a couple more steps.

She held Badly tight against her chest, praying he wouldn't bark a greeting to the woman when he saw her.

To Blaise's relief, the woman was standing across the room, staring out at an endless canvas of green fields. She held a glass in her hands, half filled with what looked like plain water, and her other hand rested against the frame, knuckles white.

Blaise realized she was staring down the road, probably in anticipation of her partner's return

Blaise hoped he'd be delayed.

She stepped off the bottom stair and the floor creaked. The woman started to turn as another laugh track blasted through the room. Then her cell rang and she seemed to forget about the creak. As she answered the call, Blaise hurried around the end of the stairs and ran toward the back of the small house.

There was a tiny half bath at the end of the downstairs hall and sunlight filtered through onto the wood floor from a room to her right. She flattened herself against the wall and peered into the room before entering, seeing only an empty bedroom with a double bed that looked as if it had recently been slept in and a few stark pieces of old furniture.

The woman's voice shifted, heading in Blaise's direction, and Badly growled, his tiny chest rumbling under her hand.

Blaise quickly ducked into the bedroom. She settled Ivy at her feet and grabbed the door, easing it closed as quietly as she could before turning the lock on the knob.

The voice stopped near the stairs. Blaise prayed the woman wouldn't go upstairs to check on them. In her hurry, she'd left the door open. If the woman even glanced that way, she'd know Blaise had flown the coop.

Blaise mentally chastised herself for being stupid.

But there was nothing she could do about it. All she could do was move forward. She glanced around the room, finding an old ladderback chair near the closet. Blaise set Badly on the floor and hurried over to grab the chair, wedging it under the knob to hopefully give her an extra thirty seconds if the woman came looking.

The two dogs set off happily exploring the room. Blaise headed for the window, pleased to see that it was only a couple of feet from the ground. She unlocked it and tugged it open, and was immediately blasted by hot air.

She looked out into the unending nothingness of the farmland surrounding them. What if they couldn't find someone to help them before the woman tracked them down?

What if the heat got to be too much?

She shoved those worries aside. The only way was forward. She had to trust that she and the dogs could find help.

Though they couldn't go anywhere near the road looking for it.

A loud scratching sound was followed by dual whines and Blaise whipped around, afraid the dogs were scratching at the door.

She didn't see them. Blaise panicked. Where had the dogs disappeared to?

Then she noticed the closet doors were ajar. "Come on you two," she whispered.

More scratching.

Zero listening.

"Miss Ivy!" she whispered in a harsher tone.

The dog's tiny face appeared in the crack between the closet doors. She was squirming from head to toe, her tail smacking softly against the door.

"What is it, girl? Did you find a way out?"

Blaise hurried over and pulled the door wide, only to find Badly scratching madly against the molding on the back wall. "You found a mouse, huh?" Blaise fought frustration as she bent down to grab him. "No time for hunting, little man. We need to get out of here."

A sharp creak sounded overhead.

The woman was upstairs!

Blaise reached for Ivy but the little dog ducked away, returning to scrabble at the increasingly scratched molding. "Come on, Ivy! We need to go."

But Ivy dodged away again and Badly wriggled free. The two dogs dug manically at the splintering wood.

Blaise's heart pounded in her chest. Footsteps pounded overhead. The woman was coming!

"Come on, you two!" she said too loudly. Then she halted, realizing she could have been heard.

Her heart was pounding so hard she almost didn't hear the muffled voice coming through the wall. "Hello? Is someone there?"

18

*D*olfe ran into Emergency and saw Clovis keeping watch by the doors into the back rooms. The nurse at the desk frowned his way as he sped past her and Clovis hit the button to open the doors. Brita stopped in the waiting room, ready to use her badge if she needed to keep Dolfe from being waylaid.

"This way," Clovis indicated they should head toward a room at the back. "He's just coming around."

"Will he be okay?" Dolfe asked, his gut churning from nerves.

"Yeah. It turns out the bullet missed all the important stuff." Clovis turned to Dolfe with a weary grin. "It just hit him in the head."

Dolfe felt himself pale before he recognized the joke. "Har, cuz."

Clovis pointed toward a room and patted Dolfe on the shoulder. "Seriously though, he's going to have some recovery time and he'll need rehab to get that shoulder useable again. But he was lucky."

Pleasance Roberts, Alf's honey, was sitting in a chair beside the bed, staring worriedly down at Alf. He was an unhealthy gray color and the whole left side of his torso was swathed in bandages from mid-torso to where his shoulder met his neck, but his eyes were open and he tracked Dolfe as he hurried over to give Pleasance a hug. "I heard you weren't successful in getting rid of him," he joked.

Some of the worry left her startling blue gaze and she chuckled. "Not this time. But I'm going to put my best man on it next time."

"Har de har har," Alf said in a scratchy voice, licking his lips. "What does a wounded man have to do to get some water here?" he asked in a decidedly pathetic way.

Pleasance let go of the hand she'd been clutching and turned away to pour him some water. "He's going to be a real pain during this recovery, isn't he?" she asked as she held the cup to his lips.

Clovis nodded. "Count on it. If it gets too bad just hit him over the head. It won't solve the problem forever but it might buy you an hour or so of peace."

She grimaced as the water trickled down his chin, grabbing a bunch of paper napkins to tidy him up. "Noted. There's already been some talk of a bell.

If that happens, I won't be responsible for my actions."

Alf chuckled. "Okay, no bell."

"Good," she said, sitting back down and grabbing his hand again.

"I'll just call you on my cell when I need something," he said with a twinkle in his eye.

Pleasance eyed the offending object on the table, grabbing it and handing it to Clovis. "Problem solved."

"Hey!"

Dolfe shook his head. "I'm glad to see he'll live." He grew serious. "Can you tell me what happened?"

Alf lay back on the pillow, his features settling into worry. "It was the wee hours of the morning. They came at us fast. I didn't expect it. There were two of them. Unfortunately, I went down first, so I have only a vague awareness of what happened. I only know for sure there were more shots fired inside. By the time I managed to get to my feet and head toward the house, they were already carrying the kennel out."

Dolfe felt the blood leaving his face and his knees buckled. "They took the dogs?"

Alf nodded. "I tried to stop them but got this for my trouble." He pointed to a large, purple goose egg on his temple. "When I came to again, I went looking for Banyon. Found him wounded and unconscious. He'd lost a lot of blood." Alf frowned, clearly worried.

"Banyon?" Dolfe asked, feeling as if he would vomit.

"My agent. I was just coming to spell him." Alf scrubbed a hand over his face, his gaze haunted. "I'm so sorry, Dolfe. If I'd known we were in danger of a breach I'd have armed up better."

Dolfe shook his head, dismissing his cousin's apology. "Can you describe them?"

"I'm pretty sure one of them was a woman. But they were wearing masks."

"Do you have any idea how they found you?" Dolfe asked.

Alf looked at Clovis, who was standing near the door, muscular arms crossed over his chest. His expression was hard and cold. He was angry.

"We have to have a mole," Clovis said.

"Not necessarily," Dolfe said. "It wouldn't have taken much digging to find out where Ty and Suz live."

"Especially for a cop," Clovis said, eyeing Dolfe.

"What are you saying?" Dolfe asked, getting irritated.

"How well do you know JJ?" Alf asked softly, his blue eyes filled with apology.

Dolfe immediately rejected the implication. "There's no way, Alf."

Alf shrugged and then paled as pain no doubt

shot through him with the movement. "I know she's your friend and, trust me, I don't want to suspect her either. But, she's the only unknown here, Dolfe."

"She did just show up, cuz," Clovis added.

Dolfe's glare swung to the big man standing behind him. "JJ wouldn't do this. It has to be someone else."

"Well, until we know who, we're going to have to exclude her from further updates," Clovis said. His glance toward his wounded brother told Dolfe all he needed to know. Clovis was going to take the heat from Dolfe to spare Alf as he dealt with recovery. Dolfe was okay with that. He fixed Clovis with a look that told his cousin they'd be continuing the conversation later. "I'll support keeping local details from JJ. But I'm still going to use her for the Miami end of the investigation."

Alf nodded, winced, and closed his eyes, looking too gray for Dolfe's comfort.

Pleasance looked at them. "Okay, you two, out. He needs to rest."

Dolfe squeezed her shoulder. "Don't worry about this one. He's too ornery to succumb to a mere bullet."

She sighed, her face filled with concern.

Dolfe looked at Clovis as they exited the room and his cousin shook his head, pointing toward the door into the emergency room lobby.

Dolfe kept silent as they retraced their steps,

finding Brita on the phone when they came through the swinging doors.

She looked excited, glancing at them as they approached. "Dolfe is here. We'll head there now." Brita hung up and pointed toward the exit. "Come on. Electronics found the rental car. Hopefully, we also found Blaise."

Blaise glanced toward the door, praying the chair would hold for a few minutes, and dropped to her knees, pressing her ear against the wall. "Who's there?" she said as loudly as she dared.

There was a beat of silence and then the sound of something brushing along the inside. "Blaise?"

Suz!

"Suz, are you okay?" Blaise ran her hands over the aged cedar paneling that covered the back wall of the closet, looking for a seam or something. There had to be a hidey hole behind the wall. She found nothing. "How do I get to you?"

"I don't know. They drugged us. We were unconscious when they dumped us here."

"Us?" Blaise expanded her search, standing and shoving clothing aside and sneezing as dust filtered off the old cotton dresses and sweaters.

"Ty's here too. But...Blaise he's hurt pretty bad."

Blaise let herself give in to a moment of despair. Could things get any worse? She immediately shoved the thought aside. Her friends were still alive. It could definitely have been worse. "Don't worry, girlfriend, I'll get you out of there."

Blaise kicked a thick-soled pair of shoes to the side and one of them hit the wall with a hollow sound. Blaise burrowed deeper into the closet, bumping up against the ceiling as it dipped sharply down toward the outsides of the closet.

She pounded the wall there and found the spot where the sound changed, hitting the area with her fist. "Suz, what's right here?"

"I don't see anything. Just boards and insulation". The brushing sound came again as her friend presumably pulled the insulation from between the boards. Suz gasped. "There's a tiny bit of light. I think it might be a door of some kind."

Blaise shoved at the wall, Badly digging into the molding at the bottom with her. Miss Ivy took off out of the closet in a shot, barking. Panicking, Blaise jumped up, bashing her head on the low ceiling hard enough for her to see stars, and then ran after her dog.

The knob on the door was jiggling.

They'd been discovered!

Blaise panicked, looking around in desperation. She glanced toward the open window and briefly considered lowering the dogs through it. At least they'd be free.

But she hated to abandon them, and she couldn't leave Suz and Ty behind. No matter what.

The door rumbled under an assault, as if the woman had either kicked or thrown herself at it. The chair beneath the knob held. For the moment. But Blaise wasn't sure how much longer it would sustain. She glanced at the window again and made a sudden decision.

Scooping up Ivy, she hurried back to the closet, pulling the doors closed and then dropping to her knees beside a still digging Badly. The molding had come loose in one spot and the little dog was chewing the edge, pulling off chunks of wood, his tail wagging happily.

Blaise dug desperately at the molding with him, hoping there'd be a space behind the wood big enough to get her fingers through. If she had something to grab, maybe she could pull the hidden door open.

A thunderous explosion sounded in the room beyond the doors. The woman had used her gun, probably to make a hole big enough to reach through. Blaise made a tiny sound of alarm as the legs of the chair squealed against the floor.

Pounding started inside the wall and Blaise realized Suz was trying to help.

A hunk of the molding came off in Badly's mouth

and Blaise saw the tarnished glow of a piece of metal. She reached for it, sliding the bolt back and giving the door a shove.

It finally moved inward, dust sifting down on her head from the top of the tiny opening. Suz's face, pale and covered in sweat, seemed to float, disembodied, from the shadows beyond.

Badly jumped happily over the short threshold and disappeared into the dark.

Blaise extended a hand toward her friend and Suz's fingers wrapped tightly around hers. "I thought we were going to die in here."

Blaise reached over and scooped up Ivy, handing her to her friend. "Nobody's dying in this house. We're going to get out of here. But right now, we need to hunker down and stay as quiet as we can."

Suz frowned, dodging Ivy's manically licking tongue. "Wait. We're not leaving?"

Blaise stood and pulled the clothing back to cover the entire rod and then grabbed the broken molding and some shoe boxes from a pile in the corner. "Not just yet. We need a minute to figure out what we're going to do. That woman out there's armed and very strong. We can't just rush her. Somebody's going to get hurt."

Suz scooted back as Blaise backed into the space, pressing the molding back into place and shoving the shoe boxes against it to hold it there and hide the broken part.

Then she took one last look at the doors, wincing as the outer door gave way with a splintering sound and the chair was thrown across the room.

She backed into the dark hidey hole, pulling the trap door closed with her, and wrapped her arms around her badly-shaking friend as angry-sounding footsteps thundered through the room.

She held her breath as the footsteps moved away, probably toward the window, and then stopped.

"Where are you, Blaise?" The woman's voice was calm. Too calm. As if she hadn't a care in the world.

Blaise closed her eyes and listened to the dogs sniffling around more deeply into the space. She prayed they'd stay there and wouldn't start barking.

"Oh, Blaise. I know you're here!" The woman's voice rose and fell in a sing-song fashion, moving around the room and occasionally getting louder or softer, sounding muffled. She was searching the room.

It was only a matter of time before she came to the closet. And the hidey hole where they'd imprisoned Blaise's friends.

19

"The vehicle hasn't moved since we found it," Bud's voice said through the speaker of Brita's phone. It was on the console between them again and they were heading out of town, into the countryside west of Indianapolis.

Bud had uncovered a stolen vehicle report for a car matching the description Paige had given them and they'd been thrilled to discover the car had a built-in tracking service installed.

Dolfe had never seen so much farmland. Acres and acres of brown fields with unplanned crops of weeds sporting yellow and purple flowers. It would have been pretty if his stomach wasn't tied in knots.

If Blaise wasn't in terrible danger.

The occasional huge piece of farm equipment, hulking in the field with alien type arms and tires as big as Brita's car waited for the cool nights and rains of Spring to give way long enough for farmers to plant their crops and kick off the growing season.

Dolfe didn't envy the farmers that season. His job could be hard, dealing with criminals and druggies, law enforcement personnel, and people whose lives had spun out of control and who weren't capable of reeling them back in by themselves.

But human nature was understandable, navigable, and subject to certain laws of behavior.

Mother Nature was a cruel taskmistress. And she followed no one's rules.

Bud's voice tore through his thoughts. "You should see the car up ahead. It's not far from your location."

Their gazes scoured the area, seeing a lot of open fields, some trees, and one dilapidated barn that looked in danger of falling completely over in a strong breeze.

But no car.

"It's not here, Bud."

"It has to be, Honeybun. Keep looking."

Dolfe's gaze landed on the barn. "Wait, I have an idea." He pulled off the road and they bounced over a short, rutted strip of dirt that apparently served as the barn's driveway. They climbed out of the truck and pulled their guns as they approached the enormous sliding doors.

One door hung at an odd angle, the track broken away on that side and jutting out from the frame.

Dolfe nodded toward the broken side and Brita veered off in that direction, pressing herself against the faded and chipped red paint as Dolfe grasped the handle on the other door and, with a nod from Brita, yanked it open.

A surprised squawk had them both lifting their guns toward the sky as a bird fluttered past Dolfe, its wings skimming his hair, and flew off with a few more choice squawks for the humans who dared to disturb its privacy.

The sunlight speared the newly breached space and lighted on a small red car abandoned in the center of the open space, amid tumbling piles of moldy hay. "We found it," Brita told Bud. "I'll call you back in a few." Brita slipped her phone into the back pocket of her jeans and strode over to the car as Dolfe split off to do a quick search of the building.

A few moments later, he'd found nothing except some rusted-out farm equipment, a lot of old hay, and a skinny cat with ragged ears who was just as vocal as the bird about them disturbing its hidey hole.

Peering through the windows, Brita did a quick visual scan of the car before opening the front door and searching inside.

She backed out as Dolfe approached, holstering her gun and grabbing her cell. "There's blood."

His stomach twisted painfully. "How much?"

She snapped several pictures of the front seat,

focusing mostly on the dash and a dark spot on the headrest of the driver's side seat. "Enough. Somebody was beaten, would be my guess." She took a step back so he could peer inside and pointed toward the dark stain on the seat and the matching patch of dark red on the steering wheel.

He nodded. "It looks like someone smashed the driver's head into the steering wheel."

He relaxed. It was unlikely that was Blaise's blood in the driver's seat. But finding the car in that barn did mean one thing. The car had clearly been abandoned. Blanchette's people had probably switched cars on that road and headed off to another location.

Dolfe's heart twisted painfully.

It looked like the trail was cold again.

Blaise fought back a shudder as the closet door creaked open.

"Are you in here, Blaise?" The woman's voice was teasing, almost playful. If she was at all worried about losing Blaise, she didn't show it.

Blaise held her breath, her arms tightening around Suz as her friend tried to move away.

Suz turned to her but Blaise couldn't see her expression in the pitch-black space.

Suz's hand found hers and squeezed once, before prying the fingers away.

Blaise reluctantly let her go.

And then immediately regretted it.

Suz pounded on the wall. "Who's out there? Why are you keeping us in here? Let us out. "

Blaise's initial panic made it hard to breathe. Her gaze fell to the spot where she knew the opening was and she waited for the woman in the bedroom to discover what they'd done and come inside.

Several tense beats of silence left Blaise feeling dizzy with dread.

But Suz's instincts had been right on. Her questions and continued pounding on the wall convinced their captor the opening hadn't been breached. She moved away without saying another word and, a moment later, Blaise heard the soft thump of the window being closed.

She closed her eyes in relief, expelling the breath she'd been holding, and then hugged her friend as the hall door slammed shut, the concussion rippling along the floors and vibrating the opening to their hidey hole.

"You're a genius, Suz Whatsnoggin."

Her friend expelled a tense gust of air. Apparently, she'd been just as worried as Blaise. "We need to help Ty. He stopped moving about an hour ago and I'm worried about him."

"Just give me a minute." Blaise shoved the small

door into the closet and crawled through, cracking the door open and peering into the bedroom to make sure they were alone.

She winced at the splintered door. From the front of the house, a screen door slammed closed, causing Blaise to jump and yelp softly, banging her head on the doorframe.

The woman had fallen for Blaise's ruse. She thought they'd gone outside.

Which meant...

Blaise yanked the door closed as a shadow fell over the window, praying the woman hadn't seen her. Her heart pounded against her ribs with nerves as the silence hovered over her. She waited, her chest tight, for the sound of the woman returning to the house to confront them.

After several moments, Blaise relaxed. The woman had to be looking for them.

She risked opening the door enough to let light into the closet, hoping some of it would filter through into the hidey hole.

Crawling back inside, Blaise saw Suz huddled over a prone form several feet into the space. Miss Ivy sat next to Tyrese's unmoving body, her big ears swiveling as Blaise crawled toward them. "She's gone outside to look for us."

Suz's face fell. "That means we won't be able to leave."

Blaise shook her head. We'll figure something

out, Suz. She moved up next to Ty. "Tell me what's happened to him?"

She cupped a hand around his chin, tears glistening in the low light. He tried to fight them off and they hit him—a lot.

Blaise placed a hand on his chest, intending to check his breathing, and he let out a long, drawn-out groan.

"He seems to be really tender in the stomach and chest," Suz told her, sniffling.

Blaise carefully lifted his torn and dirty tee shirt, grimacing at the shadows and swelling covering his flesh.

"What is it?" Suz asked, her voice wobbly with fear.

Blaise was no doctor, but she was pretty sure they were looking at the results of internal bleeding. "We need to get him to a hospital," she told her friend gently.

Suz sobbed once, covering her mouth with a shaky hand, and then fought to pull herself together and nodded. "I tried to move him but I couldn't."

No wonder. The two of them had been terrified, probably deprived of food and liquids, for hours. "I'll take his shoulders. Can you get his feet?"

Suz didn't hesitate. She crawled around him and pushed to her feet, her back bent to keep from banging her head against the low ceiling.

If Blaise's directional compass was working, the

hiding spot had been built underneath the stairs leading to the second floor where she'd been held.

Which meant it was tallest at the front.

"I'll help you pull him until we get to the door," she told Suz.

The two of them dragged Ty to the small opening and then Blaise climbed through, Suz followed her out, straightening slowly with a groan. She held her lower back, closing her eyes as she carefully twisted right and then left. "It's going to take me six months on the yoga mat to get rid of this pain and stiffness."

Blaise figured it would take a while longer than that for her friend to regain her customary cockiness after her ordeal. She didn't voice her concerns though. Instead, she gave Suz a quick hug. "We're going to be all right, Suz. You know that, right?"

"I'm starting to believe it now," she said with a smile for Blaise.

Blaise took a quick look into the bedroom before she climbed back inside the hidey hole.

She grabbed Ty under the arms and Suz grabbed his ankles. It took them several moments and a lot of sweating and heavy breathing but they finally managed to get him out of the hole.

By the time he was lying half inside the closet and half in the bedroom, his eyes had fluttered open and his handsome face had an unhealthy tone to it.

Suz kissed his lips. "We're going to be okay, Ty. Blaise is here."

He turned a hopeful gaze her way. "Dolfe?" he asked, though it clearly hurt him to talk.

She couldn't bear to tell him they were on their own. Especially since the process of moving her friend had convinced Blaise that he wasn't going to get to his feet.

And she and Suz certainly couldn't carry him.

"He's right behind me," she lied to him.

When she caught Suz's eye again, Blaise saw the pain there. Suz seemed to realize why Blaise was lying to him.

Ty grasped Suz's hand. "Leave..." He swallowed hard, his face tightening with pain. "Leave me here, Suz."

She shook her head, scrubbing angrily at the tears sliding down her cheeks. "I'm not leaving you."

He looked at Blaise, his brown eyes pleading.

She squeezed his hand. "He's right, Suz. We need to get help. The sooner we find help, the sooner we can come back and get him to a hospital."

Suz was still shaking her head.

"I'll be...fine...Suz. But I need you to go now. Bring back help."

Badly and Ivy bounced out of the closet, their tails wagging happily as they ran toward Ty. Blaise snagged Badly just before he leaped on the helpless man, but Ivy scoured his face with kisses.

"Hey, Miss Ivy," Ty said, actually smiling. "Thanks for the kisses."

Ivy's bottom wiggled as if she understood his words.

Blaise nodded. "Okay, Suz, if you want to help Ty, we need to move. Let's pull him behind the bed and cover him with the spread. They won't know he's here unless they come in to make the bed. Which I think everyone here can agree is highly unlikely."

Ty started to chuckle and then gasped in pain.

"Oops," said Blaise. "No jokes. Got it."

Ty grinned and then coughed, bright blood peppering his lips as he groaned in pain.

The sight got Suz moving. She jumped up and grabbed his feet. Blaise started to grab him under the arms but he shook his head. "No. Just drag me. It's faster."

And probably hurt a bit less, Blaise realized. "Sorry, Ty."

He shook his head. "It's all good, dark chocolate."

She hurried over and grabbed one ankle, Suz grabbed the other and they started to drag him across the room.

The agony their manhandling caused her friend was obvious, so she decided a little distractive teasing might help, "So, dark chocolate is a new one. I'm guessing you're thinking Dolfe will like that better than brown sugar?"

Ty licked his lips, grinning. "What do you think? Will he?"

"Doubtful. But I'm definitely not a fan. You know, dark chocolate is very bitter, Ty. I don't appreciate being told I'm bitter."

He licked his lips, his hands fisted on his hips. "It's true you're really more like milk chocolate, girl. But dark chocolate sounds cooler. I have a rep to maintain." He sucked air as they eased him around the end of the bed.

"Your rep is intact," Suz told him, her eyes swimming in tears. "But I'm not sure your body will be if you don't stop calling Blaise any kind of sweet. Dolfe's going to use a big pair of scissors and cut off your important parts."

He actually did chuckle at that, and then his eyes rolled up in his head and he went out again.

Suz made a terrified little sound and bent over him, her face close to his. "Ty!"

Blaise noted the rise and fall of his chest. "He's alive, Suz. I'm guessing he's just passed out from the pain. Hopefully he won't wake up again until he's in a hospital. Let's go."

Suz kissed Ty again and then stood, hurrying away as if she might not leave if she looked back.

Blaise didn't blame her. She wasn't sure she'd be able to leave Dolfe behind in a similar situation.

The dogs bounced after them as they hurried down the hall.

"What's the plan?" Suz asked.

"First we see if there's a car we can use. If there is, hopefully we can find the keys."

Because, if they couldn't find the keys, they'd be walking. And that would really slow things down. Ty might not survive that timeline.

"See if you can find a weapon of some kind," she told Suz as she hurried to the front door. She fought despair as she looked around and saw nothing drivable. But there was an outbuilding not too far away. Maybe there was a car in there.

Two tiny sets of clacking nails accompanied Suz's soft footfall from the kitchen. She was holding a very large knife and her expression was murderous. "I almost hope we see her out there," Suz muttered angrily. "I'd like to pay her back for what she did to Ty."

"Did you see any keys?" Blaise asked.

But Suz shook her head, hurrying toward the door. "No, but if there's a car, I can hotwire it."

Blaise's eyes went wide. "White girl?"

Suz spared her a mean little smile. "Hey, I have skills you don't know about."

"Obviously," Blaise responded. "Does daddy know?"

Suz blew air through her lips as she stepped outside. "Who do you think taught me?"

Laughing softly, Blaise scooped up Badly as he

made a run for the door and followed Suz and Ivy outside.

They'd nearly made it to the outbuilding when a large tree exploded in a wash of bark and splinters. Bullets tearing into the thick body of the tree and sending its insides shooting toward them, like a thousand tiny little knives.

own!" Blaise shrieked as two more bullets tore into the massive tree.

Badly wriggled out of her grip and Blaise couldn't grab him back. She barely managed to grab Ivy's collar, jerking the little dog back to her before she could take off running out of pure fear.

Suz hit the ground with a terrified scream and crawled quickly behind the tree as dirt and grass sprayed up around her feet.

Blaise didn't know if the woman was a terrible shot or if she was deliberately missing. She hoped it was the latter, because even a poor shot might accidentally hit them if she kept firing.

Suz leaned against the tree, her hands clutching the useless knife and her face as white as paper. "She's shooting at us!"

Blaise wasn't sure why Suz was surprised, after

all, the stuff they'd endured so far should have told her friend the people who had them were deadly serious.

Ivy whined and tried to jerk free of Blaise's grip. She was staring off into the tree line, where a tiny brown and black face peered at them from the shade of a big walnut tree. Blaise was torn. If she called out to Badly she'd put him into the open and into danger. If she didn't, the little dog might take off with the next round of firing and never look back.

She could lose him forever in the vast openness of the rural farmland.

"If you come out now, with your hands up, I promise I won't kill you," The woman called out. Blaise peered around the tree and saw her, hunkered down behind the corner of the house, her gun pointing right at the tree where she and Suz huddled.

"How do I know you aren't lying?" Blaise asked.

Suz turned to her, clutching her arm with fingers that were much stronger than Blaise would have guessed. "No! We can't go back. Ty will die."

Blaise reached for the knife, prying it from Suz's fingers. "Trust me." She handed Ivy over. "Hold on tight to her. She wants to run to Badly." Blaise jerked her head toward the trees and Suz's gaze slid that way. But it snapped back as Blaise shifted. "What are you going to do?"

Blaise shoved to her feet, pushing the knife carefully down the back of her pants. "I'm not a hundred percent sure. But as soon as I move on her, you run to where Badly is and don't stop. Grab him and all of you go."

Suz shook her head emphatically. "I'm not leaving any more of my friends behind."

Blaise looked into Suz's eyes, which swam with fresh tears. "You can bring back help, Suz. It's our only chance if I can't stop her."

"She'll kill you!" Suz lamented.

With a confidence she didn't really feel, Blaise shook her head. "If she'd wanted me dead, I'd already be dead. Now please do as I ask. For Tyrese." She knew that last was slightly below the belt but she had to try it. Suz didn't seem willing to do as Blaise was asking.

Her friend shook her head again but Blaise didn't give her a choice. She pulled her into a quick hug, kissed Ivy on top of the head, and then prepared to step out from behind the tree.

"Hello? I'm running out of patience here."

Blaise closed her eyes for a moment, said a silent prayer, and then peeled herself from the protection of the big tree. "Don't shoot. I'm coming."

"The other one too."

Blaise let tears fall down her cheeks, allowing her misery to show on her face. "She's dead. You killed her." The misery was quickly muted behind a righteous strain of anger, which Blaise didn't have to fake one little bit. "She didn't hurt *anybody* and you killed her."

The woman hesitated a moment and then stepped out from the house, her gun still raised to focus on Blaise's chest. "She shouldn't have run."

"Yeah, as if the result would have been different if she'd stayed."

The woman shrugged. "Too bad about your little puppies. They were kind of cute."

If the woman was trying to make nice, she'd have to go a lot further than that. "You've probably killed them too." Blaise's rage made her strides tight, her hands clench into fists.

The woman actually smiled. "You're right. They'll probably be eaten by coyotes."

The thought sucked the air right out of Blaise's lungs and she stopped, buckling over with a sob she couldn't seem to control.

Her babies.

Her sweet little dogs...

The woman moved closer as Blaise bent double, clutching her belly as she retched uncontrollably.

She was dimly aware of the small pair of scuffed work boots stopping a foot away, but she was unable to stop retching long enough to straighten and look the horrible woman in the eyes. It took the touch of hard, warm metal against her shoulder to jerk her upright, and when she came, it was with the force of a tsunami.

An unnatural power so great and so condensed into one slender body, that it was nearly an unstoppable force.

Dolfe eased on down the road, feeling his heart tear away from him with every turn of the truck's oversized tires.

His gut was on fire. He told himself it was just because of fear and worry for Blaise, but he couldn't shake the feeling that it was more.

Much more.

Without realizing it he eased his foot off the gas, his gaze locked on the rearview mirror as pain shot through his chest like a knife.

"What's wrong, Honeybun?" Brita asked. "You look a little gray."

He rubbed his chest as the truck jerked to a stop. "I think I'm having a heart attack."

She sat forward, her golden-brown gaze filled with concern. "Seriously? Do you need me to drive?"

He rubbed absently at his chest as something small and black burst out of the trees behind them and took off down the road like a tiny, black and brown rocket, big ears flopping and tiny legs pumping hard.

"Badly!" Dolfe jerked the truck door open and shot out of there like a rocket. He was vaguely aware of Brita calling out to him as he started to run.

Behind him, the truck started rolling down the road. Too late, he realized he'd never put it into Park.

There was a shouted expletive and then the truck jerked to a stop. A door slammed and feet pounded down the road behind him as the tiny little monster took a final bouncing stride and then leaped off the ground, landing neatly in Dolfe's arms and immediately covering his face with kisses.

Dolfe laughed, despite the tears rolling down his cheeks. "Hello, son. Where'd you come from?"

A slender form burst from the trees a beat later and Suz jerked to a stop when she saw them, giving a tiny cry of pleasure before taking off in their direction, a happily barking Miss Ivy in her arms.

She was shouting something, but Dolfe couldn't understand it. She was clearly upset and her words came fast and breathless as she ran.

He hurried up to her, meeting her halfway. "What is it, Suz? Where are Blaise and Ty?"

She was panting too hard to speak and Dolfe had to dig really deep to keep from yelling at her. Frustration filled his heaving chest, along with a shock of fear that he'd been so close and had almost left them behind.

Brita carefully extracted Ivy from Suz's arms and, dodging a happy pink tongue, put a hand on Suz's shoulder. "Where are they, Suz?"

The other woman straightened, pointing back to the tree line. "There's..." she swallowed hard, clearly working through more than breathlessness. "...a house. Blaise is..." She turned and clasped the front of Dolfe's shirt. "She's going to fight the woman, Dolfe. And she only has a knife against a gun."

Alarm brought tiny black spots dancing in front of his gaze. Without a word, he handed Badly to Suz. "Take the dogs and my truck. There's a police station about three miles up this road. Tell them."

He took off without another word, reaching for his gun as he sprinted as fast as he could toward the spot where Badly and Suz had emerged.

"Ivy!" Brita called out.

Dolfe barely even registered the shout, or what it meant. Blaise was in danger and uppermost in his mind was the recurring, tortuous thought that he wouldn't get there in time.

The quiet day exploded into sound. The gunshot echoed into the distance like a recurring nightmare he couldn't escape. And Dolfe whispered her name as he plunged into the cool cover of trees, his heart pounding so hard that, for a moment, he really did fear he was having a heart attack.

Blaise gave a blood-curdling scream and launched herself upward, her head cracking hard against the other woman's chin and driving her backward on a grunt of pain.

The gun went off and she stumbled several steps backward, the weapon swinging wildly as she fought to keep her feet.

Blaise reached for the knife at her back and drew it free, the fiery touch of pain telling her she'd sliced her skin as she did.

She barely noticed.

The woman had regained her balance and, though she spit a couple of bloody teeth into the dirt beneath her boots, her murderous brown gaze was locked onto Blaise and the gun was lifting toward Blaise's chest.

Blaise was determined not to give the other woman a chance to shoot her. She lunged forward, managing to punch the woman's arm with her empty hand and drive the knife downward at the same time.

But her opponent was good. She was strong and had well-honed reflexes. She lifted an arm and smashed it into Blaise's, shoving her knife-thrust off target so that it caught her on the outside of the fleshy part of her upper arm.

Blood splattered as the knife separated the

woman's flesh and the knife followed, arcing through the air from the kidnapper's counter-strike.

It hit the dust and Blaise threw herself sideways, lunging for it as the gun found her again, this time focused on the spot between her eyes.

An instant kill spot.

She grasped the knife just as a high-pitched bark broke the silence and they both turned to see Ivy galloping toward them, her teeth showing and her tail held high and rigid behind her.

The woman's gaze met Blaise's and time stood still.

Blaise's head started to shake. She clasped her fingers around the hilt of the knife, wondering if she could throw it before the gun went off.

The woman smiled and Blaise's blood turned to ice.

"No! Please, don't..." tears blinded her and she shoved to her knees. But she wasn't going to be in time.

The gun swiveled six inches to the right.

Ivy growled and came on, her tiny face the picture of rage and her satellite-like ears pinned flat against her head.

The gun focused on her tiny frame and the woman's smile widened. Blaise surged to her feet, grasping the blade of the knife and throwing it toward the woman with all her strength.

Ivy leaped into the air.

The gun went off with a terrifying concussion that seemed to rock the world beneath Blaise's feet. And Ivy yelped, her small body dropping to the ground as Blaise screamed long and loud, her heart bursting open in a blaze of fire at the center of her chest.

Then the world slowed...moments stretching immeasurably against the ribbon of time and everything brightened like vibrant blooms bursting over an ultra-HD television screen.

The woman went very still, her hate-filled gaze rising toward the distant tree line, and widening as the trees split apart and a tall, devilishly handsome man with wavy blond hair and a strong, confident stride moved into the clearing, his big hand still holding his Glock 9 and his gaze locked on Blaise.

Ever so slowly, the woman's shoulders rounded and she hunched downward, slamming into the hard earth without a sound.

Something soft and wet swept tears from Blaise's cheeks and tiny feet pressed frantically against her chest as a loud keening filled the space around her.

"Blaise?"

His worried voice, husky with fear and filled with concern, tore her from the time-warp her tortured brain had thrown her into and the world rushed back as Dolfe knelt beside her, his hands touching her arms and legs and his concerned green gaze checking her over for damage.

Something warm and soft curled into her lap and sighed, quivering with fear.

She blinked as he framed her face with his hands, tears running unchecked down her cheeks. "I couldn't stop her..."

"You did, honey, look."

The woman lay crumpled in the dusty grass, a perfect hole centered between her hate-filled eyes, now glassy with death. Blaise could see the hilt of a knife sticking from her side, right about where her liver would be, Blaise thought. "I got her?"

He wrapped himself around her and kissed her temple. "You did."

Blaise couldn't look away. "I'm pretty sure I didn't put that hole in her head."

Dolfe winced. "Yeah, I know you didn't need my help but I was there and had an extra bullet..."

Blaise shook her head. He was just trying to make her feel better. She was pretty sure the knife had landed a beat too late. But she didn't mind. At least she'd gotten to put an exclamation point on the thing. The woman had been pure evil.

"You saved Miss Ivy," he told her.

Blaise slowly dropped her gaze, surprised to find her hands frantically petting the little dog, who seemed miraculously unharmed. She immediately scooped her up and peppered the little dog with kisses, laughing wetly as tears saturated Ivy's soft coat. "Actually, I think she saved me. If she hadn't burst out of those trees like a tiny little Avenger, I'd already be dead."

Dolfe shuddered violently, but reached over to scratch the little dog behind the ears.

Ivy's back leg kicked frantically as her eyes narrowed in pleasure.

"Apparently, I'm too late," a familiar voice said and they turned to find Brita striding toward them across the yard. "Looks like, as usual, you Honey-buns took care of things on your own."

Dolfe looked down at Blaise. "Yes, we Honey-buns did, didn't we, future wife?"

She held Ivy close and smiled. The smile quickly turned to a giggle, slightly hysterical, and then morphed to full-on laughter, as she enjoyed a safe and non-judgmental moment with the man she loved and her best friend.

Sirens split the silence in the distance, rolling steadily closer at top speed.

Her head snapped up and around. "Ty! He's in bad shape."

Brita nodded. "Suz told me. I called an ambulance and she took Badly to the police station to wait for us."

Blaise took a deep breath, nodding. She prayed Ty would be all right. "He looked really bad, Dolfe. I think it's internal bleeding."

He nodded, rubbing his hand down her arm. "What do you say we get you and the dogs home?"

"I'd love that." Then she remembered the second person who'd been there earlier. "There's another guy. He left about two hours ago in a silver SUV. He'll probably be back soon."

Dolfe looked at Brita and she nodded. "Go. The local PD is on its way. I'll have all the backup I need."

"You don't have to tell me twice." Dolfe helped Blaise to her feet. She felt a hundred years old and was moving like she was. It would feel good to get home and take a long, hot shower and change her clothes.

Blaise stopped in front of Brita. "You'll be okay?"

"I'll be fine. I'm sure some of those sirens you're hearing are police."

Blaise glanced back at the house, reluctant to leave her friend behind.

"We can drop the dogs and go to the hospital," Dolfe said gently.

She nodded, feeling better. "Yeah. Let's do that." She reached out and squeezed Brita's arm. "I'll see you in a bit?"

Brita nodded. "You will."

$\mathcal{D}$olfe wished they could have stayed home, snuggling together on the couch for the rest of the day and night. But he understood her need to check in on Ty.

They'd picked Suz and Badly up on their way home and dropped her off at the hospital where they'd taken Ty. West General, which was a country hospital twenty minutes from Indianapolis.

While Blaise took a hot shower and dressed in more comfortable clothes, talking to the dogs the entire time, he took care of a few things that needed addressing.

He'd called Clovis from the car and had given him the address to the house. Brita had said she wouldn't need them, but he'd rather be safe than sorry.

From home, he'd called Godric to check on Alf.

"He's already annoying the nurses," Godric said with laughter in his voice. "He keeps trying to rip the IV out and climb out of bed. There's been some discussion of tying him to the bed."

Dolfe frowned. "Is that even legal?"

"I don't think the nursing staff cares at this point. One of them even said if she went to jail, she wouldn't have to deal with pain in the butt Honeybuns anymore. She said it would be like a vacation."

Dolfe chuckled. "It sounds like I don't need to waste any more worry cycles on him."

"Not unless you're concerned about one of the nurses putting him into an induced coma just to keep him out of trouble."

Godric hesitated. The silence throbbed with the questions Dolfe figured his cousin wanted to ask but wouldn't. At least not until the case had been put to bed and all the open switches had been closed. "Blaise and the dogs are okay?"

"Everybody's fine. Except for Tyrese, of course."

Godric made a noise. "I'm actually in my car, heading there now. I hope he's awake enough to request to be released into my care. The surgeon at West General is okay, but I'd feel better if I could do the surgery."

"You're a good man, Godric."

His cousin made a self-deprecatory noise. "Well, when your name is God, you do have certain responsibilities."

Dolfe chuckled. "We'll see you over there, then. Blaise and I are heading out now."

"See you shortly."

Three hours later, they trudged wearily into the house. They'd waited with Suz until Ty came out of surgery and then left, planning to return in the morning to see him. Dolfe placed the giant pizza box onto the island in the kitchen and pulled out beers, napkins, and a fork for Blaise's salad while she let the dogs out of their kennels and sent them into the back yard to do their business.

He noticed the way her gaze kept sliding to the spot in the kitchen where they'd found the intruder and noted the exact moment she remembered Beast.

Her gaze snapped to his. "Where is he?"

Dolfe grimaced. "Brita asked Percy to keep him. We weren't sure how long we'd be gone." Dolfe watched her carefully, unsure how she'd take the news.

Blaise finally grinned. "We're never going to hear the end of that, are we?"

Dolfe popped the tab on a can of light beer and handed it to her. "Probably not."

He indicated the food. "Do you want to eat outside with the dogs?"

She nodded. "That sounds perfect."

But before they could follow through on that plan, the sound of tires on gravel interrupted them. Dolfe's hand went to the gun at the small of his back. He hadn't put it away when they got home and probably wouldn't for a while. Being attacked in their own home had been an eye-opening experience.

One he wasn't sure he'd ever get over. "You stay here," he told Blaise. "Lock the door behind me."

She looked as if she would argue, but he didn't wait for it. He moved quickly to the door in the breezeway and glanced back, pointing to the lock.

Then he stepped outside, his gun down by his side as he watched the familiar car ease up the drive.

As the tiny car eased to a halt, Dolfe slipped his gun back into its holster. "Hey!" he greeted JJ.

She climbed out of the clown car, smiling. "I hear you wrapped up the Blanchette case."

"Well, not into a tidy bow yet. But we're close. The police are just waiting for a second kidnapper to show up. Blaise thinks he's the mastermind. With any luck they'll take him alive and we can get some answers."

She nodded, her expression filled with pleasure. "That's wonderful. With Blanchette dead, I can hopefully make some progress on my murder case too."

The screen door opened and Blaise stuck her

head outside. "Hey, JJ. How about some pizza and beer?"

"I thought you'd never ask. I'm starving."

Dolfe held the door for his friend, and she preceded him into the house. "I'd think your case was pretty cut and dried, J."

She frowned, taking the beer Blaise handed her. "Yeah, well. I looked at the photo you have of Kim Vitters and realized we have a problem."

"What kind of problem?" Blaise asked.

"The corpse doesn't look like Kim Vitters."

Dolfe chewed on that for a beat and then sighed. "Of course. That would be too easy."

JJ nodded. "I realized that, with all the hubbub over trying to locate Blanchette and bring him in, we missed a step on the victim. We ran her prints initially and got nothing."

Dolfe frowned. "That doesn't mean anything. That just means she wasn't a criminal and I'm pretty sure Kim Vitters was no criminal."

Jo shook her head. "But Vitters' prints are on file. She has a concealed carry permit."

Blaise shook her head. "I'm sorry, you lost me."

"In the State of Indiana, you have to be printed when you get a concealed carry permit," Dolfe explained.

"Are you saying Kim Vitters is still alive?" Blaise asked, clearly shocked.

"I'm saying that's how it looks. I came to tell you

that and to tell you I'm heading back to Florida. Our case there just got more complex. It appears I have my killer, but not my victim."

Dolfe nodded. "You'll keep me updated?"

"Absolutely. But I'm really hoping you were serious about that pizza. I'd hate to climb onto an airplane with an empty stomach."

J laughed at the antics of the two dogs, shaking her head. "They recover so quickly, don't they?"

When Blaise looked a question her way, she clarified. "From the kidnapping."

"Ah. Yeah. They do. Fortunately for them." She frowned.

"But you, not so much?" JJ ventured.

Blaise glanced toward the house, where Dolfe was fetching them another round of beers and getting an update on Alf. "Don't say anything to him..."

JJ shook her head. "It's not my place to comment one way or the other. I just know that what you went through must have been tough."

"It was, but not for the reason you'd expect."

JJ lifted her brows in question.

"It brought back that whole mess in Miami." She

threw a concerned glance toward the dogs. "And I was so worried about them."

"It was a bit too similar for comfort," JJ agreed. "But the good news is that Blanchette is dead. You're safe now. All of you."

If only she felt safe. "You'd think so."

They sat in silence for a moment, Blaise listening to Dolfe's deep voice rise and fall as he no doubt teased and tortured the patient.

"Have you told Suz yet?"

JJ's question brought Blaise's head around. "Told her?"

"About the barn? About it burning to the ground."

She winced. With everything that had happened, she'd forgotten about the venue. "No. She's going to be devastated. Both of them will be."

"They might surprise you," JJ offered with a smile. "I get the feeling your friend is made of pretty tough stuff."

Blaise nodded. "She is. And you're right. She's much stronger than I give her credit for."

"Any idea why Blanchette's men burned it down?"

"I'm not sure it was Blanchette's men." As soon as the words came out of her mouth, Blaise realized it was true. She had no idea why, but she didn't think he'd ordered the fire.

"Really?" JJ sat forward, her face filled with surprise and something else Blaise couldn't read.

Dolfe came through the door before JJ could ask the questions she clearly wanted to ask. He handed each of them a frosty glass with a perfect head of froth. It looked like a beer commercial.

"Pretty," JJ said, sipping it happily.

"Alf's getting released in the morning," he told Blaise, grinning.

"Wow, that was fast."

"I think it's mostly because the nurses told Godric they were going to strap him to the bed and take turns punching him if he didn't leave."

JJ spit beer and came up grinning. "Whatever happened to the Hippocratic Oath?"

Dolfe took a sip from his bottle. "Apparently, there's a Honeybun exclusion clause. Besides, that might only apply to doctors. I think you're on your own with nurses."

JJ laughed. "Good to know."

They drank in companionable silence for a moment and then JJ sat forward, settling her glass onto the table and fixing Dolfe with a questioning gaze. "Any idea who killed the guy in the barn?"

Dolfe and Blaise shared a look. He shook his head. "Not yet. But if Kim Vitters is alive, that puts her in the number one suspect position."

"I don't get it, though," Blaise said. "We saw her on video at the airport. She apparently landed and checked into that hotel. Even if she wasn't the victim, doesn't that give her an airtight alibi?"

"It sure seems to," Dolfe agreed.

JJ took one more sip of her beer. "Well, I'd better get going. Thanks so much for dinner and conversation. It was exactly what I needed tonight."

"It was our pleasure, girlfriend." Blaise gave JJ a hug. "Thanks so much for your help on this."

They stood in the driveway, watching JJ drive away. Blaise stared at the empty drive for a moment, shivering.

"What's wrong, honey?" Dolfe asked, pulling her into a hug. "You look like you've seen a ghost?"

She snuggled into him, enjoying his clean, male scent. "I didn't tell you before..."

Dolfe stiffened, the muscles of his broad back going tense under her palms. "What is it?" He gently clasped her upper arms and pulled her away so he could look into her eyes. "Whatever it is, I won't judge."

She shook her head, tears spilling down her face. With everything she'd experienced over the last couple of days—the break-in and murder, the kidnapping, finding Suz and Ty in that terrifying little hole in the wall, and then the violence of trying to escape—she'd been working on adrenaline for longer than she wanted to consider. She was suddenly exhausted. "I just wanted to let you know that, when I thought I'd never see you again..."

"Shh, it all came out okay, honey."

She shook her head, sniffling. "I love you so much, Dolfe. And I wanted to thank you for everything you give me every day. Not stuff, but the uncompromising love. The trust. And the dogs." She finished with a watery grin as he laughed, pulling her in for a hug. "You give me so much more, future wife. For one thing, I get to say 'future wife' all the time. That's tons of raunchy fun right there."

She shook her head. "You're cray-cray."

"Only about you, honey." He kissed her forehead and pointed toward the stool on the island. "Now sit. I'll get this cleaned up, and we'll go to bed."

She swatted at a buzzing mosquito, her gaze lifting to the still-broken window over the sink. "I think we need to do something about that, first."

He glanced up, his shoulders drooping. "Oh, yeah. I'd forgotten about that."

Blaise had cleaned up the glass before her shower earlier, but they hadn't had time to board it up or call for service. "I'm pretty sure we still have some boards from the raised garden project. I'll help you secure it after we're done in here. It won't take long."

He nodded, his expression sad. Dolfe was quiet as they started cleaning up the mess from dinner. Watching him work, Blaise couldn't shake the feeling that there was something on his mind.

Something he didn't want to tell her.

She moved up behind him, wrapping her arms around his waist and laying her head on his back. "What is it?"

He heaved a sigh. "I'd rather not say. It's all speculation."

"Tell me." The words came out like a command. She softened them with, "Please?"

"I just can't shake the feeling that we have more than one agenda at play here." He turned around, drying his hands on a towel. "Blanchette's piece is easy to figure out. He's...was...looking for revenge and power. But everything that's happened to us since is confusing. It's almost as if someone else were pulling the strings, either in conjunction with Blanchette or behind his back."

If what he was saying was true, then they had more than one villain. The thought made Blaise want to curl up into the fetal position and hide under a blanket.

When she frowned, he pulled her back into his arms, kissing the top of her head. "We'll figure this out, honey. There's an explanation for everything. We just need to whisk the shadows away and find it."

22

Dolfe was stirring a skillet full of scrambled eggs the next morning when his cell rang. He didn't recognize the number. Sliding the skillet with the eggs off the burner, Dolfe hit the *Answer* button. "Honeybun Investigations."

"Mr. Honeybun. It's Devon Markum."

The toast popped up, and Dolfe grabbed a slice, dropping it quickly onto a plate as it burned his fingers. "Devon. What's up?"

"I need to see you."

Dolfe put the phone on speaker and settled it onto the counter, buttering the first slice and grabbing the second. "Now?"

The teen hesitated just long enough for Dolfe to realize how brusque he'd sounded. "Sorry, things have been a bit hectic here. I'm just trying to figure out my day."

"I understand. But this is important. Can you meet me at the barn?"

Dolfe placed the buttered toast onto a plate and set it on the table as Blaise came in smelling like soap and leading the two bedroom slippers like a mother duck leading her ducklings. She grabbed a piece of bacon off the plate Dolfe extracted from the oven.

"Do you have some new information?" he asked the kid.

"You could say that. Look, I know you're busy, but trust me, you're going to want to see this."

"Okay, Devon..."

Blaise's eyebrows lifted as she divided eggs onto two plates.

"We'll be there in an hour. Does that work?"

"Yeah. An hour is okay. But if you can get here sooner, it would be better."

They wolfed down their breakfast, loaded the two dogs into Dolfe's truck, and drove out to the venue. In the harsh light of morning, the burned-out husk looked even more forlorn than it had the day of the fire.

Blaise's expression was sad, and Dolfe couldn't help thinking about their bedside conversation with Suz. Blaise's friend had insisted on knowing the worst. When they'd told her, despite the tears glistening in her bright blue gaze, she'd taken it with admirable stoicism.

Dolfe was pretty sure, looking at Blaise's expression, that she was remembering that conversation too.

"Hey," he said, reaching across the truck to squeeze her hand. "Godric called this morning. Ty's awake and talking. That's a good sign."

She nodded, smiling sadly. "That's really good. I'll call Suz later."

Devon Markum was sitting in his recreational vehicle, watching them drive into the lot. The boy jumped down from the seat and strode quickly forward, every line in his body taut with excitement.

He gave Blaise a shy smile and shook Dolfe's hand. "Thanks for coming right over. It's this way."

They walked around the remains of the building, Dolfe's nose wrinkling under the sour stench of old fire. Devon led them past the surprisingly undamaged smoker's lounge, a twist of irony not lost on Dolfe, and headed down the path toward the picturesque little creek.

"Where are we going?" Dolfe asked, one eye on Blaise. She was hugging herself, looking like she was going to cry.

"Just to the creek," the teen told him. When they reached the end of the bridge, Dolfe started across, but Devon shook his head. "This way. I hope you don't mind getting your feet wet."

Dolfe and Blaise shared a look before making

their way carefully down the short but steep bank to the edge of the water.

Devon preceded them, disappearing beneath the bridge as they half slid down the bank. Dolfe dropped Blaise's hand when they hit flat ground again and peered into the shadows beneath the bridge.

The boy had a flashlight in his hand, and he'd turned it on.

He was shining it under the bridge.

Dolfe stepped into the water and waded over, his gaze on the circular beam of light painting the underside of the bridge.

It was shoved between one of the bridge supports and the underside of the bridge itself. The packet was lumpy, a large yellow envelope secured with brown shipping tape.

Dolfe examined it carefully in place, ducking as he climbed the incline to get close. "This doesn't look like it belongs here."

"That's what I thought too," Devon agreed.

Dolfe turned to the boy and narrowed his gaze. If the envelope led to new information on the Lawrence Peck murder, he'd be grateful. But he had to wonder how and why the kid had found it.

A cynical man would think he'd planted it there.

"You want to tell me how you came upon this discovery?"

"Dolfe!"

The kid frowned at Blaise's objection. But after a beat, his young face lost the flush of irritation, and he nodded as if acceding that Dolfe had reason to be suspicious. "You remember that woman I saw running away that night?"

Dolfe nodded. "Of course."

"I thought at the time that she hesitated a minute near the bridge before running down the creek and into the fields."

Dolfe did remember the kid telling him that she'd disappeared under the bridge and had come out a minute later. He'd missed the implications of that. The small bridge shouldn't have taken a minute to pass through. "Go on."

"Well, it's been bothering me. Why did she delay here? What could she have been doing? So, I came down and took a look."

"That's some pretty good detective work," Blaise told the kid with a censorious glance at Dolfe. "We should hire you for Honeybun Investigations."

Dolfe yanked out his cell. "You didn't touch it, did you?"

The kid shook his head, his expression turning mulish. "I didn't plant this there, if that's what you're thinking, Mr. Honeybun."

"Of course, you didn't..." Blaise started. She stopped when she saw Dolfe dialing a number.

"What are you doing?" she asked.

"I'm calling Brita."

"We've got one of Lawrence Peck's fingerprints on the package," Brita told him later. "It's a strong partial."

"Nobody else's?" Dolfe asked, frowning.

She shook her head. "Nope. Which seems unlikely. I'm guessing the package was wiped down and whoever did it just missed one. It was at the very edge of a strip of tape."

Blaise frowned. "What's inside? Money? Drugs?"

Brita skimmed Dolfe a look, something skittering through her normal unreadable expression. She placed her hand over the plastic evidence bag containing the package. "It's evidence that Blanchette intended to blackmail Brick into putting forward some kind of legislation."

Blaise thought about their conversation with Alex Cox. "We heard about that, the student monitoring legislation?"

Brita nodded. "Among other things, yes. I got the impression from listening to the tapes that Blanchette thought a Federal Senator might be useful for a lot of things."

"That's how he got away with everything in Florida," Dolfe said. "He's got cops and politicians in his pocket."

"He probably blackmailed *them* too," Blaise mumbled, disgusted.

"Or paid them off," Brita added. She ran her hand over the bag again. "This is going to get a bit ugly for Brick," she said.

"Why?" Dolfe frowned. "They can't have anything real on him. Brick isn't dirty."

She shook her head. "Not Brick, no. But his assistant was getting paid to facilitate things."

Dolfe stared at her for a moment and then a light came on in his eyes. "The late-night meetings with Alex."

"Yep," Brita nodded. "They were setting your dad up big time."

When Dolfe scrubbed a hand over his face, clearly not liking what he was hearing, Blaise squeezed his knee. "Your dad's a tough old bird, Dolfe. He'll be fine."

"Yeah. But it pisses me off that Blanchette is putting him through this."

Blaise couldn't agree more.

"How's Ty?" Brita asked. "He looked in pretty bad shape when I saw him."

"Godric says he's awake and talking," Blaise said.

"That's good. Have you told them about the barn yet?"

"Just Suz. She took it like a trooper. She doesn't want to tell Ty until he's stronger."

"I don't blame her." Brita stood up and reached

for the side drawer where she kept her gun and badge. "I've got to go. I have to make a stop at Methodist Hospital to talk to the owner of the stolen red hatchback we found. It appears he was the one whose blood we found. They beat him up pretty good when they stole that car. I'm hoping I can get a description of the person who grabbed Blaise."

"Why'd they steal it?" Blaise asked. "Why not just rent another one like the one they took to our house?"

"To switch it up? Make sure we didn't know what we were looking for?" She shrugged. "Who knows? But it *did* slow us down. If Dolfe and JJ hadn't gotten a description of the car from your neighbor, we'd still be looking for a dark sedan."

"Where was the car stolen from?" Dolfe asked.

"About a half mile from the barn. I'm guessing they left the sedan at the fire to make us think Blaise was inside and then grabbed the hatchback to throw us off their track."

Dolfe nodded.

She shoved her gun in the holster. "I need to get going. After I talk to the car theft victim, I'm going to Washington so I can oversee Dresden Cooper's questioning."

"Good." Dolfe stood too, offering Brita his hand. "Let me know if I can help?"

She nodded. "Bud's in charge of the investigation into Peck's death."

"Any suspects yet?"

"We're looking at the woman who was holding Blaise and the others. We checked into her background and discovered she's been Blanchette's Lieutenant for several months."

"What about the other guy?" Blaise asked.

"He never came back to the house. I'm guessing he went back to Miami but we haven't pinned that down yet. Without even a physical description to go on, we're kind of hamstrung. We're in touch with the Miami police and they're trying to locate him on their end."

Dolfe and Blaise walked out with her, Blaise hugging Brita before she climbed into her car. "You be careful, okay?"

"Of course." Brita smiled. "You too. Try to stay out of trouble while I'm gone."

"Har," Blaise said.

They watched Brita drive away before climbing into Dolfe's truck. He glanced at her. "Lunch?"

She didn't have to think about it for long. Her stomach rumbled loudly at the suggestion. "Absolutely!"

They decided to head to their favorite Cuban restaurant in downtown Indy. Their route took them past Cox Beauty Industries, and they spotted Alex on the sidewalk just outside the entrance to the building. She was talking to a dark-haired man, her hands flying around and her expression filled with anger.

"Somebody's getting an earful," Dolfe said as they drove past.

She could only see his profile, but something about the man seemed familiar. She struggled for the memory of his face and came up blank. Then, as he leaned threateningly close to Alex, it suddenly hit her. Blaise jerked in her seat, one hand slamming against the window.

As if he'd heard it, the man slowly turned in her direction, his dark brown gaze finding hers across the distance. "No! It can't be!" she murmured, wrenching the door open as the truck came to a stop at the light.

"Blaise!" Dolfe yelled her name as the passenger side door slammed shut on his frustrated swearing.

She was vaguely aware of honking horns as she ran across the busy street, her gaze locked on the man on the sidewalk. He watched her come for a moment and then said something to Alex and took off, walking briskly. A beat later, Dolfe called out to her again, accompanied by the renewed blasting of horns that told her he'd left the truck and was following her across the street.

Alex Cox watched her come, her eyes narrowing as she clasped her hands in front of her.

Blaise glanced both ways down the street as she hit the sidewalk. He was gone. He must have ducked into a car and driven off while she was making her way across the street.

She strode quickly to Alex.

"Hello, dear..."

"Where'd he go?" Blaise demanded.

Alex frowned. "Where'd *who* go, dear?"

Blaise had to clench her fists to keep from shaking the brittle-looking older woman. She took a deep breath as Dolfe gained the sidewalk.

"Blaise almost Honeybun, you're going to be the death of me." He skidded to a stop next to her, sparing Alex a quick look. "Alex. How are you?"

Nodding her response, Alex turned her attention back to Blaise. "Are you all right? You look like you've seen a ghost."

Blaise frowned. "I'm pretty sure I have. That man you were just speaking to, where did he go?"

"That handsome Cuban man? He was looking for his girlfriend. She was a student at our school."

"Did you tell him where she is?" Dolfe asked, giving Blaise a sideways glance.

But Alex shrugged. "I wish I could have. She graduated a couple of weeks ago and we've lost touch."

"Can't you use that monitoring law you were telling us about to find her?" Blaise asked. Her tone was sharper than she would have preferred, so she tried to soften it with a smile.

Alex tensed, her perfectly made up features

sharpening like Blaise's tone. "I refuse to snoop on my students, Ms. Runa. It's un-American. I don't care what our government says."

"Even if it will get you into trouble?" Dolfe asked.

Alex shrugged. "Even if, Mr. Honeybun."

Blaise could respect that, despite how frustrating it was. "He didn't seem to be taking the news that well."

"No, he didn't. He seems to think I'm hiding her from him."

"Are you?" Dolfe asked.

Alex's gaze found his and locked on for several beats before she smiled. "Why on earth would I do that, Mr. Honeybun?"

"I don't know, you tell me."

She shrugged again. "I have no way of knowing who he really is. He could mean her harm."

"Does that mean you know where she is?" Blaise asked. She had no idea why she cared about the location of some random woman she'd never met, but her gut told her it might be important.

"Unfortunately, Bella was one of the ones I told you about who went to Florida and never came back."

Blaise blinked as she suddenly understood. She lifted her gaze to Dolfe. "Blanchette."

He nodded, looking grim. Turning to Alex, he asked, "Did that man give you his name?"

She wrinkled her face as she appeared to give the

question some thought. "I'm terrible with names, I'm afraid. I think it was Juan...or maybe Julio." She shook her head. "I'm sorry I can't be of more help."

Dolfe squeezed her hand. "No worries. You've actually helped a lot."

Dolfe tugged Blaise away, but she dug in her heels at the corner. "What are you doing? We need to grill her for more information."

"We're not going to grill an elderly woman on the street, Blaise."

"But she might know more than she's telling us..."

He tugged her into motion when the crosswalk light changed. "And what if she doesn't tell us anything," he asked her, his lips turning upward. "Should we waterboard her?"

Blaise's own lips twitched in response to his question. She tried not to think about the fact that she'd briefly considered it. "If that's what it takes."

He laughed, pulling her close and kissing her on the temple. "Come on. We need to find him."

She frowned. "Find who?"

"Detective Lopez." They stepped up onto the curb and she jerked to a stop.

"It *was* him! I'm not going crazy?" Blaise's mind spun. Jorge Lopez had helped her when she'd found herself on the run from Blanchette in Miami. He'd risked his life to help them take Blanchette down.

He was a good cop. Or at least that was what she'd believed at the time.

"No, you're not going crazy. Or, at least, if you are then so am I." He tugged his cell out of his pocket and quickly dialed a number. "Bud. Hey, could you do me a favor...?"

23

"Where's Jorge Lopez?" Dolfe barked into the phone. If the beats of silence meeting his question were any indication, the woman on the other end of the phone didn't appreciate his tone.

"Hello to you too, Honeybun."

He closed his eyes, pulled air into his lungs, and tried again. "Jo, how's the weather in Miami?"

She hesitated just long enough.

"You aren't in Miami, are you?"

"Dolfe..."

"And I'm guessing that little visit to my house last night was just to find out how much we knew?"

"Honeybun..."

"Why are you lying to me, JJ? What are you and Lopez mixed up in?"

He thought he heard a sigh.

"Stay out of it, Dolfe. This is an ongoing investigation…"

"Too late. I'm already in it, JJ. My family has been threatened, kidnapped, and blackmailed. And now I find out that Lopez is right in the middle of the whole mess. Is he dirty, JJ?"

"Stay out of it, Dolfe." Her tone was less than warm. Dolfe sensed panic in the taut delivery.

"Not until you tell me what's going on. They've already taken Blaise, almost killed my friend, and they're threatening to take down my dad. There's too much at stake here for me to stand down."

He waited as she struggled silently with her decision. A moment later, she sighed and he relaxed, hearing capitulation in the sound. "All right. Jorge is undercover with Blanchette's organization."

"Why would Blanchette let a cop get that close?"

"Because Jorge has a past. I won't tell you that story, that's his to tell, but suffice it to say that before his family left Cuba, he did some things. Things he wouldn't want people to know about."

"And Blanchette's blackmailing him?"

"Not exactly, but close enough. Jorge was fired in a hail of verbal gunfire just after you guys left Miami last year. Rumors were set into motion about his unworthiness to be a cop. He was portrayed as dirty, with skeletons in his closet."

Dolfe had a light-bulb moment. "You knew Blanchette would walk."

There was no verbal verification, but he could picture her nodding. "We engaged Plan B immediately."

"Smart."

"Well, Blanchette did have the Lieutenant Governor in his pocket."

"What you're saying is that Jorge's path into Blanchette's ranks was paved."

"To a point. But you know how suspicious and careful Blanchette is. Jorge wasn't fully accepted until he performed an important task."

Something in the way JJ said it set off alarm bells. "What did he have to do?"

"Blanchette discovered that someone in his organization was working against him. He wanted that person killed."

Silence pulsed between them. Then it clicked into place. "Kim Vitters."

"Jorge is trying to locate her."

"And he thinks Alex knows where she is."

"He's sure of it. But there's no way the old bird is going to give up her granddaughter."

Dolfe blinked in surprise. "Granddaughter?"

"Yeah. Tidy, huh? Jorge is afraid that if he can't find Vitters and fake her murder, Blanchette's people are going to grab the old lady and do whatever it takes to make her talk."

Dolfe glanced at Blaise, who was sitting at the kitchen table feeding the dogs bits of her lunch rather than eating it. His mind replayed their playful banter from earlier. "Wait, Blanchette's dead. Why would his people move forward on his vendettas?"

"The word is that even before his death Blanchette all but left the organization in someone else's hands. Ever since we scooped him up on the human trafficking charge, he's focused more and more of his energy into wrapping himself up in a cocoon of powerful, influential people. He hasn't been hands-on with the drugs, women, and money-laundering stuff for a while."

"I repeat my question. Why would this person he's given the reins to care?"

"It's just good business, Dolfe. Vitters is a loose end. If she was willing to blackmail Blanchette, she's probably just as willing to come after this second in command now that he's apparently taken control of the organization."

Dolfe sighed, rubbing his face wearily. Blaise and the dogs all looked at him, three sets of questioning gazes making him smile. "Any idea who this second in command is?"

"Not a clue. Blanchette was very careful to remain the face of everything. Whoever it is has been very good at staying in the shadows."

"Do you know anything at all about him?"

"Only that he's even more brutal than Blanchette. As proven by the fact that Blanchette is now lying in the morgue with a bullet wound between the eyes."

"And Lawrence Peck is next to him."

"Yeah. I suspect that Peck was working with Kim and Blanchette found out and had him taken care of. Unfortunately, Peck and Vitters had something on Blanchette, apparently something they were attempting to hide from him that night. And whatever it was got Lawrence killed."

"There's one thing I don't get, Jo. Why here? Why now? We're a long way from Florida."

"I'm guessing the timing was just right. That legislation Blanchette wanted squelched is coming up for a vote in the US Senate next week. Blanchette had to force Brick's hand now, or it would be too late."

"And if Vitters and Peck were blackmailing Blanchette..."

"They had to act now too. My guess is that, if they hadn't been caught hiding the evidence at Wedding Belles, they'd have already sprung the trap."

"I don't understand why they were hiding their evidence there. Why not release it directly to the media?"

"Because doing that would point the finger right at them. By hiding the evidence at Wedding Belles..."

Dolfe finally understood. "They pointed the blame and any retribution to come right at me."

"You are both an investigator and the son of the man Blanchette was trying to blackmail."

"Wouldn't it have made more sense to plant it at my office?"

"Yes. But this created a much bigger stir. Since Brick is good friends with one of the investors, the location will be tied back to him and the media will no doubt do the blackmailers' work for them creating a stink of corruption where there never was any."

Because Basil Whatsnoggin was one of Brick's golfing buddies. Dolfe sighed, nodding. "Okay, how can we help?"

"You can't. I'm trying to find Jorge now. He's gone off the reservation and I'm not sure what he's up to."

"We just saw him fighting with Alex Cox in Indianapolis."

She sighed. "Okay, it's good to know he's still in town. I've got people dusting Blanchette's yacht in North Carolina. If we're lucky, They'll find the prints of his second in command, and we can put a name and a face to him. After that, I might reach out for your help in rounding him up."

Dolfe wasn't happy with that option, but he didn't argue. Hanging up a minute later, he quickly filled Blaise in on what he'd learned from JJ.

She wasn't any happier than he was at the news.

"This person she's hunting is still out there. He's not going away because of a few little setbacks. He'll come after us again."

Dolfe wasn't sure that was true. He suspected the man had taken Blaise to keep Dolfe distracted while they set their plan against Brick into motion, but he wasn't willing to risk her safety in the event that he was wrong. "We need to find Lopez."

She nodded. "Any ideas how?"

A soft breeze skittered over Dolfe's back, the sweet scent of flowers from the back yard filling his nostrils. He had only a moment to realize where the breeze was coming from before warning bells sounded in his brain and he was reaching for his gun.

"You could just turn around," a deep, slightly accented voice said from behind them.

Dolfe's hand found the butt of his pistol and he was yanking it free almost before the man standing in the doorway could raise his arms over his head.

With happy yips, the dogs bounced over to say hello to the newcomer. Miss Ivy sat at his feet, her sweet brown gaze fixed on him and her tail wagging. Badly jumped up and placed his fat paws on Lopez's jeans-clad shin.

They acted as if they'd seen him before.

Ice formed in the center of Dolfe's chest as Lopez turned to smile at Blaise. "Hey, Blaise."

Her expression was mutinous. "You drugged me.""

Jorge flinched. "I'm sorry. But it was the only way I could keep you safe."

"Safe!" she squealed, surging to her feet. "You kidnapped me. Left me with that horrible woman. And I was almost killed when I tried to escape." She strode closer, her finger outstretched as if she intended to poke him with it.

Dolfe moved as she got too close. "Stay back, honey."

Lopez sighed. "I'm not here to hurt her, Honeybun. Believe it or not, I've done everything I could to keep her safe."

Dolfe's gun stayed focused on Lopez's broad chest but the cop didn't move, his intense brown gaze locked on Dolfe.

"I heard you talking to Jo. You know I'm undercover," he said to Dolfe. "I had to make it appear as though I was onboard with the plan."

"Did that include beating the snot out of Tyrese Miller?"

Jorge flinched. "That wasn't me, Honeybun. Desiree beat him. The woman was brutal."

Blaise shuddered and then gave a disgusted laugh. "Desiree? Really?"

Lopez shrugged, his lips turning up slightly in the corners. "I know, it's the worst kind of typecasting but as far as I know that was her real name."

Dolfe's hand tightened on his gun as rage swept him. He fought for control as spots danced before his gaze. "And the agents at Suz and Ty's house? You badly wounded my cousin and his agent might not survive."

Lopez sighed. "It's a long story."

"Shorten it," Dolfe growled out.

"We were just supposed to contain and disarm. But Desiree is blood-thirsty. I hit your cousin to save him from another bullet. I couldn't stop her from shooting the other guy. But I did what I could to staunch the blood loss before we left." He waited a moment as Dolfe considered his explanation. "Can I put my arms down?"

Dolfe nodded but didn't lower his gun. "Put all your weapons on the floor and kick them this way."

Using two fingers, Jorge pulled a Beretta 9mm from under his shirt and placed it carefully onto the floor, kicking it to Blaise. She put her foot on it and carefully shoved it behind her. Jorge pulled a deadly-looking blade with a serrated edge from a sheath strapped to his leg and extracted a small handgun from an ankle holster. He placed both on the floor and straightened, taking a step back from them.

Dolfe indicated with his gun that Jorge should kick them away and he did, sighing as if hurt by their distrust. "Don't forget I came to you, Honey-bun. I just want to talk."

"Or you wanted another chance at Blaise."

"I'd be a piss-poor cop if I couldn't sneak up on you better than this," he said with a rueful smile.

"You snuck up just fine," Dolfe muttered, angry that he hadn't seen the trap before it had been sprung.

Looking at the floor, Jorge shook his head. "Okay, I get it. You don't trust me. I did some things to the woman you love that you don't like. I didn't like it either. But I promise you that I was doing my best to keep her safe."

"I almost died," Blaise said, tears glistening in her eyes at the memory. Knowing her as well as he did, Dolfe recognized the tears for what they were. Rage. Her long body was taut with the emotion, her hands fisted at her sides.

"I know. I tried not to leave you alone there, but I got a lead on Vitters and had to follow up on it."

"What did you want to talk to us about?" Dolfe asked suddenly.

Lopez glanced his way, gaze narrowing slightly at the tense posture and the gun still pointing his way. "Can you put the gun down, Dolfe?" The question was spoken softly, soothingly, as if Dolfe were an enraged dog that needed to be handled. It pissed him off.

"I don't think so. Talk, Lopez."

Jorge shook his head. "Okay. JJ told you I'm trying to find Kim Vitters. I need to get her out of the way before El Jefe finds her."

Ivy and Badly got bored with the conversation and bounded through the door Jorge had left open, heading out to play in the back yard.

"El Jefe?" Blaise asked.

He shrugged. "Nobody trusts me enough to tell me his name. Whoever it is, everybody's terrified of him. Rumor was that even Blanchette was cautious around him."

"What did you plan to do with Vitters when you found her?"

"I have my orders from Blanchette. Until I get new orders, I can only assume they still hold under the new person. I'm supposed to eliminate the threat."

"You..." Blaise blanched. "You're going to kill her?"

"Of course not," Jorge said, looking disgusted. "But I have to make it look good."

"Like you did in Miami?"

Jorge turned gray. "That was self-defense, Honey-bun. She had a knife."

Blaise gasped, covering her mouth with a hand. "That was you? You killed the woman in the hotel?"

"It was a trap. Blanchette sent me there to kill her and I couldn't do it. I told her we needed to fake her death and she attacked me with that knife." He shook his head. "I had to defend myself."

"And in the process you got your trusted position

in Blanchette's organization," Dolfe said through gritted teeth.

"Yeah. I did." Lopez's lifted chin screamed belligerence. "Would you rather I just let her kill me?"

"You realize the outcome could be the same with Kim Vitters?" Blaise said. "This El Jefe could be testing you too."

"It's more than possible. It's actually probable. This group is heartless and cruel. A bunch of sociopaths. To tell you the truth, I've been struggling with how to handle it."

Dolfe finally lowered the gun but kept it in his hand. He leaned back against the island. "And I'm guessing that's where we come in?"

Lopez smiled. "You always were a quick study, Honeybun."

24

The man lying in the hospital bed was huge, tall, and meaty. The hands holding the television remote were twice the size of Brita's. He was staring at the television mounted on the wall across from his bed, constantly pressing buttons in a mindless search for something that could hold his interest over the numbing allure of the pain meds

She moved into the room with a neutral expression on her face, waiting for him to turn his oversized head in her direction. "Hello, Mr. Gabbert. I'm Detective Muldane, from the IMPD."

He took her offered hand, his grip warm and calloused.

"Hey, Detective. Are you here to take my statement about my car being stolen?"

He had a round halo of bushy brown hair and

matching eyebrows that could have done with a bit of trimming. His fleshy cheeks were covered in a dark stubble Brita guessed he'd have trouble keeping at bay. A thick growth of brown hair exploded over the neckline of the cotton hospital gown his huge form was straining to the bursting point.

If werewolves were real, Brita couldn't help thinking, her victim had a fighting chance of being one.

The entire left side of his face was an ugly rainbow of color, ranging from purple to red and darkening to black. One eyelid was swollen closed, and his bottom lip was split. A strange, dark purple bruise encircled both eyes. He looked a bit like a massive raccoon.

"If you're feeling up to it."

He nodded, dropping the remote to the thin blanket covering him from the waist down. "There's nothing on television anyway."

Brita could honestly say it was the first time she'd heard that as a reason for being interviewed, but she was willing to go with it. "Mr. Gabbert, can you tell me about the theft?"

He pursed his lips, the dense forests of his brows lowering over his eyes, which were a beautiful, clear blue color—at least the one Brita could see—and plucked at a string in the thin cotton blanket. After a moment, he rolled his heavy shoulders as if prepping for a bout against a heavyweight champion in the boxing ring.

He finally glanced up. "I was parked in front of my girlfriend's house, across the street, watching the house."

Brita frowned. "You were spying on your girlfriend?"

He nodded, his full cheeks going pink. "I think she's cheating on me."

Brita shook off her disgust at his admission. "Go on."

"I was focused on the upper windows, so I didn't notice him approaching. My door suddenly opened and, before I could react, he slammed a hand into the glasses."

She noted how he avoided her gaze. "Glasses?"

Gabbert compressed his lips even tighter as if he were trying to hold the words inside.

Brita waited him out.

After a minute, he said, "Field glasses."

"You were watching your girlfriend in her home with binoculars?" Try as she might, Brita couldn't keep the disgust out of her tone.

"It's not like it sounds," Gabbert said defensively.

"Let's put that aside," she ground out through clenched teeth. "For now. What happened next?"

He looked up, flinching at her tone. "I was dazed from the first hit and, before I could pull myself together enough to fight back, he grabbed the back of my head and smashed it into the steering wheel."

Brita's thumbs flashed quickly over her phone, taking down his testimony.

"I was pretty much out of it at that point. Then he shoved me back against the seat and leaned close. I think I must have misheard him, because he said the weirdest thing."

"What did he say?" Brita urged, her thumbs stilling.

"He said, don't fight back. Just play dead. And then he yanked me out of the car and rolled me to the sidewalk. I did as he said. A minute later, I heard two people talking. Somebody stepped around me..."

"Did you see them?"

"No. I kept my eyes closed like he said."

"Did you hear anything that would help us find them?"

"Clacking. Like heels on the sidewalk."

That surprised her. "A woman's heels?"

He frowned. "It might have been a woman. My ears were ringing really badly, but one of the voices was a little higher pitched. I don't know for sure."

"Describe the man."

He shrugged. "Black hair, brown eyes. Not too tall, maybe five feet ten. But he was bulky, muscular and strong. Brown skin..."

"African American?"

"No. I'd say Hispanic. He had a slight accent."

"Thanks, Mr. Gabbert, we'll be in touch." Brita slipped her phone into her pocket and spun on her heel. By the time she hit the hallway, she was running. She picked up her phone and dialed Dolfe but got no answer. She left a brief message before stepping into the elevator. "Honeybun, it's a woman. The person in charge. It's not a man."

"I have an idea for how to catch Kim Vitters," Dolfe told Jorge. "But when we do, she's not going with you. She's coming with me. I'm keeping her safe."

Lopez didn't hesitate. He nodded. "I'm okay with that. All I'm trying to do is keep her safe. And until we find out who's running Blanchette's operation, she's in grave danger."

Dolfe nodded. He looked at Blaise. "Back to Cox Beauty Industries?"

She skimmed Lopez a look that told everyone in the room she didn't trust him. "I'll put the dogs away."

The two men watched her lead Ivy and Badly into the laundry room, where their kennels awaited them with comfy foam and fleece arms. Dolfe turned to Lopez and found him frowning, his expression sad. When Lopez realized he was being watched, the expression smoothed to neutral.

Dolfe fought the urge to reassure the guy. Truth was, he was too mad himself to forgive him for his part in putting Blaise and the dogs into danger. "What do you know about this blackmail attempt on my dad?"

Lopez shrugged. "Not much. Blanchette kept the important stuff close to the vest. But about a week ago something happened that sent Blanchette on a rampage. Two of his closest advisors died suddenly of suspicious causes shortly after. The deaths were ruled accidents, but I'm pretty sure they weren't."

"Why's that?"

Blaise's soft voice filtered into the kitchen from where she spoke to the two dogs, the gentle patter of water hitting metal a counterpoint as she filled the dishes they kept in the kennel for the dogs.

Dolfe's phone dinged as a message from Brita hit the queue. He realized his cell was still silenced and decided to leave it that way. For what they were about to do, the intrusion of a call could mean mission failure. He tried her back, and it went straight to voice mail. Dolfe disconnected and slipped the phone back into his pocket.

Lopez shrugged. "I'm not a boat man myself, but if I were, I'm pretty sure I wouldn't wear a suit and tie to go sailing."

Dolfe nodded. "Agreed."

"And I'm also pretty sure I wouldn't drug myself up with Fentanyl and take to the roads on a rainy, misty night going one hundred miles an hour."

Blaise came back into the room, nodding to Dolfe to tell him she was ready.

Dolfe eyed the weapons they'd gathered up and placed on the island. He frowned thoughtfully, reluctant to do what he was about to do. Either he trusted Lopez, or he didn't.

Strange thing was, he *did* trust the cop. He just wasn't sure why.

He picked up Lopez's Barretta and handed it back to him. The smaller gun he handed to Blaise. "Only for the worst-case scenario."

She nodded. Blaise didn't really like guns. They made her uncomfortable. But thanks to hours spent at the range with him, she was a competent shot and had grown a tiny bit more at ease with them.

The deadly-looking blade he kept for himself, sliding it into the top of his boot and covering the hilt with his jeans.

When he straightened, he looked at Lopez. "Let's go."

Alex's assistant at Cox Beauty Industries didn't look happy to see them. She picked up her phone as Dolfe and Blaise came through the door. They'd left Lopez in the lobby.

Scowling in their direction, the woman announced their arrival to her boss.

Dolfe didn't even slow as he approached the assistant's desk. "We can see ourselves in," he told her in a gruff tone that didn't do anything to hide his dislike of the woman.

"Hey!" She slammed the phone down and followed them, squeezing through the door behind Blaise. "I'm sorry, Alex..."

The older woman waved off her excuses. "Why don't you bring us some coffee, Sara?"

The woman nodded stiffly and, with a final glower at Dolfe, left the office, leaving the door ajar.

Alex's smile was tight. "Have you found Kim?"

"Why didn't you tell us she was your granddaughter?" Dolfe asked.

Alex's face showed no surprise that they knew. "I'm sorry. We keep that quiet around here. Kim was..." she paled slightly, "...*is* one of my lead trainers. I didn't want the other girls to get the wrong impression. She's a lead because she's very good. Not because she's related to me."

"But we're not the 'girls', are we?" Dolfe asked.

Alex glanced at the open door and frowned. "Mr.

Honeybun, have you ever worked around a lot of women before?"

He wasn't sure how to answer that question. He worked with women all the time. He glanced at Blaise and she grinned.

"I'm talking about a place that's predominantly women," Alex clarified. "They can be very competitive and a bit...well...catty. If it had been general knowledge that Kim was my granddaughter, the other women would have made her life impossible."

Dolfe had trouble believing that, but he bowed to her opinion. He nodded, returning quickly to the reason for their visit. "Alex, do you know where your granddaughter is?"

Her expression crumpled, and tears glistened in her eyes. "I wish I did. I'm really worried about her."

"You haven't heard from her?" Blaise asked, her tone filled with surprise.

"No. And that's unlike her. As I said, I'm concerned."

The door opened wider and Sara returned with a tray that held three cups of steaming black coffee, a small pitcher with cream, and various sweeteners. She placed the tray onto Alex's desk.

"I wanted to let you know she might have been there the night Lawrence Peck was killed. She might have taken something from the venue and hidden it nearby. The police are going out there this evening to search for it."

A spoon clattered against a saucer as Sara lifted the cup, placing it in front of her boss.

Dolfe glanced at Blaise and saw her carefully watching the woman.

Alex's face went from shocked to angry as she took in Dolfe's message. "You're trying to pin Lawrence's death on her." It wasn't a question.

"Not necessarily. But the contents of the envelope she was seen carrying from the building that night might clarify her role. That's why the police want to find it."

"You're wrong. I put her on that plane myself."

Dolfe let his eyebrows lift. "Is that right? You went all the way to the gate with her?"

"Well...no...but..."

He nodded. "We have reason to believe she left before getting on that plane, Alex."

The woman shook her head, her face turning obstinate. "I don't believe it. Then where is she?"

"If the information we think she was carrying is what we believe it is, she's probably hiding out. Blanchette's organization is deep and wide."

Her hand shook as she reached for her cup. Dolfe felt bad upsetting her that way, but he needed to force her to act. She thought she was protecting her granddaughter, but she was actually putting her in more danger by leaving her out there unprotected.

"We need to go," he told Alex, settling a card in

front of her on the desk. "If you hear from her, will you ask her to call me?"

"Of course."

They left the older woman staring at his card and moved quickly through the outer office, noting the empty assistant's desk before stepping into the hallway.

When the door closed, Dolfe turned to Blaise. "Well?"

"Her ears were all but quivering. She seemed very nervous when you talked about the police gathering up the package." Blaise frowned. "Do you really believe Sara's a spy for Blanchette?"

They stepped into the elevator and Dolfe hit the button for the lobby.

"It makes a certain, twisted kind of sense. If Blanchette were going to put someone in place to keep an eye on Kim or Alex, the assistant's position would be the perfect choice."

She nodded. "True. Well," she said as the elevator doors opened in the lobby. "If she tried to leave the building, at least Jorge was in place to grab her."

In theory that made perfect sense. Unfortunately, there was one big problem.

When they walked out of the elevator into the lobby, Jorge Lopez was nowhere to be seen.

25

The lowering sun beat down on the back of her head as Blaise shifted in her spot behind the massive tree. The treetop ceiling high above their heads had cut off the worst of the heat until it moved beyond the protective covering and started to dip lower in the sky.

There'd been a gentle breeze coming off the creek, but it wasn't enough to do more than give them occasional respite from the broiling sun. If the current late spring weather was any indication, it was going to be a brutally hot summer in Indiana.

Dolfe leaned against a smaller tree next to her, his long legs stretched out to the side. He hadn't cut his eyes from the pretty little bridge even once in the hour they'd been there.

By contrast, Blaise hadn't stopped squiggling and

squirming. The hard-pack dirt beneath her butt wasn't exactly conducive to getting comfortable. And her stomach had been giving off embarrassing growls for the last half hour. "How long are we going to wait?" she finally asked him, hoping at least to draw his steely gaze from his target for the span of one breath, just to prove he was still human and hadn't morphed into some kind of unflinching robotic superhero before her very eyes.

Dolfe didn't turn as he responded softly. "As long as it takes."

She grimaced, shifting again in an attempt to take some of the pressure off her booty. "What is the point of having so much flesh on my backside if none of it is going to cushion me against long stake-outs on hard dirt?"

His sexy lips twitched. "A. I adore every inch of your perfect backside and B. We've been here less than an hour. I'm pretty sure that doesn't fall into the 'long stakeout' category."

She flinched as pain shot up her tailbone. "Whatever."

Another minute oozed by, punctuated by the buzz of mosquitoes circling for the kill and the distant chorus of a hoard of unnecessarily happy crickets. Blaise slapped at a mosquito feasting merrily on her sweaty neck and sighed. "Do you think Miss Ivy and Badly are okay?"

He finally turned to her, his expression kind but

a tinge of impatience showing in his green gaze. "They're fine, honey. They're with Beast and all of Brita's dogs."

His words did nothing to make her feel better. "Are you sure Percy's up to taking care of them all by himself? That's a lot of dogs."

"He's used to dealing with five, Blaise. He'll be fine."

She sighed, knowing he was right but inclined to worry none-the-less. She pushed her mind to other things. "What do you think Jorge is up to?"

Dolfe didn't look nearly as confident in his response to that particular question as he had about the dogs. "I'm sure he's trying to protect his cover."

"What's the point? Blanchette's gone."

"He is, yes. But there's a ton of money and power in the organization Blanchette built. Somebody's going to step in and take over for him. Until we find out who that someone is, it's going to continue to be like swatting mosquitoes at dusk in the swamp."

She fell silent, thinking about what he'd said. Doubt pulled at her, and she wondered at the source of it. "What if Jorge is setting himself up to be that next person?"

His gaze found hers again, bracketed by lines of worry. "That's my biggest concern right now. If it's him, we're in trouble. He's a cop. He knows how to avoid the usual traps, and he knows how cops think. He'll be hard to take down."

Another few minutes oozed by and the swarm of mosquitoes seemed to triple. Blaise was in the midst of a full-fledged Jihad against the hungry swarm when Dolfe went very still.

The muscles of his thighs bunched as he sat forward, pulling his legs underneath him. "She's here."

———

Brita glanced at her cell as she jumped into her car and saw that she'd missed two calls from Dolfe. She started to call him back but realized her phone was dead.

"Dangit!"

She searched through the glove compartment of her ugly sedan and found the charger, dragging it out and plugging it into the cigarette lighter. The green charging volt flashed into life on the phone's face. She tried again to make the call, but the phone was too drained to work.

Sighing with exasperation, she vowed to get a new car as she put it into gear and accelerated out of the hospital parking lot. Her old car wasn't compatible with new technology. And though she'd been guilty of lingering too long in the past, technology-wise, she was on a new trajectory and her car was holding her back.

Ten minutes later she was pulling into the

station lot when her phone rang. She grabbed for it, nearly upsetting a travel mug of cold coffee in the process. "Muldane."

"Brita, where have you been?" Bud's voice bellowed through the phone. "I've been trying to call for an hour."

"Sorry, partner. My cell died. What's up?"

"Did JJ mention a partner from Miami?"

Brita frowned. "Jorge Lopez? I met him last year. Why?"

"He was here, looking for information on the Lawrence Peck case. Specifically, on the package Dolfe and Blaise uncovered on the property."

Brita frowned. "Why on earth?"

"I don't know. But he was really insistent, to the point of obnoxious. And I...well I'm afraid he got his hands on it."

Brita closed her eyes, not liking the sound of that at all. She'd had a feeling from the beginning that JJ wasn't telling her everything. Having Lopez show up suddenly, unannounced, and start demanding information he had no right to just made Brita wonder again what the two Miami cops were up to. "How in the world?"

"I was working on it when he came into the bullpen. He must have seen me slip it under the blotter, and when he asked if we had any coffee, I..."

"You left to get him some. Let me guess, when you got back, both Lopez and the file were gone?"

"I'm sorry, Brit. I'm a dunce."

She sighed. "Let's just hope we're not dealing with a dirty cop. There's stuff in that file that could be twisted to use against Senator Honeybun. I wouldn't want to be in your shoes if the Honeybuns decide you're responsible for any problems Brick encounters from this breach." She knew she was being too hard on her partner, but *dangit*, his carelessness had the potential to destroy everything. "I'll try to reach JJ. Maybe she'll know what he's looking for." Brita disconnected without giving Bud a chance to respond, quickly dialing JJ's number.

The number rang several times and then dumped Brita into voicemail. "Jo, it's Brita Muldane. I need you to call me back ASAP. We might have a situation with your partner."

They'd heard the low rumble of some kind of vehicle a few minutes earlier, coming from the distant copse of trees. Dolfe fought the impulse to investigate the sound, his instincts telling him their best chance of building a case was to catch the target extracting the package from under the bridge.

He was about to second-guess his instincts when he finally saw her.

The figure moved swiftly across the weedy

expanse of farmland bordering the property. Watching the rapid approach, Dolfe thought the light-footed steps and small form signified a woman. But the baggy black pants and oversized hoodie turned the slight frame into an amorphous form, indistinguishable as male or female from a distance.

However, if it was a man, it was a really small one.

"Is that her?" Blaise whispered. She'd moved closer as the figure approached, her warm breath tickling his ear and her hand a humid weight on his shoulder.

"I don't know. But clearly somebody took the bait. Since it originated with Alex, I think it's safe to assume that's Kim."

A charcoal-gray cloud slid across the sky, obscuring the light of the sun just as a gust of ozone-scented wind scoured the field, sending a swirl of dust into the air and a cooling wash of air over Dolfe's face.

He glanced toward Blaise. "Stay here." Dolfe started forward and then stopped, remembering her less-than-satisfactory history with that particular instruction. "I mean it, Blaise. I want you out of the line of fire right now."

She nodded. "Don't worry. I've had enough excitement for the week."

He held her gaze a beat longer, then reached out

and tugged on a shiny black curl. "Text me 9-1-1 if anything feels hinky."

She saluted him. "Aye, aye Cap'n."

Dolfe shook his head, turning and skimming along the tree line, keeping a fringe of tall grass and brush between him and the oncoming target. He reached the end of the weedy barrier just as the figure stepped into the creek, the soft splash of water the only sound in the sudden darkness brought on by a coming storm.

Lightning speared the sky behind the bridge as the figure moved quickly downstream, heading for the pretty little bridge with the bait tucked neatly beneath it.

He reached behind him and clasped the grip of his Glock, pulling it free and waiting as the target slipped beneath the bridge. A beat later, the figure's head reappeared on the opposite side of the bridge and Dolfe became aware of an engine roaring toward them.

No!

He jumped to his feet and started running, yelling the only thing he could to stop the woman from running. "Stop, police!"

The figure's head jerked up, the hood of the sweatshirt falling back, and Dolfe sucked in a gasp, the gun wavering for a long moment as he and JJ shared a shocked stare across the distance.

The hesitation cost him. JJ took off running, the

packet tucked underneath her arm, and the four-wheeler roared into sight, a woman with long, blonde hair racing up to JJ and slowing just long enough for her to jump on board.

Dolfe finally shook off his shock and fired, aiming for the tires of the 4x4 rather than the women on board.

The vehicle swerved violently and his shots missed their mark, grazing a bumper, the frame and, by the way she jerked, the driver's arm.

Still, they made a wide turn and shot straight across the field, no doubt heading for a getaway vehicle on the adjoining road.

They didn't make it that far, a familiar figure rose up from behind a tree in the distant copse and lifted a rifle, his stance firm and unwavering as they tore in his direction.

The 4x4 slowed and finally halted, a standoff in the direct center of the island of dirt that separated all the players.

Dolfe took a step, intending to start running toward them as they were focused on Jorge.

He didn't get any farther than one step.

"Don't move, Mr. Honeybun."

The voice wobbled a bit but Dolfe knew it was more of an age thing than based on any fear. A person with a steelier spine he'd yet to meet.

"Put the gun on the ground and kick it away. Then turn slowly toward me."

Dolfe did as requested, sliding his gaze to where Blaise hid as he turned. He sent her an imploring look, demanding with his gaze that she stay hidden.

He raised his arms as his gaze slid to meet the woman standing before him. "Alex. I wish I could say I was surprised."

She shrugged, giving him a smug smile. "I'm sorry, Mr. Honeybun. I like you. I really do. But I couldn't let you shoot my granddaughter."

"There's an easy solution to that. She can just give up."

Alex shook her head, looking sad. "Kim isn't part of this, Mr. Honeybun."

He jerked his head toward the tableau playing out behind him. "You could have fooled me."

"Use your imagination," Alex said, appearing disgusted with him. "She thinks she's protecting me. As soon as I found out what she'd planned, I came here. Unfortunately, it seems I wasn't in time." She cast a sad glance toward the man in the distance, who was still holding a gun on JJ and Kim. "I knew that man was going to be trouble."

"If you want me to believe Kim isn't El Jefe, then you're going to have to give me something to work with."

Alex cocked her head. "I thought you were smarter than that."

"Okay, then let me rephrase that. I need you to

admit that *you're* El Jefe so we can clear your grand-daughter of the charge."

She shrugged. "I make it a point never to admit the obvious, Mr. Honeybun. It just insults the intelligence of everyone involved."

She lifted the gun in her hand, pointing it at his chest. "Goodbye, Mr. Honeybun. I'm sorry we couldn't have had a longer friendship. But I'll leave you with one final thought that you can carry to Hell with you. Your delightful Blaise will make a wonderful addition to my harem in the Middle East. I have several business clients from Dubai who will absolutely love her."

Dolfe's fists clenched and a shot rang out. He blinked, expecting pain and blood and seeing only the blood.

It blossomed high on Alex's shoulder. She turned ashen as she dropped the gun, stumbling back a few steps with a surprised expression on her face. She fell backward and landed hard, her head smacking against the ground with a soft thud.

Dolfe didn't have time to congratulate the shooter, because shots had started to ring behind him and, as he turned, Jorge Lopez staggered sideways and fell to the ground.

The 4x4 took off. Amazingly, it was circling around and heading back toward him.

Dolfe had only a beat to register the surprising

development before bullets rained down around the fleeing vehicle.

Kim swerved violently to avoid the intensive attack, which was sending dirt up around them like geysers. She overcorrected the unwieldy vehicle, making it tipple slightly before rolling onto its side and skidding several yards before stopping.

Dolfe looked around, trying to find the shooter. It took him a long moment, but he finally located the telltale star of a bullet exploding from the chamber of the rifle, and took off in that direction. The shooter was hiding in the same copse of trees he and Blaise had been hiding in, but much farther down. "Call Brita!" he screamed to Blaise over his shoulder as the skies opened up and torrential rain pounded down on them. "And an ambulance."

Gunfire exploded again, coming from two directions, and Dolfe saw that JJ was returning fire from behind the downed ATV.

He prayed the return fire didn't find the gas tank of the 4x4.

Sirens exploded in the distance, telling him that Blaise had done as he'd asked. Brita had probably made sure the local cops arrived quickly. It would take her a bit longer to get there from the Indianapolis Precinct where she worked.

He ran through the woods, shoving at branches and jumping downed trees as he moved toward the spot where he knew the shooter must be. He didn't bother trying to be silent, the thunder crashing overhead and the roar of the heavy rain would obscure his movements through the woods. But as he neared the area where he guessed the shooter to be, he also realized it would cover the gunman's movements, making approach even trickier than it would otherwise be.

Dolfe forced himself to slow, waiting for another volley of shots to be exchanged before moving forward again. He angled away from the edge of the woods, intending to come up behind the shooter and hopefully catch him unaware.

The shooting stopped. He stopped too, ducking down as a rhythmic thrashing sound emerged from just beneath the softening growl of the rain. The thrashing stopped. Dolfe held his position, barely breathing as he waited for the shooter to emerge.

The rain stopped as suddenly as it began.

A silent jolt of lightning lit the sky and he saw the black-clad figure huddling not three yards away, eyes skimming the trees as if sensing his presence there.

The rifle was up. The muzzle pointed in his direction.

He all but stopped breathing.

The sound of sirens grew steadily, the noise drawing the shooter's gaze briefly toward the street.

Dolfe wasn't going to get a better chance. He lifted the gun and dug into the ground with his toes, prepared to move. "Drop your weapon," he shouted, and then threw himself sideways as the shooter jerked the rifle upward and peppered the spot where he'd been with gunfire, shredding the greenery and sending flecks of shiny leaves into the air to rain down on him.

He jumped to his feet and started running, greenery shattering into molecules at his heels as he half-turned and fired blindly in the shooter's general direction.

Through the diminishing fringe of trees, he saw the red and blue flashing lights of the uniformed cops and knew he wouldn't make it across the open space in time.

So, he did the only thing he could do.

He picked a tree and dove down behind it, firing his Glock at the spot where he'd last seen the figure with the rifle.

His shots tore at the wet trees, sending bark spiking into the air and earning him a barrage of return fire.

He held his ground, knowing his last bullet was in the chamber. His spare magazine was in his pocket, the soggy denim fabric an unrelenting force as he jammed his fingers into the pocket to retrieve it. But he was half lying on the pocket and the maga-zine didn't want to come free.

The woods had darkened to the point where he couldn't see. The crickets' song rose in a hopeful crescendo around him, and in the distance shouts and slamming doors told him the cavalry was on the move.

But they'd be too late.

He heard the soft splash of a boot in the saturated ground beneath him and looked up, finding himself staring into the business end of an AK47.

A mean gaze and a cold smile found him. "Mr. Honeybun. We meet again."

He gripped the Glock, his pulse pounding as he realized the single bullet would have to be enough. But if he didn't catch her before she let the bullets fly, he'd be dead anyway.

"I'm guessing you're El Jefe's flunky?"

The insult met its mark, as evidenced by the slight tightening of her hostile gaze. "I'm her Lieutenant. But you might have noticed she's older than dirt. It won't be long until I'm sliding into the lead spot myself."

"Or maybe you could just kill her instead?" He was stalling for time, praying that, by some miracle, something would distract her for the single beat in time he'd need to fire first.

"The connections are hers, Mr. Honeybun. I haven't earned their trust or, in some cases, fear yet. But, I'm a patient woman. I can afford to wait. Learn. And make her organization my own."

"What about Kim?"

She made a moue of distaste. "What about her?"

"Maybe Alex will groom *her* instead."

She snorted out a laugh. "She's a frail, silly girl. She'd never survive in our world. But if she gives me any trouble, I'll make sure she disappears. For good."

Dolfe didn't like the sound of that.

"Now," she lifted the rifle, the muzzle directed right between his eyes.

Dolfe's hand tightened on his Glock.

"You've stalled long enough, Mr. Honeybun. It's time for you to disappear too."

The bark of gunfire preceded the bite of a bullet in the tree mere inches from Sara the Evil Assistant. She half turned, firing a bullet in the general vicinity of the originating shot.

Dolfe didn't hesitate, He rose up out of the greenery and fired his last bullet into her chest. She staggered backward but kept her feet as blood blossomed over her soggy sweatshirt.

She didn't go down.

As if she were being held on her feet by a rope, draped over the knobby tree branch above her head, she wobbled but held. Upright, and still determined to do her worst.

As a mean, bloody smile split her face, she lifted the rifle toward Dolfe.

Another gunshot exploded into the night and the woman jerked forward, falling slowly downward, to land over a fallen log, her rifle clattering to the ground beside her.

Dolfe looked up into JJ's eyes.

They stared at each other for a long moment and then Dolfe shook his head, turned on his heel, and headed toward the line of lights and uniformed officers, lifting his hands over his head to keep from getting shot.

26

They sat on the low wall of the smoking lounge and watched the EMTs carry Jorge Lopez toward the waiting ambulance. Dolfe had spoken to them as they'd prepped him for the journey and the consensus was that he'd be fine after a lot of rehab. He'd taken a through and through in his right thigh. Painful, and it would definitely slow him down for a while, but he'd recover fully.

Blaise glared at JJ across the lounge, her brown gaze boring holes into the other woman's heart. Dolfe didn't envy JJ when she tried to explain why she'd gone behind their backs and nearly gotten everybody killed.

Dolfe had spoken to Lopez about it for a moment as they readied him for the trip across the field. He'd insisted they were only trying to get Alex to show her hand, knowing that only her grand-daughter's safety would be a strong enough motive for her to show up.

Apparently, Lopez had found Kim after all, hiding in a guest room at the back of her grand-mother's well-protected home on Meridian Street. Set on a green and rolling five acres, the entire prop-erty was surrounded by a ten-foot-high rock wall, topped with wrought iron spikes. Access to the prop-erty happened only through a large iron gate at the drive. And the gate was guarded by guys with high-powered rifles.

The Miami cop had apparently used his reputa-tion as one of Blanchette's hand-picked guys to get past the armed guards at the gate. Lopez insisted it had been a fairly easy trick to find the girl after that.

Surprisingly, Kim welcomed his approach, proclaiming that her grandmother had all but kept her prisoner on the lush estate and angry about her grandmother's role in the organization. She believed Alex had killed her fiancé and she asked Lopez for help in bringing her down. Believing he was truly one of Blanchette's thugs, she offered him informa-tion about a certain Senator as payment for his help.

At that point, Lopez knew Kim wasn't in danger from the new head of the organization, but he did see an opportunity to use her to trap Alex.

Lopez admitted to Dolfe that he'd taken Brick's

file from the police because he needed to verify the information she'd fed him.

When he saw the transcripts of Blanchette's tapes, he knew they had to stop Alex.

"Dolfe?"

He looked up to find JJ standing there, fingers twining nervously before her. "I don't think now's a good time, Jo."

She nodded. "I know. I just wanted to tell you that I'm sorry. We were trying to close the case before any more people were killed."

"Well that worked out great, didn't it?" Blaise snapped out. "One dead, two injured, and you nearly got yourself and Kim Vitters killed too. Nice work."

She held up her hands. "I know you're mad..."

"Mad?" Dolfe straightened away from the low wall. "We passed mad a while back. You put all of us in danger, Jo. You lied to me about everything. And you created a much more dangerous situation than if you'd just counted Brita and me in on everything."

"I know. I just wanted you to know I'm sorry. Jorge and I have been under a lot of pressure to shut down this ring."

"Well at least you can check that off your list," Blaise said. "I can't believe I considered you a friend."

JJ flinched as if struck. "I know you won't forgive me. But I promise I didn't know about all the stuff Jorge was doing. He hasn't communicated with me for over a week." When Dolfe and Blaise just stared at her, faces clearly expressing their disgust, JJ shook her head. "I really am sorry." She turned and walked away.

Brita approached a minute later.

Dolfe pointed toward the retreating cop. "You're just letting her walk?"

"I have no choice," she told him. "Word came down from the top. She was acting on orders from the Governor of Florida. He's throwing a lot of power behind making sure she and Lopez come out of this unscathed."

"Damn politicians," he growled.

Brita nodded. "I heard what Lopez said to you. So, you know why they did what they did."

"I guess, though I still don't understand why they didn't loop us in."

"Yeah, I know what you mean. At least we have this contained for now," Brita said.

"Brita, Kim Vitters knew all the stuff about Brick. What if the tapes we uncovered aren't everything?" Dolfe asked.

"I'm going to Miami next week. We're going to turn Blanchette's home and places of business inside out looking for the source of those tapes."

"Somebody in his organization taped him without him realizing," Blaise offered.

"Yeah. I get that," Brita said. "As of right now, we're working on the assumption that it was

Lawrence Peck. Apparently, Blanchette was pressuring him to set up a sting on Brick."

Dolfe's eyes went wide. "He's the one who was working with Brick's assistant, snapping the photos of late-night visits with Alex and all the rest?"

"Yes. He apparently got some incriminating audio of Dresden Cooper that would sink your father if it was released to the press."

"How much were they paying Cooper?" Dolfe asked on a growl.

"More than most people could resist, I'm afraid," she responded. "I've requested a search warrant for Peck's and Alex's homes. Hopefully, we'll recover the original audio and, if we're lucky, there will be clarifying audio of Dresden that will exonerate Brick."

"One thing I don't understand," Blaise said, "is the whole murder in Miami. Who was the woman murdered in Kim's hotel room? How did she get there? And why did we think Kim was there in the first place?"

Brita sighed. "That's a little tricky. But from what I've pieced together from JJ and Jorge, Alex told Peck to send Kim out of town that night, to keep her safe. But when she found out he'd stupidly sent her to Miami because he had family there, she contacted Kim and told her not to get on that plane. Alex sent a woman from the school to the airport and they traded IDs..."

Dolfe's eyes widened as he realized who it must

have been. "Kendra Baxter, the cosmetology educator who looked so much like Kim."

Brita nodded. "Baxter pretended she was Kim, flew to Miami, and took a room in Blanchette's hotel, per Alex's instructions. Alex figured that if Blanchette did the worst and took out Baxter, he'd make the same assumption the police had, and believe he'd killed Kim. Alex figured that would keep her granddaughter safe until she had a chance to neutralize Blanchette. But Alex found out later that Blanchette wasn't in Miami. He was here."

"It didn't stop him from ordering Jorge to kill the woman in Kim's hotel room," Dolfe said.

"No. And Blanchette didn't know that Kendra would fight back when he sent Jorge to kill her. She'd apparently had a rough childhood living among the drug gangs in Los Angeles and was pretty adept with a knife when she needed to be."

Dolfe scowled. "Lopez told us it was a trap and that he'd killed her in self-defense."

Brita shrugged. "He probably did. And considering he probably believed he'd be dealing with a spoiled little rich girl, Kendra's viciousness probably did make him feel like he'd been set up."

Blaise sat back down on the low wall, leaning back on her hands. "Tell me what happened here? Why did these people destroy Wedding Belles? Why was Peck killed here? And who was the woman who ran from the place that night?"

"And why were Blaise and the dogs kidnapped?" Dolfe added.

"I'll answer the last one first. It wasn't JJ if that's what you're thinking," Brita told him. "She wouldn't have deliberately put you and Blaise in danger."

"You could have fooled me," Dolfe ground out.

"She says she never expected Sara Rodgers to come and start shooting people. She thought Alex would come alone to protect her granddaughter. The fewer people who knew Kim had touched the evidence against Blanchette the better." Brita seemed to be holding in a grin.

"What's so funny?" Dolfe finally asked.

"JJ said she figured if you couldn't hold your own against a seventy-year-old woman, you deserved to get shot."

"Har de har," Dolfe said, but his lips twitched with humor. "Turns out it was Blaise who saved my butt." He reached over and squeezed Blaise's hand as she beamed.

"That was a pretty good shot, wasn't it?" she asked him.

"Perfect shot, honey. Just like I taught you. Except you're supposed to take the kill shot." He pointed to his chest, over the heart.

She frowned, tugging her hand free. "I intended it to be a kill shot. Not everybody can be a sharp-shooter like you guys."

Brita chuckled. "The shoulder worked fine. She

dropped the gun and she'll live to hopefully sing like a canary about Blanchette's organization."

"Okay, so who *was* responsible for kidnapping me, Suz and Ty?" Blaise asked. "Those were Blanchette's men at our house that day, right?"

"Yes. He'd just arrived in town. He had suspicions about Alex already and figured he could kill two birds with one stone. He'd get his revenge on you and give Alex a stark lesson on what happens to people who displease him."

"But Alex found out what he was doing and came to the house where they'd taken me?" Dolfe guessed.

"Or Blanchette summoned her. We'll probably never know. The guys who were there with Blanchette are either dead or have disappeared."

"She's the one who killed him?"

"According to Kim, yes. The girl heard Alex bragging about it to her assistant, Sara Rodgers, a.k.a. Sarina Rodriguez. She's wanted in Mexico for several murders, BTW."

Dolfe remembered the feeling of staring into the woman's cold eyes. "Then I definitely won't lose any sleep that she's gone."

Brita nodded. "Alex and Sara were working on winning the allegiance of Blanchette's main people. His infamous temper and cruelty were helpful in their managing to woo a considerable number of his inner circle to them. Including Peck. Though his relationship with Kim had already been working to draw him away at that point. But that's how Alex was able to clear the house of his bodyguards that day and kill him."

"It doesn't pay to be a donkey's backside to people," Blaise said cheerfully.

"Amen, sister. As to the other things you wanted to know about...I don't think destroying this place was their first choice. When Desiree Frank followed Lawrence here that night, she suspected he was hiding evidence against Blanchette. But she and her men couldn't find it. Sara managed to grab the package, unseen, and run with it while Blanchette's guys worked Peck over."

"They were looking for the package," Dolfe said, nodding. "That's why the place was torn apart?"

"Yes. They'd seen Peck come into the building with it but he didn't have it when they confronted him. Desiree didn't realize Sara was there until later and couldn't have known she'd taken the evidence."

"The assistant was the woman who Devon Markum saw running away that night?" Blaise asked.

"Yep. And later, when they were unable to find the package, Desiree instructed them to burn the place to the ground to ensure it would be destroyed."

"Only they hadn't counted on Sara hiding the evidence under the bridge."

"That was pretty smart, actually. They could get

to it if they needed to, but if any of Blanchette's people accused her or Alex of anything, they wouldn't find the proof that either of them had been behind the coup."

In a flash of understanding, Dolfe realized just how clever it was. "The trail would lead directly to Peck and, if the evidence was discovered here later, to me."

She nodded. "They wouldn't mind you taking the blame at all."

"Then, that's it?" Blaise asked, jumping to her feet. "We can go home?"

"Yeah. Just be extra cautious for a while, until we're sure there aren't any more cockroaches that will scurry out of the woodwork."

"Will do," Dolfe assured her.

"We'll drop by your house and get the dogs, if that's okay?" Blaise said hopefully.

"Why don't you leave Beast there until tomorrow," Brita said, grinning. "Percy's decided to give him a bath tonight. I can't wait to see *that* circus. I'll post the video online later."

An enormous, furry head rested against her shoulder as Beast leaned over the seat between them. Blaise buried her face in Beast's sweet-smelling fur, fighting tears. Brita and

Percy had done a great job with the big dog, he seemed much calmer than when they'd brought him home and a whole lot happier.

They'd also given him a bath—posting the hilarious video online as promised—trimmed his nails, and taken him to the vet for all his shots. And best of all, he was currently sporting an enormous Superman collar that made Blaise smile.

He was like a new dog. But one thing definitely hadn't changed. He still seemed heartwarmingly sweet on Blaise. Her face was sopping wet from all the swipes of Beast's wide, pink tongue across her cheeks. Even Dolfe had received a few well-aimed kisses from the happy dog.

Hearing her sniffle, Dolfe turned a worried gaze her way. "You know, we can keep him. I'm sure he'll do fine with the bedroom slippers."

She shook her head, swiping angrily at the tears flowing down her cheeks. "This is better. He'll be loved and safe and he'll be an only dog. I think Beast will thrive there."

Dolfe reached over and scratched the big dog behind his ears, grinning when he heard the thump of a big, hairy foot against the back seat. "He's kind of grown on me too. Hopefully we can come visit him."

Blaise nodded, kissing Beast's wide nose as they pulled into the driveway and looked at the tidy metal pole barn. The front door was open and a pile of moving boxes and construction odds and ends poked out of the top of a small dumpster near the street. An unassuming gray sedan with a few rust spots on the back bumper sat in front of the window nearest the door.

A lone hanging plant, vibrant with red geraniums and bright green ivy, hung from a hook in the eaves in front of the window. Probably a homecoming gift from Devon's mom.

Dolfe climbed out of the truck and opened the door to the back seat, grabbing Beast's leash and waiting for the big dog to hop down. He hit the ground with a wagging tail and his big nose lifted, nostrils flaring as he glanced toward the building and gave off a deep-throated, *woof!*

Blaise walked around to the front of the truck as the door to the building opened wide, the familiar form of Devon Markum appearing in the breach. The kid's jaw was bristly with a few days' growth and his clothes were rumpled, spotted with dirt, and looked as if he'd been crawling around on the floor of a mechanic's shop.

He glanced at Blaise and then Dolfe, and finally, his gaze slid to Beast.

A wide smile split his face. He held out his hands. "Thor!"

The big dog bounced with excitement, straining the leash until Dolfe released him. He lumbered to Devon, happily jumping up to put his massive paws on the boy's shoulders and drenching his face with kisses.

Devon laughed as he hugged the dog. "I was so worried about you," he murmured into the dog's fur. He looked at Blaise. "Where's he been? I thought Smythe took him to the pound or he ran away."

"We've had him." Blaise blinked away her tears, pulling the folded sheet of paper out of her pocket and walking over to hand it to the young man.

He looked at the paper. "What's this?"

"Mrs. Smythe is giving him to you."

His eyes turned suspiciously shiny as the big dog dropped to his haunches and leaned against Blaise's leg. She reached down and scratched behind his floppy ears.

Reading the quickly scrawled note with Sally Smythe's signature at the bottom, Devon shook his head. "This says she gave him to either of us." He frowned. "You don't want him?"

"I do, actually. But I think he belongs with you."

Devon glanced at the dog. "I can't believe it. He's really mine?"

"He is." The joy on Devon's face helped loosen the tightness in Blaise's throat. "As long as we can come visit him sometimes. I've grown kind of fond of the big oaf."

Devon laughed, nodding. "He grows on you. He deserved so much more than Smythe would give him." The smile died. He looked up. "Do I need to worry about him? Mr. Smythe?"

Dolfe dropped an arm around Blaise's shoulders, shaking his head. "I had a conversation with him and told him what was going to happen. He... agreed...this was the best thing for the dog."

Blaise barely repressed a snort at that one. The man had actually demanded they pay him for the dog, despite the fact he'd hated Beast and wanted nothing to do with him. But Blaise was happy to pay him for Beast's freedom. If only to take the tightness of worry from Sally Smythe's face.

Devon watched Beast sniff around the building, a wide smile on his face. "I can't thank you enough."

"We did it for the dog," Dolfe said. "You care about him and will take care of him. He deserves a good home."

"And you deserve to have a dog who cares about you too," Blaise said. "But if you ever realize you can't take care of him properly..." she said.

He nodded. "I'll take good care of him. My parents are backing me in my business and I've already got several clients lined up. We'll be fine, Thor and me."

The rest of the tightness left her throat and Blaise swallowed the ball of tears there. "Good. But I'm serious about coming to see him. We owe him big time. He saved my life. He's a really special dog."

Dolfe nodded, squeezing her shoulders.

"Besides, he has a baby brother and a sister who'll want to check out his new digs."

Devon perked up. "Your dogs?"

Blaise nodded, pulling out her phone and showing Devon the main screen, which sported a goofy picture of Badly and Ivy playing in the back yard.

"They're so cute," the young man said, glancing speculatively at Beast. "Do you think he'd like a friend? I've been thinking about going to the pound and rescuing another dog."

"I think he'd love that," she said, her eyes welling up again. On an impulse, Blaise pulled the young man into a hug. "I'm so happy that Beast..."

"Thor," he corrected quickly. "I hate that name. He's no beast."

"You're right," Blaise said, nodding. "He's a perfect gentleman." They shared a smile. "Anyway, I'm glad you're going to be his friend."

"Thank you." He offered his hand to Dolfe. "I owe you."

"The only thing you owe us is to take good care of that dog." Dolfe cast a speculative gaze over the building. "Now, let's talk a little business..." He dropped an arm over the kid's shoulders, leading him toward the door. "How good are you with lawn mowers? Mine has a spring that keeps popping off..."

Blaise watched them disappear into the building,

Beast...no...Thor trotting happily after them, and sighed with contentment.

Life was beautiful again.

Then her phone rang and she looked down to see Suz's name on the screen. Expelling another sigh, she hit *Accept*, and braced herself for a harsh return to reality. Apparently, it was too much to hope she could escape the drama of real life for very long. "Hey, girlfriend."

"Hey. Listen, Ty and I are meeting the Insurance guy out at the venue in a half hour. Is there any chance you and Dolfe could be there?"

Blaise smiled, settling back against the heated metal of the truck's hood. "We wouldn't miss it for the world."

READ MORE GAINFULLY EMPLOYED MYSTERIES

Did you enjoy Risky Venue? If so, you might want to check out Book 1 of the *Gainfully Employed Mysteries*.

Please enjoy Chapter One of Homicidal Holiday as my gift to you!

***It was a simple holiday getaway...a chance to regroup
and figure out how to move forward after losing the
man of her dreams...then she witnessed a murder on the
beach...***

Dolfe Honeybun broke up with Blaise Runa because
her party girl ways were driving him to distraction.
Unfortunately, out of sight does NOT mean out of
mind. And when his favorite party girl sees something she shouldn't and finds herself being chased
by a cold-blooded killer, reason shuts down and
Dolfe's heart takes over. If only he can get to her in
time!

HOMICIDAL HOLIDAY

Dolfe Honeybun stood in the shadows and watched his ex-girlfriend flirt with a tall, annoyingly good-looking guy on line at a popular nightclub. She looked spectacular as usual; her long, slimly curved form lovingly embraced in some kind of shimmery white material which didn't cover nearly enough of her.

He frowned as the man she was speaking to leaned forward, whispering something into Blaise's ear as his hand slipped over her hip and stopped on her firm, round behind. Dolfe's pressure spiked and he was moving forward before he could stop himself.

He crossed the street to the blare of horns, almost entirely oblivious to oncoming traffic. Red flares were flashing in front of his eyes and his hands were clenched into fists. As he plummeted heart first into complete loss of control, Dolfe took some comfort in the fact he hadn't pulled his gun.

It didn't matter that Blaise deftly, and with a smile, removed the man's hand from her butt. It didn't even matter that she walked away. Because the other guy's lust-saturated gaze followed her sexy sway down the sidewalk, her heels click-clacking rhythmically on the concrete as she walked.

Dolfe decided at that moment the man had to die.

He headed straight for the cocky, overdressed buffoon who was accepting knuckle bumps from his friends by way of celebrating that he'd copped a feel from the gorgeous black woman with the million-dollar smile.

Dolfe would rip him into such small pieces his friend Brita Muldane, the cop, wouldn't even be able to find the body.

The weasel turned as Dolfe stormed toward him, his unintelligent blue eyes widening at the look on Dolfe's face. He took a step back as Dolfe reached for him.

Dolfe's ears roared. He could taste every beat of his heart as his pulse surged to the danger zone. And adrenaline had him by the throat as he grabbed pretty boy's expensive tweed coat by the lapels and dragged him off the ground.

"Hey!" the guy's friends coughed out. But when Dolfe turned his murderous gaze on them, they lifted their hands and stepped back. Apparently judging their friend to be unworthy of having their own blood spilled.

Somewhere on the edges of Dolfe's awareness a familiar click, clack, click, clack intruded, the sound speeding and getting louder as it got closer.

He shook the offensive pup like a rag doll and pressed his face close. The young punk stank of expensive cologne. He was darn lucky he didn't smell like Blaise.

That would have signed his death warrant for sure.

Click, clack, click, clack...

The guy tried tugging Dolfe's hands from his coat without any success. "What the hell, man?"

"You think that's the right way to treat a lady?" Dolfe growled into his face.

The guy blinked under every word, as if he were being pelted with buckshot. "What lady?"

Dolfe's growl deepened and the guy's heels lifted another inch from the ground. "Wrong response, punk."

Click, clack, click, clack...

"Hey come on, dude," the guy whined. "Blaise is just a friend."

"You always run your hands all over your friends' asses?" Chuckling from the guy's disloyal friends abruptly stopped as Dolfe skimmed them with a hostile, green glance. When they were properly quelled, Dolfe refocused his hostility where it belonged. "You want to feel up *my* behind?"

More chuckling.

Click, clack, click, clack...

The guy grimaced. "I don't play for that team, dude."

Dolfe shook him. "But I thought you always felt up your friends. I'm thinking you and me are friends."

"Darn it, Dolfe!" A soft, long-fingered hand gripped his arm, tugging on it. "Let him go."

Dolfe inhaled deeply, her exquisite scent spearing his senses and rolling like warm butter over his nerves. "Stay out of this, honey. The guy dissed you. I'm takin' care of it."

She tugged harder. "Dolfe Honeybun, you let go of him right now and come with me."

He finally turned to look at her and forgot to breathe. He'd almost forgotten how beautiful she was...how delicious she looked and smelled. He frowned, turning back to the punk. "Learn respect you little jerk." He dragged the guy off the ground another half inch just to drive home his point and then flung him away.

The punky kid stumbled backward several steps, his friends catching him before he landed on his ass.

Dolfe turned away and immediately forgot him. He grinned. "Hey, honey. You look stunning as always."

Blaise glared at him, her long, slender arms crossed over her chest. Her pretty brown eyes flashed with anger. "Let's take a little walk, shall we?" She started down the sidewalk, her four-inch-high spiked heels click-clacking angrily against the concrete.

Dolfe winked at the disgruntled punk and started after her, his gaze sliding over the crowd of males to ensure nobody else got any ideas about disrespecting his girl.

He blinked, his stomach twisting with disappointment. Scratch that. Blaise was now his ex-girlfriend. They'd broken up the week before. Primarily because of the very thing he'd just interrupted.

Blaise hit the corner and stopped, turning back to him with a decidedly unhappy look on her beautiful face. The golden light from the streetlamp illuminated her delightful form, making her look like an ebony-skinned angel with fire in her veins. She fairly vibrated with rage. Her whole frame was taut with it, her delicate jaw working over the words she no doubt wanted to fling his way.

She didn't even wait for him to reach her before she launched. "What is wrong with you? What are you doing stalking me?"

Dolfe drifted to a stop and shoved his hands into his pockets, holding her fiery gaze. He was fully aware he'd acted badly, but he didn't care. He'd do it again in a heartbeat.

She didn't seem to require a response from him anyway. She was too busy pelting him with her angry verbal assault. "We broke up, remember? We're no longer an item, you and I. We're finished, *kaput, finito.*" She stepped closer, poking him in the chest with every word. "I don't answer to you anymore and if I want to flirt with another guy I'll do it all day long. *Capiche*?"

He lifted an eyebrow and crossed his arms, telling himself the tearing sensation in his chest cavity was just the aftermath of a bad lunch burrito. Unfortunately, he knew better.

She was flailing his heart into tiny little pieces. "I'm sorry, honey. But I'm not gonna just stand around and watch some punk manhandle you on the street."

She took a deep breath and expelled it, obviously striving for calm. "I had it handled, Dolfe."

He shook his head. "No, no you didn't. You sweetly removed his hand and smiled at him. Kneeing him in the crotch would be handling it. What you did was just short of a promise."

"Shut up, Honeybun."

He twisted his lips against a cocky response and glanced away, knowing she deserved better. She had a right to be mad. "I don't regret what I did."

"I'm sure you don't. That's the problem."

He covered the last of the distance between them and wrapped an arm around her tiny waist, pulling her close. She gasped in surprise and struggled against his grip. "No. The *problem* is that I can't stand the idea of you with another guy. The *problem* is that you should be in my bed right now, writhing and moaning underneath me." Her eyes glittered with unshed tears and he suddenly felt guilty for dragging them both through the mire again. Dolfe lowered his head so that her lush lips were close... too close. Close enough for him to feel the soft hitch in her breath that told him she wasn't nearly as disinterested as she pretended. "The *problem* is that you make me crazy and the longer we're together the crazier I get." Dolfe touched her lips in a soft, prolonged kiss and then forced himself to step back. "I wasn't stalking you." He scrubbed a hand over his chin because he needed to do something with it. If he didn't, he'd be grabbing her up again and he wasn't sure he'd be able to let her go a second time. "I'm working."

She frowned. "I'm supposed to believe you just happened to show up at the same club where I was?"

Dolfe turned away. "Believe it or not. I've been here for two hours, watching for the most likely cheating spouse of my client." He looked around. "I'll walk you to your car. Where did you park?"

She stepped past him. "I'm going back to the club."

Anger spiked and Dolfe gritted his teeth against it. She was right. They weren't together anymore. It sucked planet-sized lemons but it was the reality he'd have to get used to. After all, it had been his idea to split. He didn't respond as she walked away... didn't trust himself to speak. Instead, he followed along behind to make sure she got safely inside, the click, clack, click, clack of her heels pinging against his nerves like bullets. And doing just as much damage to his heart.

"Are you sure you're up for this?"

Blaise turned to the man sitting next to her, forcing a smile onto her face. "Of course. Why?"

Dugald Richards shrugged, his dark chocolate gaze sliding over her, assessing. "You don't seem very excited about our trip."

Blaise reached over and squeezed his arm. The bulging flesh was like iron under her fingers. It reminded her of Dolfe. She barely kept from sighing, biting her bottom lip instead. Everything reminded her of Dolfe. "I'm just a little tired." She *was* tired, in fact she'd been tired for two weeks, since Dolfe had told her he couldn't be with her anymore. She was starting to think it was depression. Which was why when her best friend since high school asked her if she wanted to come to Florida with him over Christmas she eagerly agreed.

Maybe some sun and partying would make her

feel better. The plane's engines roared as they prepared to land in Miami and the pilot came on the intercom to verify that they would be on the ground in ten minutes.

Still, the prospect of parties just didn't give her the jolt of excitement it used to. It was the constant partying that had come between her and Dolfe. He was a serious man. A man whose job as a private investigator meant he was always dealing with the seedier side of life. Dolfe knew intimately how dangerous the world could be. He lived it every day. He'd seemed fascinated by her carefree, party girl ways in the beginning. But after a few months, her almost manic need for fun and frivolity started to rub him the wrong way.

Blaise knew he had a point. She was careless at times. Unthinking. But she was young and beautiful and she wanted to enjoy it while she could.

Unfortunately, she wasn't enjoying it anymore.

Scrunched into the comparatively tiny Business Class seat, Dugald wrapped his long fingers around her hand and squeezed. "Reggie and the gang are meeting us at the hotel in an hour. We'll have dinner and drinks on the terrace and then go to a party they say is *the* big event of the season." He tried to stretch his long, long legs and grimaced as his knees bumped up against the seat in front of him.

Blaise dug for some enthusiasm and tried to focus it into her answering smile. "That sounds perfect. I want to walk on the beach every day while we're here. And eat seafood until it's coming out my ears."

Dugald laughed his baritone laugh. "None of that fishy stuff for me. I'm gonna eat Cuban food until my eyes turn the color of peppers."

The steward started down the aisle, collecting trash and telling people to close their trays in preparation for landing. Dugald adjusted his seat into the upright position as the steward lifted a sandy blond eyebrow at him. Her friend saluted and made the guy laugh. Blaise grinned. He was always making people smile. It was his best skill other than playing basketball, which he'd done professionally for six years until the Indiana Pacers had cut him from the roster the previous year.

Dugald had taken the change with his usual grace and good humor. He'd always wanted to open a restaurant, he told Blaise. So that was what he'd done.

Not surprisingly for anybody who knew him, *Dugald's* was on its way to becoming an Indianapolis favorite. Partly because it was a favorite spot for the Pacers players and management to hang out. And partly because of Dugald himself. Like Blaise, her friend loved people and he was good with them.

She'd been a little surprised when he'd asked her to come with him to Florida. The holiday season was a busy time in the restaurant. But Dugald had a good manager he trusted, and he said he needed a break.

Lord knew Blaise needed one too. She only hoped the time away would help her forget the way Dolfe's hands had felt on her body...or the decadent delights his sexy mouth performed on her.

Blaise's body tightened on the thought and her mood took a dip. She pushed the painful thoughts away. Dolfe no longer wanted to be with her. He'd moved on. And she was determined to move on too. She'd even formed a plan for how to do that, and her current trip might be just the thing she needed to put that plan into play, turning Dolfe Honeybun and their short but incendiary relationship into a distant memory. As Blaise left the 737 and stepped into the busy Miami terminal, taking Dugald's muscled ebony arm, the thought made her feel a little bit better.

Check out the entire series here: https://samcheever.com/books/#gainfully

ALSO BY SAM CHEEVER

If you enjoyed **Risky Venue**, you might also enjoy these other fun mystery series by Sam. To find out more, visit the **BOOKS** page at www. samcheever.com:

Gainfully Employed Mysteries
Honeybun Heat Series
Silver Hills Cozy Mysteries
Country Cousin Mysteries
Yesterday's Paranormal Mysteries
Reluctant Familiar Paranormal Mysteries

ABOUT THE AUTHOR

USA Today and Wall Street Journal Bestselling Author Sam Cheever writes mystery and suspense, creating stories that draw you in and keep you eagerly turning pages. Known for writing great characters, snappy dialogue, and unique and exhilarating stories, Sam is the award-winning author of 80+ books.

To learn more about Sam and her work, visit her at one of her online hotspots:
www.samcheever.com
samcheever@samcheever.com